Tomorrow's Promise

DIANE GREENWOOD MUIR

Cover Design Photography: Maxim M. Muir

ISBN-13: 978-1501042331
ISBN-10: 1501042335

Don't miss the first books in
Diane Greenwood Muir's

Bellingwood Series

All Roads Lead Home – Bellingwood #1
A Big Life in a Small Town – Bellingwood #2
Treasure Uncovered – Bellingwood #3
Secrets and Revelations – Bellingwood #4
Life Between the Lines – Bellingwood #5
Room at the Inn – Bellingwood #5.5
A Season of Change – Bellingwood #6

CONTENTS

THOUGHTS AND THANKS

For a book that was never intended to be, this story brought changes to Bellingwood that were a little unexpected ... at least they were before I wrote them. Then, it was if they had always been part of the story. A new (and she's gonna be fun) character, a semi-regular character who gains more of a foothold, and two wonderful little babies.

The readers who keep Bellingwood vibrant helped choose the names of Joss and Nate Mikkels' babies and I couldn't be happier with the choices.

Cooper Oliver's name came from suggestions by Sandy M. Gardiner, Marci Abel and Robin Miller. Sophia Harper's names were proposed by Bonnie Roupe-Lazuka, Sue Wigand, Ruth Slaughbaugh and Jeanne Baenen Benck.

~~~

I could never stay on track without trusted friends who read my manuscript and remind me that life isn't lived in a bubble. There are so many different perspectives through which we read books. As these wonderful people edit, fix and comment through the process, I learn about writing, Bellingwood, myself ... and what friendship is truly about. They are extraordinarily unique individuals who offer themselves to me for a period of time to make my writing better.

Thank you to Rebecca Bauman, Tracy Kesterson Simpson, Linda Watson, Carol Greenwood, Alice Stewart, Fran Neff, Max Muir, Edna Fleming and Nancy Quist for all they do to make these books happen.

~~~

This book had one – almost – blooper. I caught it one night and when I did, I sweat and panicked and then laughed and laughed. I wrote it, proofread it, my readers read it, I edited through several times and none of us noticed it: a boy with a broken arm can't (shouldn't) play Twister. But, I tossed a fun scene up in the air and hoped it came back down without breaking apart. Whew. But I had to tell you – what fun would it be if I kept it to myself?

CHAPTER ONE

Polly stood in the middle of the living room doing her best to hold back tears. Goodness, she cried at everything, all the time. How had things gotten so out of control? More importantly - how was she going to pull it back together in time? The worst thing ... it was her own stinking fault.

Her best friends from Boston - Sal, Drea, and Bunny - would arrive in less than three hours and Polly had to clean, get beds ready, and then pack for her own trip. There wasn't enough time between now and eternity to pull that off. They had each laughed when she told them they didn't need to come to Iowa for this party. Polly was the last one anyone expected to be married and they were going to celebrate.

Bunny Farnam had pouted, too. The poor girl desperately wanted a family, but couldn't find the perfect husband. That was Bunny-speak for a man who would pay for all of her dreams and never complain. Sal Kahane was trying the long-distance thing with Polly's veterinarian, Mark Ogden, and Drea Renaldi had been dating the same man for as long as Polly had known her. They were perfectly happy, living two separate lives.

Sal and Bunny had been a little miffed with Polly when they discovered she'd gotten married on the sly. Both had hoped to be bridesmaids if it ever happened, but as soon as the party was announced, they'd set aside their disappointment and promised to come to Iowa and have fun.

Polly flopped down on one of the sofas in the middle of the room. Spreading out across the top floor of Sycamore House had seemed like a great idea at the time. She grinned to herself. In truth, it just created more space for her to make a mess. She tried to keep things neat, but it wasn't in her nature. She always seemed to be picking up at the last minute. Henry was usually pretty great about helping, but he'd been so busy lately, she was just glad when he showed up for dinner.

The last couple of months had flown by. The first wing of the hotel out on the highway was finished and was ready for occupancy. The caretaker's house was close to being complete and before they got too much further, she and Henry needed to find someone to manage the place.

Every person Polly had hired at Sycamore House had dropped into her lap. She kept hoping someone wonderful would show up again. After this stupid trip was over, she and Jeff Lyndsay might have to actually work at finding the right manager.

Stupid trip. No, that wasn't fair. It was her honeymoon and she was excited. Yeah. That was it. Excited. When Henry had first talked about going away, she was. They'd spent hours deciding which route to take and where to go and stay. The hotels for the beginning of the trip were all booked and they knew what sites they wanted to see along the way. Now that it was nearly here, Polly was having a hard time getting past her anxiety. She knew that once they got out of town ... oh, about fifteen miles ... she'd relax and start having fun. If she could just make it to that point.

Polly bent over to pick up an empty cardboard box and dropped it beside the pile in front of the sofa. She was never going to be ready. And it was her own fault.

She and Henry tried to tell people they preferred not to receive gifts, but they showed up anyway. He explained to her very gently that people were generous and she needed to accept it. They'd set up a fund at the bank for Sarah Heater's hospital bills, asking friends to contribute in lieu of gifts. The fund was filling up nicely, but gifts still arrived every day.

Lydia also insisted on a gift table at the party. She and Henry needed nothing, but Lydia, Beryl, and Andy had taken her to Des Moines to register for the special things that newly married couples should have. If they hadn't been with her, she might never have chosen a china pattern, much less crystal and silver. Polly refused to register at Victoria's Secret, even though Beryl made lewd remarks every time they passed the store. The wicked glint that never left that woman's eyes was a little unnerving.

Yep, she was pretty sure this was going to kill her. Polly reached over, and taking the box cutter in hand, ripped through the boxes in front of the couch and stacked them into the largest box. First thing finished. Now, no more whining and complaining. It was time to get over herself and get busy.

A beautiful crystal vase and a wooden clock sat on the table in front of her. The bookcases lining the front wall had just been installed two days ago. They were still empty, so now was as good a time as any to start.

Polly looked at the floor behind one of the chairs and wrinkled her forehead. Why was a pair of Henry's jeans out here in the living room? She didn't remember him taking them off and dropping them. The poor man had been falling asleep after supper. He'd been pushing pretty hard to get things wrapped up before he left town.

Rats. This just wasn't the right time to be taking this trip. Polly tried to talk him out of it as recently as last night, but Henry insisted that they needed to get away from everything. She didn't have the heart to argue with him, he really did need a vacation.

A knock at her front door broke Polly's reverie and she set the vase and clock on a shelf before opening the front door.

"What are you doing here?" she asked Lydia, Beryl, and Andy.

"We figured you might need help," Lydia said. "You can tell us to go away, but we're here to do whatever you need."

Polly felt herself relax. "How did you know?"

"You've been busy these last few weeks and Henry looks absolutely exhausted," Lydia said. "

"And it's not that 'happy to be exhausted because my wife is wearing me out' kind of exhaustion, either," Beryl grinned. "Now are you going to let us in or do we have to get on our knees and beg to clean your house?"

Polly backed away from the door. "I have no idea how you do this," she said. "I've never known anyone who takes as much time to make sure that I'm okay as you do."

"If your mother or your Mary were alive, they'd be here, wouldn't they?" Lydia asked.

"Yes, but you have your own kids to take care of. And grandkids," Polly protested.

"And you're our friend," Andy said. "You have a big weekend coming up and you shouldn't be stressed. We couldn't help with the wedding. The least you can do is let us help you with this."

"Okay." Polly let out a breath. "Thank you. I'm not going to stop you. I'm in trouble here."

"I'll start in the kitchen and dining room," Lydia said. "Is that okay?"

Polly swept her arm toward the door leading to her old apartment. "Have at it. I think I cleaned most everything last night, but one more run-through wouldn't hurt."

"Let me deal with these boxes," Andy said. "What if we take your china and silver into the office? You two won't be using that for a while, will you?"

They had turned Polly's old bedroom into an office for Henry. Polly's closet had been emptied into their bedroom, so there was a little space available there.

"Thank you," Polly said. "That will help. I just need to clear the clutter out of the main room."

"Have you made the beds in the guest rooms?" Beryl asked. "I can do that." She scowled down at the two cats who had flopped beside her feet. "You two can't help, though." She nudged Luke's bottom with her toe. He didn't react. "Every time I make my bed,

Miss Kitty thinks it's the greatest game in the world. I usually end up sprawled across the bed in a wrestling match with her."

"Me too," Polly said. "I try to shut them out of the bedroom, but they sit outside the door and whine. Sheets are already sitting on the beds."

Each woman left for a different part of her home. They never ceased to amaze her. Even after a year and a half, she still couldn't figure out how she'd gotten so lucky.

She bent over to pick up Henry's jeans and there was another knock on her door.

Rachel was standing there. "I'm sorry to bother you, Polly. I know you're busy this morning, but there's a man downstairs who says he needs to talk to you. Jeff isn't here and I didn't want to send a stranger up to your apartment."

Jeff Lyndsay was probably at the hotel. If she looked at her calendar, Polly was certain he had it on the schedule.

"Is this person in the office with Sarah?"

"Yeah. I put him in the conference room. Was that okay?"

"That's perfect. Thank you." Polly looked at the jeans in her hand. "Does he look like a salesman?" There wasn't much she hated more than being interrupted by someone trying to sell her something. Jeff was much more tolerant, but he knew how to get rid of them more efficiently than she did.

"I don't know," Rachel said. "He didn't give me a business card or anything."

"Yeah. He probably wouldn't."

"Maybe he's not a salesman. I don't know. He's not dressed up and he asked for you specifically, not the manager or owner."

"Okay, thanks. I'll be down in a few minutes."

Rachel left and Polly went into the kitchen. "Lydia?"

The woman was bent over, trying to rearrange pots and pans in a lower cabinet and jumped when Polly said her name.

"Whoops ... I must have really been into my work," she said. "What's up?"

"There's someone downstairs who needs to talk to me, but I feel guilty about leaving you three here to clean my house."

"Don't worry it, dear. You take care of whatever you need to and we'll keep working. It's really not that bad. You could have done it yourself in a couple of hours."

"You and I both know better than that," Polly said, laughing. "I'll be back."

She trotted across the living room to her bedroom and tossed Henry's jeans into the laundry basket. If this was a smarmy salesman taking her away from her day, she was going to be furious.

Polly went into the bathroom and checked herself in the mirror to make sure she looked relatively professional. Nope, not at all. Jeans and a t-shirt, her hair was pulled back into a pony tail and she hadn't bothered with makeup this morning. Oh well. If you walk in without an appointment, you can't expect perfection.

CHAPTER TWO

Rachel was right. The man wasn't dressed in a flashy suit at all, but was wearing a plaid shirt tucked into his jeans. He turned the chair and stood to greet her.

"Miss Giller?" he asked.

"Yes, how can I help you?"

He gestured to the seat he'd been in and moved to another chair, waiting for her to sit down. "Miss Giller, I am certain that my name will mean nothing to you, but I was a friend of your dad's in college. He and I lost touch over the years, but I find myself in the precarious position of needing your assistance. Being as how you are Ev's little girl, I'm hoping you carry his heart and soul in yours."

Before she could respond, he reached into the back pocket of his jeans and drew out several pieces of paper that had been folded together. He flattened the sheets on the table before pushing them in front of her.

They were pages from her father's college yearbook. She remembered looking through it when she was much younger. It had always been strange to think of her dad as a college student and it fascinated her to see him from a different perspective. The first was a picture of her dad's fraternity. She shuffled to the next sheet and smiled at the photograph of her dad in a laboratory, wearing goggles and bent over a Bunsen burner. Another picture from the yearbook showed him stretched out on the lawn, leaning back on his elbows, grinning up at the photographer.

Polly put the pages back on the table and looked at the man who was facing her. He could well be her father's age. He was slim and wiry, his tanned face lined by years of working outside. His fingers were long with very pronounced veins running across his hands and there was pain and weariness in his eyes.

"Who are you?" she asked.

The man reached across the table and pushed the pages apart, then pointed to a boy standing across the lab table from her father. "That's me, Curtis Locke." He pointed at the picture of the fraternity, touching the face of the same young boy who had slung his arm around her father's shoulder. "We were friends. He was my best friend back then."

"I see," she said. "Why are you here today?"

He took the pages back from her and ran his hand across the photograph in the laboratory, then folded them back up and clutched them. "I need your help. Not for me, but for my baby girl. Ev told me that if I ever needed anything, he'd be there. It looks like I'm too late to find him, but I hope you might be able to help me. I don't know where else to turn."

Polly held his gaze until his eyes shifted back to the pages he held. "Tell me what it is that you need, Mr. Locke."

"Call me Curt, please," he said. "No one calls me Mr. Locke unless they're giving me a paycheck. Do you believe that I knew your Dad?"

"I don't understand why it took you so long to look for him." she asked.

He sat back in the chair. "Your dad left college and started farming. My number got called up. Viet Nam. I didn't come back with all my marbles. I called your Dad one night, just to reconnect. He didn't mean anything by it, but when he told me what a great life he was living with his pretty wife and cute little baby girl, I didn't feel like I had the right to mess it up. And I would have messed it up. I ruined everything else in my life back then. I couldn't tell him how screwed up I was - he would have tried to rescue me. He didn't need my problems. So, I never called again."

He was afraid she wouldn't believe him and it showed. Polly knew there were many heartbreaking stories about vets and the difficulty they had reintegrating into society, but had never come face to face with it. Eliseo tried to tell her that he might experience problems because of PTSD, but he'd conquered so much before she met him that he seemed more like a superhero than a wounded vet.

"What have you been doing for the last forty years?" she asked.

"I've been in and out of jail and then I finally found a good reason to straighten up. I met a woman and you could say she helped me find my way. There was no use telling her no when it came to cleaning up my act. She wouldn't put up with it. I never figured out why she stuck, but we had four children. I haven't made an easy life for her or the kids. She's back in Colorado with our youngest. Our only girl, the second from the youngest, has disappeared. We finally found out she was in Iowa and the only person I knew here was your father. When I got to Story City, though, I found out that he had died."

He sat forward and put his hand on the table, reaching out. Polly put her hand on top of his and he said, "I'm sorry for your loss, Miss Giller. Your father was a good, good man."

"He really was," she said. "I wish you'd had an opportunity to know him again. But why do you think I can help you find your daughter?"

Curt sat back again and seemed to fold in on himself. "I have no one else. She's nineteen and left on her own." When he looked up again, tears filled his eyes. "I'll take the blame. I wasn't home enough to tell her she was a good kid. The only thing we ever did was yell at her for screwing up. She was a normal teenager and we just couldn't let her be. I know that drove her away, Miss Giller, and now I have to make sure she's safe."

"Do you know where she is or who she's with? Iowa is a pretty big state."

He took another piece of paper from his wallet and handed it to Polly. "Her mother talked to one of Jessie's friends and got a name." He shook his head. "But how many Dennis Smiths are there? We don't know what he looks like or how old he is or what town he lives in. We don't even know if they're still here."

"When did she leave home?" Polly asked.

"She's been gone two months. We kept thinking she'd come home or call, but she left her cell phone at the house." He stopped. "I'm sorry. This is a lot to ask of you."

Polly let out a breath. "It's a lot, that's for sure, and I'm not an investigator by any means. But I do have friends who might be able to help. Have you got a place to stay?"

"I stayed in Story City last night. I can go back there."

She smiled to herself. Jeff wasn't going to believe this one. "Let me make some calls. Have you had anything to eat? Would you like coffee?"

"I'm fine. I just want to find Jessie and tell her that she doesn't have to cut us out of her life. I want her to know we love her, even if I screwed everything up."

"Her name is Jessie Locke and the man she is with is Dennis Smith, right?"

"Yes."

"Tell me more about Jessie's friend and what she knows."

"Maggie. She told us Jessie was coming to Iowa. The guy has a job here somewhere."

"Maggie hasn't heard from her either?"

"If she did, she isn't saying. Those two girls were best friends and if Jessie asked her to keep quiet, she would. The last couple of years have been difficult for my girl. I tried to take the blame for everything that was going on in the house. It was just easier."

"And Maggie would keep this information from your wife?"

"When Jessie left, she and her mother had a terrible row. She called her mother some awful things and Kelly told her to get out and stay out."

"I'm sorry," Polly said.

"We figured this would pass, just like every other bad thing did with that girl. She was always pushing us. Maybe it all accumulated to where she couldn't deal with any more. All of that mad and hurt bubbled up and she left."

"I can't believe you never met this boyfriend."

"She wouldn't bring him around, said we'd embarrass her. We don't have a lot of money and the house isn't anything special. She always wanted it to be fixed up and fancy. It's got solid walls and is clean, but there's nothing fancy about it. When she was in junior high, she brought a friend over once and the girl laughed at the dining room table because it wasn't very pretty. Jessie never invited anyone over again. Kelly and I did our best, Miss Giller. It was just never good enough for the girl."

"Let me make a few calls, Mr. Locke," Polly started and he interrupted her.

"Please call me Curt."

"Okay, I'll try." She stood and walked to the door. "Sycamore House is a big place and there are a lot of things to see. There is a garden on the corner and you can walk down and talk to the horses and donkeys at the barn."

"Thank you, Miss Giller."

"If I have to call you Curt, you might as well get comfortable with Polly. And please, if you go back this way," she was already walking out the door of the office and pointed toward the kitchen, "you will find Rachel, the girl who came up to get me. She's in the kitchen and can pour you a cup of coffee or serve you breakfast. I'll find you after a bit."

He walked toward the front door and went outside. Polly turned back to Sarah Heater, who was working through a pile of contracts. She had cleared nearly all of the stacks of paper from Jeff Lyndsay's office over the last two months, slowly getting them digitized and filed. Her health was on hold as the chemo continued to work in her body. Some days were horrible and she could do nothing other than stay in bed. Other days weren't quite as bad and she did as much as possible.

Sarah's nine year old daughter, Rebecca, had placed herself in charge of her mother's care once school let out for the summer. Today, though, Sylvie Donovan had taken her son, Andrew, and Rebecca down to Des Moines. They were due back in time for Sylvie to finish preparations for the evening's wedding reception. She'd had a day off from classes and since Sarah was feeling so well, Rebecca had consented to an outing.

"Is that someone you know, Polly?" Sarah asked.

"He knew my father, I guess. I've never met him, but it sounds like he needs help."

Sarah smiled up at her. "You are certainly the person to come to when someone needs help."

"I don't know how this happens," Polly dropped into the chair in front of Sarah's desk. "I'm about to call Aaron. Maybe I should put this on speaker so you can hear him. You know he's going to think I found another body."

"Oh, do!" Sarah's face lit up. "I want to hear it."

"Well first, you're going to have to listen to Jeff sigh at me. I need to ask him if the rooms are ready at the hotel."

"There's a room available upstairs here," Sarah said. "The last guest cleared out Wednesday night and Rachel already has it cleaned. There's one girl coming in this afternoon and then we don't have anyone due until ..." She clicked through a screen on her computer. "Not until next Sunday."

Polly grinned. "Oh, I love that you have that information. We'll see what torment Jeff tries to put me through."

She pressed the button to call him and turned the speaker on.

"Good morning, Polly. Do you have your apartment all cleaned up for your friends?" Jeff asked.

"I'm working on it, but I need a huge favor."

She could practically hear his eyes roll back in his head and looked over at Sarah, who had clapped her hand over her mouth to keep from laughing out loud.

"You need a room for someone, don't you?" he grumbled. "Don't you know that we are a business and trying to make money?"

"So there's nothing available? Nothing at all?"

"You try my patience, boss lady. Let me do some digging and see what miracle I can work for you this time."

"You're like my own personal Scotty," Polly said.

"Your what? Like a Scotty dog?"

"No, you muggle. Scotty from Star Trek. He always over-exaggerated the trouble it was going to cause him to get the ship up and running for Captain Kirk. He wanted to look like a hero."

"I am a hero. I always find room when you need it."

"And you'll find a room for me this time, won't you."

Jeff let out a deep, long sigh. "There's a room upstairs and you know it. You're sitting there beside Sarah, aren't you?"

"What makes you say that?" Polly chuckled into the phone and Sarah released the laughter she'd been holding back.

"Sarah, you are supposed to make me look good," he said. "You aren't supposed to spoil my fun."

"I'm sorry, sir," Sarah said, simpering. "I'll do better next time."

"Go ahead and set Polly up with what she needs. I'm meeting the last inspector in fifteen minutes and will be back in a while."

"Thank you, Jeff," Polly said sweetly. "You rock."

"You're darn right, I do. We still need to talk about that raise."

"Come see me next week."

"Yeah. Even I know you'll be halfway to Arizona by then."

"Hmmm. Imagine that. See you later."

She ended the call and Sarah said, "That was fun. Now what?"

"Now I call Aaron and make him sweat a little."

Polly pressed another button to call the Sheriff and switched the speaker back on. She hoped he wouldn't disappoint her. Sarah sat forward to listen, as Aaron answered.

"Polly Giller, you've done it again, haven't you," he said. "Bellingwood is going to run you out of town one of these days. I'm surprised more people aren't running and screaming when you walk down the street. Where's the body this time?"

She held her finger up and grinned at Sarah. "I'm in the same building as your wife, Aaron. Do you want me to get her involved?"

"You leave her out of this. In fact, if there is anyone else around you right now, tell them to get away from you."

"She's upstairs in my apartment, you rat. And there's no body. I have something else I need to ask you about."

"But you never call me directly unless you need me to come rescue you from the dead," he said, laughing.

"I'm investigating a missing person."

"I thought we talked about this," he said. "You aren't supposed to do that kind of work. In fact, you're not supposed to be doing anything this weekend except get ready for a party and then get the heck out of town."

"I know, I know. That's why Lydia is here. She's helping me in my apartment. But I just had something come up and I need your help."

Polly stood and smiled at Sarah. Sarah waved her away and turned back to her work while Polly walked into her office and shut the door. She turned the speaker off and said, "An old friend of my father's showed up this morning and needs help finding his daughter. I told him I would make some calls. I don't know what else to do."

"Tell me what you know," Aaron said.

She gave him the little bit of information she'd received from Curt Locke. "I know it's not much and maybe there's more to the story from his side than he's telling me. But, he pulled the 'I knew your dad' card and I couldn't say no."

"I guess I can understand that. She's an adult now and can make her own decisions, but if we find her, maybe we can give the family a little reassurance. Let me do some digging. I might send Stu up to have a chat with him. He reads people well and can tell me what he thinks about the guy. Do you know where he's staying?"

Polly paused just long enough for Aaron to laugh at her. "You're putting him up at Sycamore House, aren't you?"

"Maybe," she said. She hated that her friends knew her so well.

"Got it. Let Sarah or Jeff know that Stu will be coming to talk to him and I'll sic Anita on this."

"Thank you, Aaron."

"Are you going to let me do the Father-Daughter dance with you tomorrow night?"

"Please tell me you're kidding."

"Well, if I have to be kidding, I guess I am. I just thought it would be nice for you to have someone to dance with when Henry is dancing with his mother."

"We're not doing all of the traditional stuff, Aaron."

"That doesn't surprise me at all. Okay, tell my wife that ..." he stopped. "No, don't tell her anything. I'll tell her myself. Good-bye, Polly."

"Thank you. I really appreciate this."

"I appreciate that you didn't call with a body."

"Bye, Aaron." Polly looked at the time. There was none left. Her friends would arrive in less than an hour.

She went out to the main office. "Sarah, I'm going to find Curt Locke and tell him to see you about his room. Aaron is going to send Stu Decker up to talk to him. Will you have his details?"

"I'll take care of it, Polly. You go on. You've got people coming in this morning, right?"

"I have to hurry!"

Polly ran out the front door, looking around to find Curtis Locke. She finally saw him standing in the garden and ran over. He looked up as she approached.

"Hi Curt," she said, a little out of breath. "I have a room available here for you. Just go back into the office and speak with Sarah. I called a friend of mine who is the local sheriff. He will see what he can find, but is going to send one of his deputies up to ask you more questions. There might be something you know that you don't realize you know. Stu is a good guy."

He stood there nodding while she rattled on. When she took a breath, he stopped her. "Thank you. I don't know that I can afford to stay here, though. This is pretty fancy."

"Don't worry. That's why I have this place. It seems like most of the time the rooms are filled with my friends and family. I'm sorry I can't spend more time with you right now, though. I have a group of friends coming in from Boston and need to finish preparing for them. Take your time out here and when you're ready, Sarah will tell you how to get to your room."

"Thank you, Miss Giller. You are your father's little girl."

"I'd like to find a moment to talk to you more about him sometime," Polly said.

"I'd like that too."

She patted his arm and turned to go back to Sycamore House. Then, she realized she needed to call Henry and tell him what was happening. Things had been pretty quiet around here for a while. It was probably time for something to erupt. He needed to be reminded that marriage to her was filled with craziness on a fairly regular basis.

CHAPTER THREE

Even though she'd only been gone for a short time, Polly's friends had done wonders. Henry's plans for transforming the upper floor of Sycamore House into a home included removing the entryway that he'd built when she first moved in, leaving the doorway open. The old living room was transformed into a media room for Sylvie's boys and Rebecca and they'd shifted the dining room table further from the kitchen, opening up the space.

Beryl was leaning across the peninsula, attempting to steal a muffin from Andy's hand and Lydia was at the sink washing dishes when Polly walked in.

Andy looked up and snatched the muffin back from Beryl. "Now you're in for it," she said, pointing at Polly.

"What?" Beryl spun around and laughed. "Well Mama Merritt made plenty. I don't know why I can't have one."

"You've already had one. How you stay so skinny with all the food you eat, I'll never know."

"It's called good livin', sweetie and I'm full of it."

"You're full of something," Andy muttered.

Beryl danced over to Polly. "Your house was in pretty good

shape up here, Miss Thing. I call that needless worrying."

"I'm so sorry that I went away though. You three are amazing."

Lydia dried her hands on a towel as she turned around. "Who was that man in the garden?"

"An old friend of my father's," Polly said, smiling inwardly at the fact that Lydia missed nothing. "He asked me to help him find his runaway daughter. I called your husband."

"You don't have time to search for a girl who doesn't want to be found," Andy said. "Your friends are coming and you have a party and honeymoon to prepare for."

"I know." Polly hopped onto a bar stool and reached for a muffin. They were still warm. "I can't say no to him, though. How awful this has to be for their family."

"Why is he bothering you? He should have gone to the police."

"She's an adult and left home on her own. It sounds like this is tearing him to pieces." Polly breathed in the scent from her muffin and said, "The poor guy. He's one of those people who believes he's responsible for every bad thing around him, and then he does things to perpetuate that belief."

"What do you mean?" Andy asked.

"Well, he got messed up in Viet Nam., When he came back, he decided not to contact Dad or his old friends because he thought he'd screw up their lives. It sounds like he just spiraled downward. When he finally met a woman, his job kept him away from home and when he was home, he wasn't easy to be around."

"And you're going to try to rescue him, aren't you, missy," Beryl said.

"Well, not him, exactly, but how could I say no to helping his daughter? He came to Iowa looking for my father and when he discovered Dad was dead, tracked me down. Dad would have helped him - I find that I can't say no to this."

Lydia gave Polly a quick hug. "And that's why we come over to help you out when you're in a panic."

"But you take care of more people than I ever will," Polly protested. "When do you just relax and spend time with your own kids?"

"My kids find me whenever they need me," Lydia said. "Honestly, I think they're glad I can't meddle in their business every day. You shouldn't worry about me."

"We worry all the time," Beryl admonished her friend. "But it doesn't do us any good. You still insist on taking care of us."

Polly glanced at the time. "I'd love for you to stay and meet my friends. I have to take a shower and change, though. Will you let me take you all out to lunch?"

Lydia smiled and said to Beryl and Andy. "See, I told you this would pay off." She turned back to Polly. "We'd love to. We'll finish in the kitchen and eat more muffins."

Polly took another bite of the muffin in her hand. "I'll take Obiwan outside and be right back." The dog heard his name and followed her to the back door. As she passed the closet, she grinned at the boxes which had been neatly stacked and tagged. Yes, Andy had done her job quite well.

Leia and Luke were perched on the cat tree looking outside intently, barely acknowledging her.

"What 'cha seeing there?" she asked, joining them at the window. Eliseo was bent over in the garden, pulling weeds. Beautiful rows of green sprouts were coming up through the dirt. It was exciting to see that immense space behind Sycamore House become useful. He and Ralph Bedford had enjoyed working with Demi and Daisy, preparing the ground and then planting. Eliseo promised her loads of sweet corn and tomatoes as the season progressed. This didn't look anything like the little vegetable gardens she remembered seeing in the city.

"Come on, Obiwan. I can't dawdle today. Too much going on." He followed her down the steps and out through the garage. When he saw Eliseo, he took off at a run.

"Obiwan. Stop." Polly commanded. The poor dog ground to a halt and turned around as if to ask what her problem was. She jogged to catch up to him and put her hand on his collar. "You can't get into the garden."

"Good morning, Polly," Eliseo said. He walked over to the two of them and knelt down to nuzzle Obiwan's neck. The dog wriggled with glee, even though he'd seen Eliseo early that morning at the barn.

"It's like he was never going to see you again," she said, laughing. "The garden looks beautiful."

"Stay right here," he said and waited until she put her hand back on Obiwan's collar. Eliseo strode back to the garden, bent over and pulled something out, then reached into his back pocket and drew out a handkerchief. He was polishing what he held as he walked back, then handed Polly a deep red radish. "Do you like them?" he asked.

"I love radishes! Mary used to make radish sandwiches for me all the time."

He handed it to her and she took a bite. "Oh, that's wonderful. These are ready now?"

"Jason and I are going to spend some time this afternoon out here. We have several things ready. Quite a few different greens and some lettuce. It's going to be a fun summer."

"I can hardly wait." Obiwan tugged at her hand and she said, "I'd better get him away from here. Thank you, Eliseo."

His face lit up with a smile and he turned back to the garden.

"Come on, Obiwan. You have to hurry."

The dog looked back at Eliseo, and before she had to yell at him again, made an obviously conscious choice to follow Polly to the trees lining the creek bed. Rain had filled the creek, so they wandered through the trees down to the horse's pasture. All four horses and the two donkeys trotted to the fence line to greet her and she talked to them as they followed her around the perimeter. When she and Obiwan headed back to the house, she watched as Nat ran back to the fence at the tree line, rearing and neighing for the others to follow him.

There were a couple of balls in the pasture that the donkeys especially liked to play with. Some days she loved nothing more than watching her big animals enjoy themselves in the summer sun, but today wasn't that day. There was too much to do.

"Let's go back, buddy," she said. "I have to get all prettied up. The girls will be here soon."

"I'm back!" she called out when she opened the front door. "Gonna take a shower and be right out."

When Polly stepped out of the shower to get dressed, she heard more voices in the front room.

"Crap," she said to herself. "I knew it." She ran into the bedroom and breathed a sigh of relief at her preparedness. Last night, she knew that today would be harried, so she'd laid out clothing to wear. All she had to do was dress. She ran back into the bathroom to put makeup on and blow out her hair. Giving herself a quick grin, she stuck her tongue out at the mirror image and took a deep breath. She was going to have fun.

She worried they might not really recognize her. These last two years she'd discovered a new independence. Her friends in Bellingwood knew her as Polly Giller, independent business owner and finder of dead bodies. Even though it might be strange to those who had known her before, this was who she was now.

Drea and Bunny knew her as a very different person. Independent, yes, but so much had changed. Polly felt more certain of herself than ever before. This was her territory, these were her people. This was her life and she desperately wanted these girls to allow her to be the new person that she'd established.

"You've got this, Giller. You're married. You have your own home. You have friends who love you and animals who adore you. The girls will love it, too. Trust them."

Taking another deep breath, Polly entered the living room. Sal saw her first and jumped up to run across the room.

"I love you!" she cried, "and I love what you've done up here. Polly, you make me so proud." Sal grabbed her into a hug and whispered, "Bunny is terrified that you don't like her anymore. Pay no attention to her hysterics."

Polly pulled back and smiled up at Sal, "I love you too. I'm glad you're here."

Drea had stood as well and walked toward the two of them. Sal released Polly, who ran into Drea's arms. "I've missed you, my friend," Polly said. "It's so good to see you."

"You look amazing. Life in Iowa is good for you. I've never seen you so beautiful and happy," Drea responded.

Bunny was sitting on the couch with her back to the bedroom, glancing surreptitiously over her shoulder as Polly greeted her other two friends. Polly decided to ham it up completely and after letting Drea go, dashed to the sofa, rolled over the back of it and dropped her head into Bunny's lap. "You're here! I've missed you so much!" Polly smiled up at her friend.

"You silly goose." Bunny was giggling as she reached around Polly and pulled her into a hug. "I forgot how much fun you are."

Polly sat up and said, "Have you all introduced yourselves?"

"Yes, but they didn't have time to tell us any stories about your life in Boston," Lydia said. "You came out too soon."

"How was your trip?" Polly asked. She gave Lydia a glare, then followed it with a smile.

Sal laughed. "Oh! It's such a small world!"

Polly raised her eyebrows. "What do you mean?"

"We brought one of your guests up with us. She was having trouble getting a rental car in Des Moines."

"Right when you were at the rental counter?"

"Well, it seemed like she'd been waiting for a while. When I was talking to the rental agent, she overheard and asked if she could get a ride. She seems like a nice young girl. Some photographer from Montana. I asked where she was staying and she told me Sycamore House. I couldn't believe it."

"That's crazy!" Polly exclaimed. "You flew in from Boston and she came in from Montana and you met at the same car rental counter?"

"Well, they're all kind of together in the same place. She was sitting on a bench, pretty frustrated."

"I can't believe she hadn't planned better. Who comes in to a little town in the middle of Iowa without having a car ready?" Bunny asked.

"Don't you dare get snotty about it, missy," Sal interrupted. "You didn't do the planning for this trip, I did."

"Whatever," Bunny snipped.

"And with all of your luggage, we were barely able to fit Polly's guest in the car."

"I was the one who had to sit in the back with her. You crammed me in there with her suitcases. She was dumping things all over the place."

"Girls, girls. The trip is over. Miss Wexler has been delivered, we're here and settling in. I think we can let it go," Drea said. "It's time to focus on Polly's marriage, don't you think?"

Bunny reached across and took Polly's left hand to look at the ring. "I can't believe you got married before me," she said. "Your ring is beautiful."

"Thanks," Polly said, smiling. "It was my mother's. Dad kept it and Henry had it cleaned and adjusted for me."

"That's total perfection," Bunny said. "I'll never find someone like your Henry."

Sal leaned over the back of the couch to interrupt. "When are we going to get to spend time with your honey-bunny?"

Polly took her hand back and looked up. "I thought we could all go out tonight. Is Mark free?"

"He'd better be. I'm taking all next week off to play hausfrau, so he promised to make sure he had his evenings free."

"He's a small town veterinarian," Polly said, with a hint of warning in her voice. "You can't be mad if someone needs him."

Sal grimaced. "I can be mad, but it won't do me any good. Don't worry. I'll be a good little princess." She patted Polly's back. "So, are you taking us to the Diner? I was telling Drea and Bunny that they just couldn't miss this wonderful piece of Americana."

Before Polly could speak, Sal continued, "And I promise you that I've been good. I told them that you wouldn't put up with any cute remarks about how quaint Bellingwood is. These are normal people and you love them."

"I wasn't going to say anything," Polly said. "But you're right."

She looked over at Lydia and Andy, who were trying hard to contain their laughter. Beryl had given up and was snickering as loudly as possible.

"What?" Polly asked.

"You keep everyone in line," Beryl said. "Even your friends are a little afraid of you."

"No one's afraid of me." Polly was chagrined. "You're not, are you?" She looked up at Sal.

"I'm a little afraid," Sal replied.

"I'm always afraid, but you give me courage," Bunny said.

They turned and looked at Drea. She grinned. "I have two brothers. I have no fear."

"And they're gorgeous." Polly fanned herself. "So gorgeous."

"Stop it," Bunny scolded. "You're married. Leave some for the rest of us."

Polly patted her knee. "Your day will come, sweetie. You just have to quit worrying about it so much."

Bunny didn't respond right away, but when she stood up, she said. "So, you hooked Sal up when she came out to Iowa. Do you have a hot date for me tonight?"

"Umm. No?" Polly was so shocked she wasn't sure what to say. She looked at Sal and Drea for help, but they both shrugged their shoulders as if to disavow any responsibility for the girl's behavior. It had been so long since Polly had spent time with Bunny, she'd forgotten how self-centered the poor thing was. Neither Sal nor Drea knew her very well. She'd always been Polly's friend and they only knew Bunny peripherally.

"Why not?" Bunny whined.

"Sweetie, you are only going to be here for a couple of days and tomorrow night you can dress up in your best dress and dance with all of the single men at the party. I promise."

"Tonight's not going to be as much fun if you have a date and Sal has a date."

"That reminds me. I've invited our friends, Joss and Nate Mikkels to go with us, too," Polly said.

"That figures," Bunny said. "Another couple."

"You can be my date," Drea said in a deep voice. "I'll put my hair up and look macho. Will that help?"

"Oh well. It's just another in a long string of lonely nights for me. Whatever. Which room is mine?" she asked dejectedly.

"You will be in here," Polly said, walking toward the front room. "Drea, you're in the middle room. Lydia decorated them and I don't know which is my favorite. They're both beautiful."

Bunny stood in front of a pile of suitcases and looked over at everyone. "Could I have a little help, please?"

Sal let out a loud, dramatic moan. "I had to carry those things up the stairs for her. She was afraid she'd break a nail if she carried anything heavier than her purse."

"It's not often that you're supplanted as the diva in the group, Sal Kahane. Manual labor, eh? You might as well just give up and move to Iowa!" Polly followed Sal and picked up a suitcase. She wasn't prepared for it to be quite so heavy. "Bunny, you're only here for the weekend. How could you pack so much?"

"I didn't want to forget anything. The suitcase Sal is carrying has all of my shoes for the weekend."

Polly turned around and looked at Lydia, Beryl and Andy. They were close to tears from holding back laughter.

Beryl was done in. "Shoes! She has a suitcase for shoes! Two days and she has a suitcase for shoes."

Drea snapped the wheels down on a small black suitcase and flung a satchel over her shoulder. "In here?" she asked, heading for the door to the middle bedroom.

"I'll be right there," Polly said.

"Oh, take your time," Drea said drolly. "I think I can handle this on my own. Is that the bathroom?"

"It is, but I think I'll show you to a different one." It suddenly occurred to Polly that she couldn't imagine Bunny and Drea sharing a bathroom. Fortunately, the one off her old bedroom was available and she knew Drea would be fine with a few extra steps.

Polly and Sal dropped Bunny's luggage inside the door, and Sal leaned against Polly. "How ya doing?"

"I'm fine," Polly said. "At this point, I'm just ready for the party to get started."

"Bunny," Sal said. "Are you changing for lunch?" She winked down at Polly.

"Of course! I feel like I've been dragged behind a four-horse team for hours," the girl said blithely. "This is casual, right?"

"Right," Polly said. "Very casual. Jeans and a t-shirt casual."

Bunny fluttered her hand, effectively dismissing them. "I'll be out in a few minutes. I just want to freshen up. It's absolutely lovely that you have a sink in here, Polly."

They backed out and Polly pulled the door shut. She and Sal fell into each other in a fit of giggles.

"I'd forgotten about all of that," Polly whispered.

"Girls," Lydia scolded. "Be good."

"Oh, this is us being good. We could be so much worse," Sal said.

Polly knocked on Drea's door.

"Come in," Drea called.

"Bunny is changing her clothes. You have a few moments if you want to do the same," Polly said.

"Is this okay?" Drea gestured at the clothes she was wearing - a sharply pressed pair of black jeans and a red, floral blouse.

"It's perfect. I just wanted you to know you have time."

"I'll bet I do," Drea laughed. "She's a piece of work. No amount of Dramamine could relax me enough to put up with her chatter. If it had been later in the day, I'd have just gotten drunk." She stepped forward and gathered Polly in her arms. "I'm glad to see you so happy. My family all sends their love. In fact ...," she released Polly and went to her satchel. "Mama wanted you to have this."

Drea handed Polly a wrapped package. "Go ahead. Open it. It isn't new. It's been part of our family since they were in Italy. Mama wanted me to tell you how much she loves you and how happy she is that you have found a wonderful man."

She shook her head. "I'm almost certain there might have been a sideswipe at me since I'm not married yet, but this is for you."

Polly carefully separated the tape from the paper and set it aside. "Oh my," she gasped as she opened the box. "I remember this. It's from her table!" She unfolded a white lace table runner that had been in Drea's home. Her eyes filled. "This is beautiful. Thank you."

"Mama always thought of you as her adopted daughter," Drea said. "I have a few other gifts in here for you, but those can wait. I wanted to do this one while we were alone."

"Thank you and give your mother this for me." Polly kissed Drea on both cheeks and pulled her into a hug.

"Okay, enough emotion. Let's go out and see how long Bunny keeps us waiting. Your friends probably think that she's the most ridiculous person they've ever met."

"They know their share of crazy," Polly said. "I'm just excited that all of you finally have an opportunity to meet each other."

The two girls re-entered the living room to gales of laughter.

"What are you telling them?" Polly asked Sal.

"We were just talking about the flight out from Boston. There was a little old man who insisted that he was going to sit with me. He kept trying to hold my hand, telling me that he'd never flown before. Fortunately, we left him in Chicago."

Polly and Drea sat back down on the sofa, waiting for Bunny to emerge.

"I'm getting kind of hungry." Beryl tapped her watch impatiently. "How long is this going to take?"

"I don't know," Polly said, sighing. "I'll check." She got up and walked toward Bunny's room, hoping the girl would just open the door and come out. When she got there, she rapped twice. "Bunny, sweetie? We're starving. Can you hurry it up?"

"I'm almost there. I want to be perfect. You never know who I'll meet."

"It's a diner, sweetie. Just hurry."

Bunny flung the door open and danced around Polly. "Am I casual enough?" she asked. She was wearing stilettos, a pair of pale yellow capris and a layered, flouncy yellow top. Her hair had been teased into submission and she wore a pair of hoop earrings that were at least three inches in diameter.

"You'll do," Polly said, trying not to look too shocked. "Let's get something to eat. I want to hear everything that has been happening in your life." She took Bunny's arm and propelled her to the front door. "Sal, will you drive? We won't fit in my truck."

"Absolutely," Sal said. "Let's head out." She turned to Lydia, Andy and Beryl. "Thanks for being so patient."

"As long as I get food, I won't get murderous," Beryl said. "And I'd better get food soon."

"Beryl," Lydia warned, in her best mother voice.

"What? I'm starving!"

CHAPTER FOUR

Polly paced back and forth late that night while Henry lay back on the pillow with his hands behind his head. "Just come to bed," he said. "You can't fix anything by worrying about it."

"Were you even there? I wanted to smack the twit," Polly said. "What is her problem? I do *not* remember it being this bad."

"You dealt with her, Polly. She settled down."

"But, everyone was uncomfortable. I couldn't wait to get out of there. The one weekend I want to enjoy my friends and little Miss Twit-face has to come into town and make it all about her."

"Polly, you have to let this go. No one else was as exasperated by her behavior as you were. Even Mark and Sal ignored her."

"But, she was practically in his damned lap. She knows they are a thing, but did she care?" Polly turned on him. "No. As the only unmarried man at the table, he was going to damned well pay attention to her. Damn it, Henry. I want to drive her little ass down to Des Moines tomorrow and put her on a plane back to Boston. I don't want her ruining any more of this weekend."

"I'll bet that after the public scolding you gave her, she'll be on her best behavior."

Polly flopped belly-down on the bed beside him. "I'm so embarrassed. I was just so mad. When she ran her hand through Mark's hair, I was done."

"You know. Sal probably could have taken care of it herself and since Mark wasn't encouraging anything, she wasn't worried. Even I saw that."

"But, I'm her friend. Or at least I'm supposed to be. I've seen Bunny play these games before. She doesn't play them to participate. She plays to win and isn't satisfied until the object of her attention has dropped everything else to be hers. Then she finds some reason to hate him and moves on."

Henry turned onto his side and ran his hand up and down Polly's back. "You know, I was reading an article a few weeks ago about people who were toxic friends. You might want to decide that Bunny isn't worth your effort. You are a better friend to her than she is to you."

"No kidding," Polly said and rolled her shoulders under his hand. "This afternoon we had to hear all about her life. We had to hear about how much she hates her job and how she is never going to find a husband and will never have babies of her own. Not once did she ask about you and me. If Drea or Sal asked a question, it was all I could do to get a sentence or two out before she latched on to something that related to some other thing going on in her life and change the subject back to her. It didn't matter at all that we are celebrating our marriage this weekend. Everything was about me not finding her a date for dinner tonight. Can you even believe it? She can't freakin' be happy for me without making me feel guilty for not taking better care of her."

Polly felt angry tears leak out of her eyes. "I'm so damned mad. I just want her gone. Why did I have to invite her?"

"Because you are much too kind-hearted and she's been a close friend." Henry gave a small chuckle. "I was going to say that you were much too nice, but after that tongue-lashing you gave her at dinner, nice isn't a word any of us will use to describe you."

"I wasn't that bad, was I?" Polly whimpered, feeling chagrined at what she had done.

"Those times you took me out?" Henry said. "Those were gentle love-taps compared to what you did tonight."

Polly flopped her head on the bed. "I'm a terrible person." She looked up at him. "Did I upset everyone?"

"No honey." Henry stroked her back again. "You said exactly what we were all thinking. None of us had the courage to speak up and when it was over, we were pretty much relieved that her antics stopped. Nobody thinks less of you. I promise."

After putting up with Bunny's self-centered behavior at lunch and then her whining for the rest of the afternoon, Polly prayed she'd be better was out with a large group. They had gone to a sports bar in Boone. It was the same place that she'd gone with Joey when he had been in town, but it had gone through several different owners and the Giggling Goat was now some generically named bar. The food was fine and the alcohol still got them tipsy, but it wasn't as much fun without the crazy name.

When they were seated, Bunny managed to arrange it so she sat beside Mark Ogden. All through dinner, she flirted with him - playing with his clothes and his hair. She kept sliding closer and closer and when he moved away so that he could put his other arm around the back of Sal's chair, Bunny didn't stop.

Mark's face had been priceless. He was so worried that Sal would be upset. He had yet to learn that Sal simply didn't play games with other women. When she was in a relationship, she just plain didn't worry. Sal Kahane was so fully confident in herself that she knew someone as silly as Bunny couldn't compete. She had flicked Bunny's hand off his back a couple of times and when Bunny, a little drunk, had climbed into Mark's lap to get to something across the table, had pinched the girl's backside.

Drea, Henry, Joss and Nate Mikkels had all tried to ignore what was happening. Sal waved Polly off once, quietly shrugging her shoulders and patting Mark's arm. The others tried to have fun. Drea and Joss had hit it off and everyone was fascinated that Polly and Henry were driving his classic Thunderbird on their honeymoon. They were even more surprised that Joss and Nate were planning to go with them in their 1962 Chevy Impala. The two couples were driving to Joplin to pick up Route 66 and head for the Grand Canyon. What better way to travel on the "The Mother Road" than in classic cars? When they got to the Canyonlands in Utah, they were renting Jeep Wranglers, but until then, classic vehicles were their mode of travel.

Drea asked about air conditioning. Especially since they planned to drive through Texas, Arizona and New Mexico. It was the middle of June, for heaven's sake. Polly had batted her eyes at Henry. This wasn't a new conversation. They had gone back and forth between taking his truck with all of its conveniences, and taking the car. But it was something he wanted desperately to do, so she'd relented and purchased lightweight clothing and several fun hats. If they were driving in the heat of the summer, they were driving with the roof down.

Then, Bunny climbed into Mark's lap and Polly went ballistic. She physically lifted the girl off of a very surprised Mark and dropped Bunny back in her own chair, then stood over her, shaking her finger.

"You stupid, selfish, bitch," Polly had said. "It wasn't enough that you made everyone carry your crap and wait on you today. We also had to listen to you go on and on about yourself. Now you embarrass yourself by coming on to someone who is obviously not interested. I've had it. You should apologize to every single person at this table, but you won't because you believe the world revolves around you. So, keep your damned hands to yourself and keep your mouth shut."

Bunny had the grace to look chagrined. She muttered "I'm sorry" and then pouted the rest of the evening. Polly knew her outburst had effectively killed the fun, but the strain on everyone's faces while Bunny was out of control was apparent. Bunny sniffled and snuffled in her seat and pushed back from the table, in order to make it obvious that she wasn't getting close to Mark. Every once in a while, she sent a grim look Polly's way.

After Polly took a few deep breaths and calmed herself, she apologized. "I'm sorry for coming unglued, guys. I didn't mean to wreck the evening."

Since no one was willing to make it any more difficult for Bunny, they had simply acknowledged Polly's apology and pretty soon, the evening broke up. Drea and Bunny rode with Polly and Henry in his truck and the ride home had been silent, except for texts constantly coming in from Sal and Joss, who were apparently laughing hysterically at what had happened.

Bunny had sulkily gone to her room and Drea had given Polly a hug, telling her that the little fool had it coming and Polly was the only person she knew who had the balls to say it out loud.

Polly crawled up and put her head on the pillow beside Henry's, then caressed his face. "Maybe I was mad at her because this weekend was supposed to be for us and she was intent on stealing the limelight. It's not like I don't know that about her. She always has to be the star. Maybe I was just jealous."

"Honey, you don't do jealous. At least not like that. She was making all of us uncomfortable and Mark wanted to crawl under the table. Since she was your friend, he wasn't sure how to handle it. I suspect he breathed a huge sigh of relief when you shut her down. A little sulky behavior on her part isn't going to destroy the weekend for me, don't let it affect you, okay?"

"Them's easy words to say," Polly remarked. "Them's not so easy words to live."

"Tomorrow, you're going to be busy with your friends. If you let Bunny ruin your weekend, you'll be sorry for a very long time. Just ignore her and act like her bad behavior doesn't even exist."

"You say that like it's a new idea. Bunny doesn't let people ignore her, but I'll try. At least I have a lot of people around here who don't care about her."

"Exactly. If you want more entertainment, sic Sylvie on her. You know how she puts up with bad behavior."

Polly started laughing and let out a snort. "That's perfect. She's managed more than her fair share of nasty wedding behaviors." She hugged him. "I love you and I'm sorry that I screwed up the evening."

"I keep telling you - you didn't. Bunny did. No one is mad at you."

Then Polly sat straight up. "I didn't tell you what happened this morning! I had to call Aaron."

Henry groaned. "I'd have heard about a dead body. What happened?"

"This guy showed up who knew Dad in college and he needs my help finding his runaway daughter."

Henry pulled back. "He needs your help? How do you plan to manage that with a party and a honeymoon?" He raised the right side of his upper lip and growled. "You aren't going to try to talk me out of this trip again, are you?"

"No, I won't do that. At least I hope not. That's why I called Aaron. Hopefully Anita finds enough information so they can track the girl down."

"Good." He breathed a sigh of relief. "How did he find you?"

Polly told him everything she knew about Curt Locke and his daughter, ending by saying that the man was staying at Sycamore House until they knew something more.

"I swear, Polly," Henry said. "They come out of nowhere to find you. I don't understand how this happens."

She chuckled. "I keep telling people that it isn't my fault."

"It might not be your fault, but I'm beginning to wonder if you weren't implanted with a rescue magnet."

"But you love that about me, right?"

Henry reached across and wrapped his arms around her, pulling her against him. "I love everything about you. Now, have you calmed down enough to be able to sleep?"

"I'm almost there," she grinned. "I might need a little more attention from you, though."

"But there are people sleeping right next door," he said in a stage whisper.

"I know how you insulated these walls. And I promise to be quiet."

"You're a bad girl, Polly Giller."

"You said you loved everything about me. Were you lying?"

"Not at all."

CHAPTER FIVE

"Are you awake? Do you smell that?" Henry whispered to Polly the next morning.

"What? Smell what?" She turned over and pulled the sheet over her head. "I don't want to smell anything. Let me sleep."

"Somebody's cooking in your kitchen," he said in a singsong voice. "Don't you think you should find out who?"

"I don't care. I don't have to get up today. Eliseo told me that it was the beginning of my vacation and I didn't need to come to the barn or do anything." Polly growled from beneath the sheet. "Why won't anyone ever let me just sleep in?"

Henry peeled the sheet back and grinned down at her. "You're the one who invited your girlfriends to stay here rather than rent them a room in Boone."

When he leaned over to kiss her, Polly licked his lips instead. "It's not my fault the inspectors haven't sent the certification for the rooms over at Sycamore Inn." She pulled the sheet back over her head and whined, "I just want to sleep in one morning. Just one morning." Then she sat up. "You and Nate aren't going to let us sleep late this week either, are you? You're going to make me get up early every morning so we can drive somewhere else."

"There's no air conditioning in the T-bird, honey. You'll want to get up early. We'll get off the road and into an air conditioned hotel room every afternoon before you turn into a beast."

"Why didn't we just go to a resort in Cancun or something?" Polly felt a full-blown whine coming on.

"I offered. You told me you'd be bored on a beach. This was your idea."

"Hmph," she groaned and swung her legs to the side of the bed. "It's your job to tell me when I have bad ideas. You're supposed to love me that much."

Obiwan jumped to the floor, wagging his tail and the cats followed suit.

"I love you more than that," Henry said, laughing. "I love you enough to save my own skin."

Polly tossed her pillow at him and stood up, then put her robe on. "Do I look presentable enough?" she asked.

"You're my pretty Polly, no matter what you look like."

"That's not the right answer, but thank you. Can I go out there looking like this?"

"Yes. You're fine. A little messy, but you did just wake up and it is still early. I'll take the dog outside. You go find out who's making good smells in the kitchen."

Polly opened the door of the bedroom and both cats skittered out. "I'll feed them while you take the dog out. And thanks," she said, pulling the door closed.

Padding across the living room to the kitchen, she realized Henry was right. Something smelled wonderful.

"Good morn ..." Polly stopped in surprise. Bunny was standing at the sink, washing dishes by hand. "What are you doing?" Polly asked.

"Making breakfast. I figured I owed you all something since I was such a ninny yesterday." Bunny dried her hands on a towel she'd tucked into the belt of her pants, crossed the room, and drew Polly into a hug. "I'm so sorry. Everything was making me jealous and you know how I can be. I promise to be good for the rest of the weekend. I didn't come all the way out here to act like a whiny crybaby. Will you forgive me?"

"Of course. Already done. What are you making? It smells wonderful."

"I didn't know how to get to the grocery store, so I rummaged around in your refrigerator and cupboards. Is that okay?"

"For smells like this, you can do anything you want." Polly followed her back into the kitchen and opened the cupboard door to get cat food. "I didn't know I had enough food to make anything that smells this good. What did you come up with?"

"You had bacon and sausage in the freezer and plenty of eggs and cheese. Can it be a little surprise?" Bunny giggled a little.

"Absolutely. But that is your sausage gravy in the pan, right?"

"You're going to love it."

"Oh, Bunny, you've always been the best cook of all of us. Someday you're going to find a man who loves you and treats you right."

"I know. I'm just tired of being a bridesmaid. Then I come out here and you don't even need me to do that."

"I'm sorry, sweetie. I really am. But I couldn't not marry Henry. You know that, right?"

"I do. And I'm really not complaining. I promise."

"How long until breakfast is ready?"

Bunny looked at the timer on the stove. "Just a few more minutes."

"Let me start the coffee and I'll knock on Drea's door to see if she wants to get up this early."

"These will wait, too. Don't hurry anyone."

Polly wasn't sure what had happened to her friend overnight, but she was grateful for the change in attitude. She went back across the hall and knocked on Drea's door and said quietly, "Are you up yet? Bunny made breakfast."

Drea opened the door, dressed in a pair of hot pink pajamas with her hair bundled on top of her head. "Bunny?"

"She's acting almost human this morning," Polly whispered. "I'm encouraging it."

"I'm going to the bathroom and then I'll be ready to eat. Really?"

"I know!"

They walked back across the living room laughing. Drea gave a little wave to Bunny, who was setting plates out on the dining room table. She escaped into the bathroom as Obiwan came tearing in the front door. He pulled up short when he saw Bunny moving around, then turned and looked at Polly.

"I know, bud," she said. "It's breakfast. I think there's room for you though." The cats had retreated into the office and were perched on their ledges, keeping an eye on the activity both inside and out.

Henry strode in and took in the situation. "It smells wonderful. Miss Bunny, did you get up early and make breakfast?"

She giggled again, "Yes I did. I thought it was fair payment."

"Can I help with anything?" he asked.

Polly stepped over Obiwan to get his food and fill his bowl. When she was finished, she handed the coffee pot to Henry. "Bunny, you still don't drink coffee, do you?"

The girl looked at her in shock. "Not that horrible stuff. I can't bear it. I'll be fine with juice. I made a fresh pitcher. It's in the refrigerator." She reached into the oven and took out a pan of round balls of dough, then scooped them into a basket she'd lined with a dish towel.

When everything was on the table and they were all seated, she said, "These are breakfast biscuit drops. They're filled with bacon, scrambled eggs and cheese. And this is my specialty." She pointed at a steaming bowl of sausage gravy." They waited a moment, staring at her until she said, "Eat up!" and passed the basket of biscuits around.

Henry ladled gravy over his biscuits and then put his finger in it to taste it. "This is like yours, Polly."

"She taught me," Polly said. "Bunny was always the cook."

"It's nothing," Bunny said. "I love blending flavors ..." she glanced down at her outfit, a hot pink t-shirt under a floral blouse and a pair of turquoise shorts. It all seemed to work well together.

"And colors, too, I guess."

When they finished eating, Polly picked up plates to take them to the kitchen and Bunny stopped her, "No. I'll take care of it."

"But you cooked," Polly protested.

Drea stood and said, "Bunny and I will clean up. You two get ready. Today is all about you."

Henry and Polly looked at each other and put their plates back on the table. "Thank you." She walked around the table and bent over to hug Bunny from the back. "I'm so glad you came out to Bellingwood and I'm sorry I was so hard on you last night."

"I deserved it. I was being selfish," Bunny said. "But I'm going to try to be better for the rest of the weekend. I promise."

When they got back in their bedroom, Henry sat down in a chair. "Well, wouldn't it be nice if a good talking-to would fix everyone!"

"No kidding," Polly said, laughing. "But trust me, it didn't fix her. It just slowed her down. She won't be able to help herself and before the weekend is over, I'll be glad to see her get on a plane and fly out of here. I love her, I really do. She acts like a brat, apologizes and does something wonderful like this, then acts like a normal human being until she just can't stand it any longer."

"Well, it was still nice to see her try this morning."

"And I shouldn't be so hard on her. I do love her."

She sat down beside him. "So, who's taking the first shower?"

"We could ..." he looked at her and grinned.

"No. Not with my friends out there."

"They'll understand," he pleaded. "We're celebrating our wedding today."

Polly laughed at him. "You go ahead, you nut. I'll find something to keep me occupied."

With a big sigh, Henry stood up and slowly loped across the floor. He got to the hallway leading to the bathroom and turned back to give her a last, sad-faced look. "You're sure?"

"I'm sure," she said, laughing. "Now get moving!"

He smiled back and went on in to the bathroom. She heard the water turn on and reached down to pat Obiwan's head. "It's nice having him live here with us, isn't it, Obiwan?" The dog's tail thumped as he wagged it back and forth.

Polly sat down at the secretary. She unplugged her phone and swiped it open, wondering what might have happened overnight.

There was a text message from Anita Banks, the young woman who worked in the Sheriff's office. She was an amazing whiz with computers and Polly had tried to set her up with one of the young men living in the apartment over the garage - Doug Randall. There had yet to be a productive date between the two of them and the last time Polly tried to pin Doug down as to what was going on, he brushed her off and changed the subject. She wished she knew what was happening. Oh well, none of her business.

Good morning, Polly. Give me a call sometime this morning if you could. I have some information for you. I'm working in the office today but I can't wait to see you tonight.

Polly made the call.

"Hi Polly," Anita said.

"Good morning, what's up?"

"The Sheriff told me I should call you about Dennis Smith."

"You have something already?"

"I think so. There are a bunch of Dennis Smiths in Iowa, but after doing some digging, I found one that is the right age. He lives in Oelwein. I talked to a friend over there and this guy was living in Colorado for a while and came back a few months ago, but she wasn't sure whether or not he had a woman with him."

"What do you think I should do about this?" Polly asked.

"If it were me, I might call him first. And all of this information is available on the internet. You could have found it, maybe paid something for the search. Just call and ask if the girl is there."

"I suppose that wouldn't hurt," Polly said. "If he doesn't know who she is, he'll tell me."

"Exactly. Unless he's done something wrong, I don't think you want to get the police involved yet. I'm glad to help you get this far, but ..."

"I get it. No problem. This is awesome." Polly checked the time, it was only eight thirty. "I think I'll wake him up."

"On a Saturday morning? You probably will unless he's working."

"You don't have that information, do you?"

Anita chuckled. "I do. He works at an auto parts store." She gave Polly the name and number of the shop and they hung up.

Polly entered the home phone number in her telephone and hovered over the screen, trying to decide if this was the right thing to do. She could just give the information to Curt Locke and let him deal with it, but it would be horrible if he screwed it up in his panic to find his daughter. She swiped the phone and took a breath. All she could do was try.

The phone rang three times and a groggy voice answered, "Hello?"

"Is this Dennis Smith?"

"Yea, who's this?"

"My name is Polly Giller. I'm looking for Jessie Locke. Is she there?"

"Why do you want to know?" He was starting to wake up and got defensive.

"Could I speak with Jessie?"

"No."

All of a sudden, Polly was listening to dead air. He'd hung up.

"Well, damn," she said out loud.

"What's damn?" Henry asked. She turned her head and looked at him. He was so handsome. She smiled. He wasn't drop-your-jaw gorgeous like Mark Ogden, but he'd definitely do. His shoulders and upper body were well-defined from working construction all day long and even though his arms and face were much darker than the rest of him, he made her heart beat a little faster when he took off his clothes.

"Damn, you're a good looking man," she said.

"Well, thank you!" He did a little pirouette and the towel he'd wrapped around his waist nearly fell off. To ensure his cool factor, he stumbled at the end of it and grabbed the towel before it hit the ground.

"Yeah, that's my man," she said. "Suave and debonair."

"I try," he said and tossed the towel back into the bathroom. "So what were you swearing about?"

"I talked to Anita and she gave me a phone number of a Dennis Smith in Oelwein. I called him and he hung up on me."

Henry took a deep breath and then pursed his lips. "You're going to get involved in this, aren't you?"

"Maybe?" She tried a flirty smile and realized it wasn't going to work. He knew her too well.

"What are you going to do next?"

"First I think I'll call him back. Let's see what he does with that."

She re-dialed the number and waited. It went to voice mail. She tried it twice more and the third time he answered.

"What in the hell?" he asked.

"I'm sorry to bother you, but I really am looking for Jessie Locke. Is she there?"

"I told you no. Leave me alone."

"Look, I'm just trying to find this girl and her friend gave me your name." Polly heard movement and then the sound of his footsteps.

"She's not here," he said. His voice sounded muffled as if he were covering the phone with his hand.

"Was she there?"

"She left. I kicked her out. She's gone."

"Gone? Is she still in Oelwein?"

I don't know."

"When did she leave?"

"Last week. She got all weepy about her mama and I told her to get over it. Now leave me alone."

"Wait!" Polly said. "Does she have a phone number or a job in town? Where's she staying?"

"I don't know. I'm not responsible for her."

"Do you have a phone number for her?"

"No. Now get off my phone, bitch."

"Yeah. That's helpful. Do you talk to your mother with that mouth?"

"My mother doesn't ask me too many questions."

He hung up again and Polly put her phone down on the desktop. "Well, now what?"

"What's up?"

"He said that Jessie left and he's not responsible for her."

"More detective work?" he asked.

"I'd better get a shower before I do anything, don't you think?"

"Probably," he said. "Do I need to remind you that you have a party to prepare for?"

"I know, I know," Polly said distractedly as she walked to the bathroom. "I wonder what kind of job Jessie would try to get?"

"Why do I even bother," Henry muttered.

Polly spun around, ran back to him and hugged him, "Because you love me. I'll be out in a minute."

CHAPTER SIX

"Ready!" Polly announced, prancing out of the bathroom wearing nothing but a smile.

Henry stammered and finally got out, "For what?"

"Whatever the day brings."

"I didn't see this coming when I asked you to marry me. I'm the luckiest guy in the world!"

"Darn tootin.' What have you been doing out here?"

"Uh. Uh."

Polly put her hands on his shoulders and turned him so his back was to her. "Now, try to think again."

"Yeah. Okay. Your phone rang. It was Lydia. I answered it."

"That's fine," she said. "What's up?"

"She says you're supposed to stay up here this morning until Joss comes and you aren't supposed to ask questions."

Polly chuckled. "I wonder what they're planning. They weren't happy with me ignoring pre-wedding fun. But it's not like I needed wedding showers or a bachelorette. I'm just not into that."

"Well, apparently when Joss comes to get you, Nate is taking me to my bachelor party."

"At least I don't have to worry about you getting all drunked up for a wedding at this hour on a Saturday."

Henry turned back around and hugged her, sliding his hands down to rest on her hips. "Should I worry about you?"

"With Lydia and Andy in the room? Doubtful!" She butted him with her hip. "Now back off, Mister Handsy. I have to get dressed." Polly ran her hand over the dress she had purchased for the evening. It was a strapless, silk chiffon gown in a beautiful deep sea blue. She could hardly wait to wear it. When it had arrived, she'd run upstairs and tried it on while Henry was out on the jobsite. Polly could hardly believe the wonderful opportunities she had at Sycamore House to wear beautiful gowns.

After listening to Aaron extol the virtues of owning a tuxedo, she and Henry had decided to purchase one for him. This wouldn't be the last time he had cause to wear it. Polly had always known that a well-fitted tuxedo made a man look good, but when Henry came out of the fitting room, good wasn't quite the word she wanted to use to describe him. He looked delicious.

Not knowing what her friends had planned for her this morning, Polly dressed simply in a pair of khaki pants and a fun, purple blouse she'd found. She slipped into a pair of flip flops and then sat down on the bed. "Now what am I supposed to do?" she asked him. "When is all this fun taking place?"

"Joss and Nate will be here at ten. Maybe you should go play with your other girlfriends."

"I'd rather stay in here and play with you, sexy," she said and pulled him to the bed.

He grinned and stood in front of her, then leaned over and cupped his hands around the back of her head and kissed her. "You only married me for my body, didn't you," he said.

"Well, that and your woodworking skills." Polly giggled and snorted. "It's all about the wood." Then she laughed out loud and clapped her hand over her mouth. "I'm terrible!"

It didn't take but a moment, and she was laughing again. "No, I'm not terrible. You men are! Everything is about sex with you, isn't it. You drill and you screw and you hammer and pound."

"You are just putting that together now?" Henry sat beside her and pulled her into his arms. "I love you, my sweet Polly. Sometimes you are completely naive."

"Not naive, just slow," she said. "I can't believe it. I married a carpenter and everything he does is a euphemism for sex."

He shook his head. "Yes. I love you."

"You can't tell anyone that I just put that together today. Promise? Sanctity of the marriage bed and all that?"

"You're going to make me promise to not tell people about this conversation?"

"Please? I'll be so embarrassed if they think I didn't get it before today."

"Okay. I promise. But you have to promise that when you decide to tell it on yourself ..." he looked at her and gave her a scowl. "... and I know that you will, I get to be in the room. Because otherwise, it just wouldn't be fair."

"I promise."

"Polly?" Drea's voice came just before a knock on their door.

"I'll be right there," Polly said.

"No, it's okay. Bunny and I are heading out with Sal. She's here to pick us up. We'll see you in a little bit, okay?"

Polly walked over to the door and opened it. "What's going on?" she asked innocently.

"Don't you be pushing us, missy," Sal said from the front door. "We have big plans."

Drea hugged her. "We'll see you soon." She looked Polly up and down. "And you look great!"

"Thanks. I'll see you later." Polly watched them leave and then went out into the living room. "We're all alone again," she said to Henry. Now what should we do?"

He came out and looked around. "It's really quiet in here. And that seems weird."

"They've only been here for a day."

"But there's always something going on. Between the kids and our friends and Doug and Billy and Rachel, it doesn't stay quiet very long."

"Maybe that's what we should do for our honeymoon. Lock the doors and not let anyone in. We can just enjoy the quiet."

"We're going to the Grand Canyon, Polly. Stop trying to talk me out of this. You'll have a great time."

"I know. I know. It's just that I'm going to miss everyone and I'll miss Obiwan and the cats and all of the animals at the barn and I'll have to sleep in strange beds and ride in a car all day and be around strange people ..."

Before she could go any further, he said, "But you'll be with me. Surely I'm enough."

"Well of course you are. I'm just being a whiny butt. I've never been much of a traveler. I still can't believe I moved to Boston to go to school."

"I can't either," he said. "But at least it got you to Bellingwood."

"I suppose. But now that I'm here, I really don't want to go anywhere."

"I've waited my whole life to have someone travel with me. You're going. Even if I have to buy you a camper so you can take all of your animals and your stuff with us."

Polly swatted his arm. "Now you're just being silly."

"Am I?"

"Maybe we should have rented one for this trip. Do you think we can pull that off?"

He looked at her in shock. "Are you kidding me? We're leaving Monday morning and now you decide that you want to rent a camper? Tell me you're kidding."

"Only kind of. I don't really want to stay in campgrounds. I want to stay in motels. I just want to take everything and everybody with us."

Henry put both of his hands on his head. "I love you more than life itself, Polly Giller, but sometimes you give me a headache."

"I know. It's just pre-trip jitters. I get like this every time I go somewhere. I'll be fine and we'll have a great time. I promise. We just have to get me on the road."

"Okay. Then I won't worry. But this isn't the last conversation we're having about the trip, is it?"

"Nope." She grinned and started walking to their front door.

"What are you doing?" he asked.

"Look at the dog," she said. "Someone's coming up the steps."

Obiwan had gotten up and walked to the door, wagging his tail. By the time she got there, a quick rap was heard.

Polly opened the door to Joss and Nate.

"Come on in." Polly stepped back and gestured to the room.

"We're here a little early," Joss said. "We've got some bad ..."

Nate interjected, "...and good ..."

She grinned at him and finished the sentence, "news."

"What's up?" Polly asked.

"Well, we can't go to Arizona with you. We have to cancel our side of the plans."

"Why?" Polly's heart sank. Something was wrong.

It must have shown on her face because Joss placed her hand on Polly's forearm. "No, that's the good news. We're getting a baby this week!"

"You are!" Polly pulled Joss into a hug. "I'm so excited. What day? Where? What's going on? Do you know if it's a girl or a boy? When did you find out?"

Joss took Polly's hand and led her to the sofa, while Henry strode across the room to Nate, "Congratulations, man. I know you've been ready for this."

"We really have," Nate said. He puffed out his chest. "I'm gonna be a dad."

"Tell me everything. Don't leave anything out," Polly said. "When did you get the call?"

"They called this morning." Joss looked up at her husband and her eyes glistened. "I can't believe it's going to happen. I couldn't let myself think about it. I had to prepare, but I couldn't believe it." She started to cry and Polly reached out and took her hand.

Henry looked around desperately, found the box of tissues and dropped them on the table in front of the two girls. Joss sniffled and used a tissue to wipe away the tears.

"We've got time. You two sit down," she said, pointing at the chairs.

Being the obedient men that they were (Polly smiled to herself realizing how easily they fell apart with a few tears), they sat exactly where Joss had pointed.

"I'm fine." Joss took another tissue and clutched it in her hand. "They called this morning. There was a couple who planned to adopt a baby that was due this week, but something happened and they backed out. So we got the call. It could be any day."

"Where do you have to go?" Polly asked. "Is it close?"

"We're going to Omaha. And since we've already taken vacation for this week, we don't have to worry about our work schedules."

"Do you know if it's a boy or a girl?"

Nate smiled and said, "We told them we didn't care. I think they know, but we want to be surprised."

"Are your parents coming out?" Polly turned to Henry. "This is a lousy time to leave Bellingwood. I keep telling you."

He laughed and said, "I knew we weren't done with that conversation."

Joss put her hand on Polly's knee. "You can't cancel your honeymoon. Nate and I feel bad enough that we aren't going. We aren't even sure when the baby is going to get here. The case worker says she is due tomorrow, but you just never know."

"Are you going to meet the mom?"

"She doesn't want anything to do with us, so no. It sounds like she just wants this to be over."

"I can't believe that I won't be here for you," Polly said.

"You'll be back in two weeks. Nate and I will have time to get comfortable with a baby in the house. Our parents will come out and make a big fuss and then when you get back, you can come calm me down. It's really going to be okay."

Polly stood up. "Well, then I have to give you this before I leave. Because that baby won't stay little very long." She went back into their bedroom and came out with a wrapped gift and handed it to Joss. "It's really silly."

"Polly, you and Lydia already threw me a baby shower and gave us a bouncy seat. You didn't have to get anything else."

"Really. It's silly. But I want a picture," Polly said, laughing. "Go ahead. Open it."

Joss opened the small package and laughed as she pulled out two onesies with the Sycamore House logo on the front. "You're right. This is totally silly. But we will take a picture of the baby in one of these right away. Be watching for the announcement of our new family member. Thank you, Polly."

"I can't wait to meet your new little one," Polly said. "I'm disappointed that I won't be here when you come home." She heard Henry take a loud breath. "I know, I know. We'll be having fun."

Joss looked at her watch. "It's time to go! Today is your day. I just needed to tell you before everything got going."

"I'm so excited for you." Polly hugged her again. "Can we tell people or not?"

"Let's not do that today," Joss said. "I wanted you to know why we weren't going to travel with you, but we're supposed to celebrate your marriage today and I'm still feeling a little leery that it won't actually happen."

Polly stood up again. "It's going to be great. I just know it." She walked over and took Henry's hand. "I hope you have fun today. Be good, okay?"

Nate stood up beside his wife. "We aren't going to get in too much trouble and we'll be back in plenty of time to get him dressed for the evening."

Henry glanced at Nate, curiosity in his eyes. "Aren't we going to help set up the auditorium?"

"Oh right!" Nate clapped Henry on the back, laughing loudly. "I guess we'd better get moving then."

The four went down the steps and Henry and Nate left by the front door. When Polly tried to follow them, Joss stopped her. "Nope. We're not going that way. Come with me."

She opened the door to the auditorium and stepped in. Tables toward the front of the room were filled with women she'd come to know since moving to Bellingwood and hot pink seemed to be the color of the event. There were pink and white balloons and hot pink cloths on the tables. A fountain was flowing with pink liquid and cupcakes were decorated with pink and purple frosting. A bright purple drape covered a pile of something on a table off to the side and Polly wasn't surprised to see her closest friends dressed in pink and purple.

"We had to have it here so Sarah and Rebecca could be part of things. And there were so many women who wanted to come, we needed a large space," Joss whispered.

"I can't believe that I put this blouse on," Polly said. "I match."

Joss grinned. "Everyone in town remembers your purple undies." She unbuttoned the black tunic she was wearing to reveal a purple t-shirt. "We had to do this one more time for you."

Lydia was waving madly from the front of the room. "Here's our girl!" she said. "Come on in, Polly. We've been waiting."

A smattering of applause greeted Polly as she and Joss walked to the front. "I'm a little embarrassed," she said. "I wasn't expecting a party."

"Well, of course you weren't," Beryl said. "But it's what we do."

Polly looked around the room and smiled at people she'd grown to know so well. It felt as if she'd always known these women. They were entwined in her daily life and some had become close friends. They'd each shown up at different times, but the connections were strong.

"Where's Sylvie?" she asked, looking around again.

"In the kitchen," Lydia said. "She'll be here in a minute." She raised her voice. "This morning we're not going to subject Polly to any games. If you know her at all, you know that she'd hate that. There are a few things we want to share with her and then we'll have a relaxed brunch together. Help yourself to the champagne punch or coffee and we'll get started."

Some of the women already had glasses of the pink punch at their tables and the noise level in the room rose as the women milled around, drinking champagne and chatting with each other.

Rebecca ran up and hugged Polly. "Mom said I could come today but I can't have any punch."

"No," Polly said, smiling down. "No champagne for you. But I wonder if Sylvie has some punch in the kitchen without champagne. Would you like that?"

"Yes, please! Mom would like some of that, too, I think. She's just drinking water."

"Let's see what we can find." Polly took Rebecca's hand and headed for the door to the kitchen, waving at Lydia and Andy. "We're going to get some virgin punch."

Sylvie, Hannah and Rachel were scurrying around in the kitchen when Polly and Rebecca got to the window.

"You three shouldn't be working this hard," Polly said.

Sylvie looked up. "Of course we should. We're almost ready. Do you need something?"

"Rebecca and I were wondering if there was any punch without champagne in it. She'd like a glass and I think Sarah would, too."

"Certainly." Sylvie stopped in her tracks. "We should have thought of that. I have a pitcher right here in the refrigerator, all mixed up. Others might want some. I'm so sorry."

"No problem! We've got this." Polly carried the pitcher back in, passing Bunny, Drea and Sal. "What are you three doing?" she asked.

Sal smiled. "We're the waitresses."

"What? I didn't ask you to come out here to do that?" Polly was stricken.

"Stop it," Sal said. "We've been talking to Lydia for the last month and this was part of the plan. Just quit worrying about it and enjoy your day. We're here to help you have fun, not the other way around. Now go. Have fun."

Polly shook her head and took the pitcher over to the table filled with drinks and poured a cup for Rebecca. "Oh," she said. "And one for your mom." She poured another and put the pitcher down. Rebecca took the two cups back to the table and Sarah smiled over at Polly.

"Ladies," Lydia called out. "We want to get this part out of the way so you can enjoy your food. The girls are going to begin by bringing around breads and muffins. The main dish will be out in a bit."

Polly watched helplessly as Sal, Drea and Bunny; Sylvie, Hannah and Rachel carried in baskets and placed them on the tables. She would have hired someone so her friends could just relax, but Sal told her to back off, so she said nothing.

"While you are enjoying yourselves, Polly would you come here please?"

Polly smiled weakly and went up to stand beside Lydia.

"We know you didn't want a wedding shower and you didn't get a bachelorette party. You also said you don't want a lot of wedding gifts, so all of us in this room have come up with some things that we hope you enjoy."

Lydia nodded to Beryl, who handed her a purple gift bag. "We bought this for you. Beryl always threatened to take you to Victoria's Secret if those purple panties were your idea of fancy." Lydia drew out a purple teddy and Polly felt her face flush bright red. "Since you and Henry are leaving on Monday for your honeymoon, be sure to pack this."

Polly's mouth opened and closed a couple of times, then she just ducked her head and shook it in disbelief.

"The next thing is something we've been searching for. Helen Randall had to ask Doug for help. He called us old ladies and insinuated we should have been able to find it on our own. But he was a good boy and hooked us up."

Andy handed Polly a wrapped package. "Go ahead. Open it. We're all dying to see it."

She held it while Polly ripped the paper off, revealing a Star Wars R2D2 droid robot.

"Are you kidding?" Polly asked. "Does this really work?"

"All of the reviews say so. We thought this would be more fun than kitchen kitsch," Lydia said.

Polly laughed. "This is perfect! What fun!" She put it down on the table in front of her.

Helen Randall grinned and said. "Doug put batteries in it, so it's ready to go."

"Send it around and let everyone look at it," Polly said, and she spoke up, "Thank you all. These are really fun gifts. This isn't like any wedding shower I've ever been to and I like it so much better."

"We're not done," Lydia said. "That table back there is filled with gifts for you."

"Oh no, you shouldn't have."

"Ladies?" Lydia nodded at Andy and Beryl.

They lifted the cloth and revealed a table filled with books.

"What is this?" Polly asked.

"Since you didn't want gifts, we talked to Joss and decided that we are going to become friends of the library. All of these books were on a wish list that she created. Everyone here bought a couple of books and we are donating them to the library in your name. I hope that's okay."

Polly started shaking and her eyes filled with tears. "This is perfect. I couldn't have asked for a better gift. All of you?" She looked around the room and the women were nodding.

"Andy's in charge of organizing us and we're going to work with the Library board to raise money for some of the big repairs that need to happen in the building. Joss is ready to put us to work."

"Wow." Polly looked for her friend. Joss was beaming. She had so much to be happy for today. This was perfect.

"Thank you, everyone." Polly put her hand on a pile of books. "These are perfect gifts. Thank you all for coming today."

Lydia glanced back at the kitchen door and then said, "That's all the business we have. I think it's time to eat. They're ready for you in the kitchen. Shall we let Polly go first?"

Polly shook her head. "No, I'll go last. I can wait." She whispered to Lydia. "I had a big breakfast. Y'all are killing me."

Lydia took her arm and drew her aside. "I know you didn't want your girlfriends to work, but they weren't looking forward to making small talk with a bunch of people they didn't know. I tried to stop this, but no one was having it."

"I can't believe they're not just relaxing."

"They didn't want you to feel like you had to entertain them. You have a lot going on this weekend."

"But they're here to see me, not stand around in a kitchen."

"I tried."

"They're impossible. You all are. But I love the R2D2 droid. I've wanted one of those for years, but at some point I thought I'd gotten too old."

While the women were filing out of the room to go through the line at the kitchen, sirens wailed as they came into the parking lot of Sycamore House. Polly was already moving when she heard them stop at her front door.

CHAPTER SEVEN

Eliseo was holding the side doors open when Polly reached the front hallway. Two EMTs and Jeff came in the front door and headed that way.

"What happened?" she asked. "Who's hurt?"

Jeff pointed the EMTs to the addition. "Take the elevator to the second floor. He's in the first room. The door is open."

"Curtis Locke? What happened?" Polly asked.

Jeff moved toward her. "I think it's a heart attack. He called my cell phone and said he was feeling sick. He just wanted to know if he could get some soda. After a few questions, I knew I needed to come over. When I got here, I called for more help."

"You came in from Ames to deal with this?"

Jeff glared at her. "I was with your husband. Remember? Wedding fun?"

Lydia put her hand on Polly's shoulder. "I'm going to tell the girls what's happening and keep them contained. We don't need to be out here making a scene. Come back when you're finished."

Polly nodded and followed Jeff toward the addition. "Thank you for coming right over. How would we have ever known?"

"He probably could have made it downstairs, but somehow I believe that having him bust into the auditorium clutching his heart might have been a little more dramatic than you needed."

She swatted him. "You're awful."

"I know. I made Nate come. He's the only one of us who has any medical training and even though he thought I was insane, he came anyway. He's still upstairs with him."

"Thank you again. I'd feel terrible if something happened to the poor man. Where are you guys partying anyway?" She finally took a good look at him. He was a mess. His clothes were always immaculate, but today he was dressed in an old t-shirt and jeans and there was paint splattered on his face and forearms.

"What in the world have you been doing?" she asked.

"I've never been to a bachelor party quite like this one." He looked up as the EMTs came through with Curtis Locke on a gurney. Nate was following them, looking just as messy as Jeff.

The man on the gurney reached out for Polly as they wheeled him past and she walked with them toward the front door. He grabbed her arm, "Find my little girl, please. Don't let me die without knowing she's safe."

"Do we have your wife's phone number?" Polly asked him.

"Just find my Jessie. You have to find her."

"I have a few ideas where to look. I will do my very best. Can we call your wife?"

He nodded and the young man pushing the gurney said, "We have to go. We're taking him to Boone."

"Find Jessie," Curt Locke said one last time.

"Tell me you have his wife's phone number," Polly said to Jeff as the door closed behind the EMTs.

"Sure, it's in his file. Do you want me to call her or will you?"

"I'll make the call. It's my responsibility. But before I do, will the two of you tell me what you are putting Henry through this morning? You look like you've been painting. Are you really making that poor man do construction at his bachelor party?"

"Trust me, he's not doing anything today," Nate said. "We're doing all the work."

"What do you mean? What are you doing?"

"Wanna see?" Nate asked.

"Of course I do."

Nate took out his phone and swiped it open and then handed it to her with the photo gallery open. The first picture she saw was Henry sitting in a chaise lounge with two blow-up palm trees behind him and a large umbrella over his head. He was wearing a Hawaiian shirt and a pair of shorts and was drinking something pink with an umbrella in it."

"This is hilarious," she said. "What's going on?"

"Keep scrolling through the pictures. The story is all there."

As she went through the pictures, she realized that they were at the library. "Today has a theme, doesn't it?"

"Yep. Since you girls are raising money and buying books, it fell to us to do the dirty work. We're repainting the outside trim today. But keep going."

Polly scrolled to another picture and realized that Henry's mother and another woman were in moo-moos and his sister was in a grass skirt. They were serving drinks to Henry from a homemade Tiki bar.

"You chose to work rather than have a bachelor party?"

"What else were we going to do on a Saturday morning? And the poor man is already married, so it's not like wants to get himself in trouble." Nate grinned and took his phone back. "A few of us have been talking about working at the library anyway. We thought it would be fun to make our favorite construction guy sit on his tail while the rest of us worked. His mom and sister got in on the planning and came up with the Hawaiian theme."

"I wondered why they weren't here," Polly interrupted.

"Yeah. They were worried you might be upset, but figured that once you knew what was going on, you'd laugh."

"We should probably get going," Jeff said. "We promised to pick lunch up on the way."

"Where's the phone number for Curt Locke's wife?" Polly asked.

"Oh, right. Sorry." Jeff motioned for her to follow him into the office and he flipped through some papers on the desk that Sarah was using in the main office. "It's on the computer, but I'm not going to ask you to figure out the system today."

"You know I'm not a tech moron," Polly complained. "I can learn that."

"But you don't want to, so you're just as bad."

"Whatever. Just give me the number."

He handed her a printout of the room information they had for Curtis Locke. "Let me know if they're staying here. If I need to find another room, I can."

"Thanks Jeff. What time are you all coming back?"

"Most of the setup crews will be here by three."

She watched them leave, and called the number on the sheet of paper in front of her.

It rang a couple of times and a young man's voice answered. "Locke residence," he said.

"Hello. Is Mrs. Locke available?" Polly asked.

"She's outside. Who should I say is calling?"

"Tell her this is Polly Giller in Iowa."

"Just a minute."

Polly heard silence then, "Mom! Some lady from Iowa is calling. Mom!"

It took a few more moments before, "Hello, this is Kelly Locke, who is this?"

"Mrs. Locke, this is Polly Giller from Bellingwood, Iowa. Your husband is staying with us here at Sycamore House ..."

"Is something wrong? Is he okay? What's happened?"

"Mrs. Locke, we think your husband has had a heart attack. He's on the way to the hospital in Boone. I'm so sorry to have to call you with this."

"No!" the woman responded, her voice rising. "What am I supposed to do? I can't come out there. I don't have a place to stay and I have my son. Is it bad? Was he alive when they took him?"

Polly waited as the woman sobbed on the other end of the call. "Your husband is in good hands. The doctors will take care of him. He was talking to me before they left in the ambulance."

"Thank goodness." She held the phone away from her mouth and yelled. "Ethan, turn that music off. I need quiet to think. Your dad had a heart attack in Iowa. Please stop!"

Then the call went dead. Polly looked at her phone. Yep, the call had been ended.

It rang again and Polly answered it.

"I'm sorry," Kelly Locke said. "I must have disconnected us. I'm not sure what to do. I have to be at work on Monday. I told him not to go after that girl. She'll find her way back when she's ready. And now this. Tell me where this hospital is?"

"It's in Boone. I can find a phone number for you."

"No, that's fine. I'll find it myself. You're the one helping him find Jessie, right?"

"Yes, ma'am."

"He said you were the daughter of a college buddy of his. It's nice of you to help him. I told him there were a lot of people in Iowa and he might not have any luck. But he said you put him in touch with a deputy."

"Yes, and this morning I did find the young man that she came out here with, but I haven't had a chance to tell your husband yet."

"Have you talked to Jessie?"

"He says she's not there any longer."

"She left him? That girl isn't going to be happy anywhere. Well, I hope she figures this out."

"It sounded like she was going to try to get a job somewhere. Can you tell me what kind of jobs she's had before? That might make it easier for us to figure out where she's gone."

"I don't know. She didn't have a lot of gumption, so she only got menial jobs. Why wouldn't she call us?"

"If you'd like me to put you in touch with the Boone County Sheriff's Department, they can help you work through this, Mrs. Locke. And I'd be glad to make some more calls, but I'd really like to have some idea where to start."

"I understand that. Let me make some decisions here and I will be in contact with you later on today."

"Your husband's room here at Sycamore House is still open. If you want to stay here, you're more than welcome to do that or there are a couple of hotels down in Boone."

"Thank you, Miss Giller."

"It's Polly. Call any time. Let me know what else we can do for you. Goodbye."

After the call was finished, Polly went into her office and sat down at her desk. The day was already out of control. It wasn't even noon and she was ready to hide. She opened her computer and searched for malls in Waterloo and Cedar Falls. Maybe Jessie had been able to get a job at one of the shops there. It wouldn't hurt anyone if she made a couple of quick phone calls. She opened the directories and beginning with what she thought was probably the largest mall, Crossroads Center, calling one shop after another, asking for Jessie Locke. Twenty minutes passed and no one gave her a positive response.

"Polly?" Drea stood in her office doorway.

"I forgot!" Polly exclaimed. "I'm so sorry. I got wrapped up in something and completely forgot that I was supposed to be somewhere."

"What are you working on?" Drea sat down in front of Polly's desk.

"I'm calling stores in Waterloo, looking for that guy's daughter. He left here in an ambulance and I feel awful, knowing that she's all alone."

"How old is she?"

"I think he said she was nineteen. Old enough to know better, but still young enough to make stupid decisions."

"You don't think she'd make really stupid decisions like prostitution or drugs, do you?"

Polly shrugged her shoulders. "I don't know what to think. I don't know these people at all. This guy was a friend of my dad's from college."

Drea looked at her in confusion.

"I know. He must have married a much younger woman. It sounds like it took him a long time to get his life back together after Viet Nam. But now he's had a heart attack and his wife has a job and a kid at home and she doesn't know whether to come out here or not and ..."

"And you are supposed to be celebrating this weekend, not taking on the cares of the world."

"But he has no one else and Dad would have helped."

"You're right, but come on back to the party. Here's the deal. I promise that this afternoon, you can put all of us on the phones and we'll call every store in Waterloo or wherever it is and try to find this girl. If we help, then will you try to relax about it?"

Polly grinned across the desk at her friend. "Do or do not, there is no try."

"Then Yoda, you will relax about it because we are helping. Come on, let's get back to the party. There are a lot of ladies in there that I don't know and pretty soon Bunny is going to lose control."

"What do you mean?" Polly stood up, laughing.

"She's going to start begging them all to find her a husband. It will be embarrassing. She already cornered a couple of them and asked if they were bringing their sons to the party tonight."

Polly grabbed Drea's arm as she went past her. "Oh, for pity's sake, let's hurry, then. Bunny on the loose is dangerous for Bellingwood."

CHAPTER EIGHT

"Friends are the best," Polly said, a little sloppily. She took a drink of the wine Sal put on the table in front of her. They were in her apartment again, laughing as Sal regaled them with tales of her mother's latest attempts to find her an appropriate husband. Bunny had tried to interrupt a couple of times, asking why Sal wouldn't pass off the rejects to her, but Polly scowled at her and she finally got into the spirit of things.

They'd finished brunch and once the guests had left, quickly set up for the evening's festivities. Polly and Henry insisted that it be simple. The most important part of the weekend was time with friends. Off-white muslin tablecloths with squares of dark blue layered across the top, set the color and tone for the evening. Candles placed in the mason jars she had purchased for last year's hoedown were set on mirrored glass in the center of each table. It had nearly killed Jeff to leave it so sparse, but Henry backed her up. They hired a band for dancing and Sylvie was cooking dinner. She was thankful her husband didn't have extravagant taste. It was one thing to create lavish parties for Sycamore House, but for the two of them, simple was much more appropriate.

Once the setup was complete, Lydia, Beryl, Andy and Joss joined them in the conference room and office. All eight of them spent two hours calling retail stores in the Waterloo / Cedar Falls area looking for Jessie Locke. They had no luck, but left the Sycamore House phone number with as many people as would take it. Polly had hoped that they might stumble across the girl. Watching Curtis Locke's pleading eyes as he left with the EMTs had been tough.

She was so thankful that she and her father had always said the words, "I love you," before ending any phone call. Polly was crushed when he died, but at least she didn't feel guilt over unspoken love. In the darkest nights when she was all alone, tears still fell when Polly thought about how much she missed her dad and how she wished he was here to be part of this crazy life she'd created. He would have enjoyed every single thing at Sycamore House, from the gardens to the animals, the rebuilding to the people. Oh, how she wished he could have known Henry.

Henry came home after she and the girls had gotten comfortable. He was still wearing his Hawaiian shirt and shorts and plopped two blown up palm trees just inside the front door. "Just in case you want to have a luau," he said and headed for his office. Polly was just drunk enough to be silly.

"He's pretty hot, isn't he?" she asked. "I'd do him in a second."

Drea started chuckling and took the wine glass from Polly's hand. "You might have had a little too much today. You need to pace yourself, there's a long night ahead of you."

Polly bared her teeth, growled, and snatched the glass back. "I am pacing myself." She stood up and her legs felt wobbly, so she handed the glass back to Drea. "Okay, you're right. You're always right. But, I'm going to go pat his butt. I've missed it today."

The three laughed as she went through to his office. He was sitting on the edge of his desk with the phone to his ear and tilted his cheek for a kiss. Polly wrapped herself around him and slid her hand under the tail of his shirt, drawing her fingers up his back. Henry looked at her in shock, then mouthed, "What are you doing?"

"This," she whispered and licked his earlobe, drawing her tongue down his jawline.

"I'll see you tonight, Leroy," he said. "Thanks for taking care of this."

He ended the call and put the phone down on his desk, then grabbed Polly's arms. "What in the world are you doing, woman?"

"I might have had too much to drink," she giggled. "I don't think you should let it go to waste."

"Can't we save this for later when everyone is gone?"

"This is the moment, buddy boy. If you wait any longer, I'll just fall asleep." She leaned in and kissed him. "You don't want me to go to sleep, do you?"

"I'm going to have to chance it." He picked her up and turning around, set her bottom on the desk where he'd been seated. "What are your girlfriends going to think?"

"They've seen me drunk before. They know what I'm like."

"Well this is a new one for me. I'm not prepared to do this in the middle of the day with them in our living room."

Polly stuck out her lower lip in a pout. "You're no fun. I think I'll call you a fuddy duddy."

"You can call me anything you want, but you only have a couple of hours until you need to be dressed and downstairs. You should spend this time with the girls who have flown all the way out here from Boston to see you."

Her lower lip pushed back out and she said, "You're trying to get rid of me, aren't you? You don't love me anymore, is that it?"

"Absolutely. You found me out." Henry reached around her and hugged her close. "I love you more every day, Polly Giller. Now go be with your friends and slow down on the wine."

She hopped down and kissed him. "Okay, if you're going to be a fuddy duddy, I'll go away."

"Believe me, I'm getting you drunk on our honeymoon. I want to experience this Polly when no one is around to compete with me."

When she got back to the living room, Sal placed a large glass of ice water in her hands and said, "Drink. All of it. If you're going to keep up tonight without falling asleep on everyone, you need to start flushing this stuff out right now. I didn't realize you were such a lightweight."

"I'm not a lightweight," Polly protested.

"Uh huh. And I'm a Baptist."

Polly had enough presence of mind to put the glass down on the table before she started laughing. Sal Kahane was a very liberal Jewish American Princess from Boston and the farthest thing from religious she could imagine. Drea and Bunny chuckled a little until her infectious, unreserved laughter had them howling with her. The phone ringing on the table beside Polly finally stopped their hilarity.

"Hello?" she said, trying to control the final giggles that threatened to consume her.

"Miss Giller? This is Kelly Locke. My son and I are on the road. We'll be in town late tonight. Should we just go to Boone and get a hotel?"

Polly shook her head, trying to regain some sensibility. "No, come on up to Bellingwood. It's only another twenty minutes. There's a large party going on here at Sycamore House until one o'clock. Will you be here before then?"

"GPS says we should be there about eleven thirty. I shouldn't ask this of you. Don't worry. We'll stay in Boone."

"Don't be silly. Your husband's room is still available and I'll be downstairs when you come in. Just ask anyone you see for Polly Giller and they'll find me."

"Are you certain?"

"Absolutely."

"Thank you. Have you heard anything else about Jessie?"

"I'm sorry. We haven't. We spent time this afternoon calling all of the retail shops in the malls and plazas in the area. No one had heard of her. I'm not sure where to go next, but I'm not giving up."

"Thank you. I'm not used to others knowing our troubles."

Polly smiled. This was what Sycamore House was all about and sometimes she got so caught up in things she forgot why she'd named it for that gorgeous tree in the first place.

"Don't think anything about it. Whatever I can do to help, I will. Drive safely and we'll see you tonight."

"Thank you again."

Polly ended the call and put the phone back down, then picked up the glass of water and took a long drink. When she looked up, her three friends were staring at her.

"It's your wedding party tonight," Sal said.

"So?"

"So, you're getting too involved in someone else's problems. You should be celebrating."

"Her problems don't go away just because I'm having a party. Her husband has had a heart attack and her daughter is missing. Really missing. Do I need to further elaborate?"

Bunny put her wine glass down. "I don't know how you do it, Polly."

"Do what?"

"Make me feel so guilty."

"How did I do that?" Polly looked at the other two and they seemed to be in agreement with Bunny. "What?"

"You're always so nice. None of us would have even taken the time to talk to that guy yesterday, much less invite him to stay in our place and then call hundreds of people. You make me feel like a heel just for living."

"Oh stop it. You all have your things that you do. And if someone needs you, you're right there." She turned on Drea. "When my friends called and told you that Joey had taken me, you dropped everything and brought in your brothers to rescue me. Then you took me home and made sure I felt safe that night."

"But you're my friend. I wouldn't do that for strangers."

"If I called you on Monday and told you that someone I knew was in desperate need of your help, you'd take care of them, wouldn't you? If one of your brothers told you that they had a friend who needed help, you'd take care of them. Right?"

"I suppose."

"I'm not anything special. I just do what I have to do. This woman isn't going to interrupt my party tonight. She's going to show up and I'll ask Jeff or Eliseo to help her find her room. Then tomorrow after I've slept off whatever amount of alcohol I've consumed, I'll see if there's anything else I can do to help her before we get on the road on Monday. I'll show her what I've done and maybe she and her husband can search for their daughter now that she's in Iowa. It's no big deal."

Sal sat down beside Polly, nudging her closer to Drea so that she could have more room. "It is a big deal, Polly. You're a big deal. And we love you." She wrapped an arm around Polly and hugged her. "You're pretty special."

Bunny sat down on the table in front of the three of them and leaned in for a hug. "You are special, Polly. You're the only person in the world who loves me even when you tell me to get over myself. And I still love you even after you do that. Because you're always right."

"Is this some weird pre-wedding party huddle, too much wine, or have I walked into something scary?" Henry asked.

The girls popped apart and Polly gave a startled giggle. "Something scary. What's up?"

"Oh, nothing. I'm going to take a shower so the bathroom is ready for you later."

"Ohhhhh," Polly's three friends moaned as a group.

"He's so sweet," Bunny said. "I wish ..." before she could finish her sentence, she stopped and smiled at Polly. "I wish every man on earth were as wonderful as he is."

"He wouldn't mess around with me a little while ago," Polly said in a stage whisper to her friends. "He's a fuddy-duddy."

"Well, thank goodness!" Drea said. "I know what you're like when you get tipsy." She turned around and looked at Henry, who had turned bright red. "We feel for you. Do you want us to corral her while you shower? She might lose control again."

He shook his head and walked away from them to the bedroom, then turned back to them, unbuttoned the top two buttons of his Hawaiian shirt and spread the lapels apart. "Fuddy-duddy this," he said and turned on his heel before opening the door to go into the bedroom.

"Oooooh," they moaned in unison.

Polly smiled. "You might think that because he's such a good guy, he's boring."

"Apparently not," Bunny said, fanning herself with her hand. "That was a nice looking chest, too."

"All mine," Polly said.

Sal stood and said, "I'd better go back to Mark's so I can get ready. He's not as polite and wonderful as Polly's boy."

"Yeah, but he's gorgeous. He can get away with some of that," Bunny said.

"He is that," Sal acknowledged. She bent over and hugged Polly. "We'll be back before it starts. If you need anything, I'll be around."

"Thanks." Polly stood and followed her to the front door. "Thank you for everything."

"See you tonight."

Sal left and Polly put her hand on one of the plastic palm trees. They were ridiculous. What in the world would she do with them?

"If I time this right, I could take a twenty minute nap before I have to get ready," Drea said. "Bunny, what about you?"

Bunny looked back and forth between the two of them and said, "Oh, I have plenty to do to prepare for tonight. You go on, Polly."

Polly grinned. "I love you two. See you later." She swooped up her glass of water and went into the bedroom. The shower was running, so she sat down at her desk and composed a text to Jeff Lyndsay, telling him about the arrival of Kelly Locke and her son tonight.

CHAPTER NINE

"Oof," Polly moaned, trying to shift her legs while not disturbing the dog or cats. She pried her eyes open and saw that dawn was barely breaking. There was still plenty of time to sleep. Taking a few days off from being at the barn was going to spoil her.

The party last night had been loads of fun. She and Henry ate wedding cake and toasted each other with champagne. They'd danced and spent time with friends and family. A few of Henry's college buddies had shown up out of the blue and she was finally introduced to nearly all of his extended family. They'd come in from all over Iowa. She had no idea there were so many.

Her aunt and uncle hadn't come over for the party and neither had any of their children. Polly wasn't surprised and as a matter of fact, was just as relieved. Spending time trying to make small talk with people who had told her how little they liked her wasn't how she wanted to spend the evening.

Kelly Locke and her sixteen year old son, Ethan, arrived about eleven thirty, completely exhausted. Jeff showed them to their room and they were going to the hospital early this morning to spend time with Curt. From all accounts, he would be fine.

"You're over there thinking again, aren't you?" Henry whispered.

"I'm just enjoying the fact that I don't have to get up."

"I can't believe you don't have a hangover."

Polly chuckled. He didn't know that she'd quit drinking following her afternoon silliness. A glass of champagne for the toast and she'd spent the rest of the evening drinking water. The last thing she ever wanted to do was be drunk at a party she hosted. She'd experienced that once after college and it was awful. Several of her guests had gotten out of control and she'd been too drunk to deal with it. A fight ensued and Polly had done her best, but one friend had gone home furious, another two friends quit speaking to each other after that night and she felt guilty for all of it. From that time forward, she stayed in control unless someone she really trusted was there.

"You had more to drink than I did last night," she said, turning over to face him.

"That's what you think." He kissed her on the nose. "I had one glass of champagne. I wanted to make sure everyone else was having a good time, so I didn't think it was smart to get drunk."

"We're a pair," she said, laughing. "That's exactly what I did."

"One night this week we are going to just have to get totally smashed together. I want to see you all tipsy and frisky again."

"Can you believe that after all this time, we've never gotten drunk together? I guess we're too old for that now."

"We have at least ten more years before we're too old, right?"

"Yep, we're still baby bunnies, innocent and sweet. But it really stinks having to be honorable and reliable all the time."

Henry leaned up and looked down at her. "Were you ever a party animal?"

"I had my days. Sal and I had a lot of fun in college and then there were a few rousing parties after that, but these last few years I've had other things to do." She swatted his hand out from under his head. "I haven't had time since I moved to Bellingwood. And who goes out and gets drunk with the Sheriff's wife? What about you?"

"Well, of course." He wrinkled his forehead at her. "What do you think? That I've always been Saint Henry?"

"It seems like it. The Terrible Trio at the winery look up to you, so that tells me you didn't do a lot of drinking in high school. All of those guys who work for you respect you a lot, so that makes me believe you don't get out of control much these days."

"No. College was my time, and let's just say I'm very lucky to be relatively intelligent. I don't know how I made it out of my freshman year with any grades at all. Fortunately, I didn't damage my grade point so much that I couldn't rescue it the next three years. I learned how to do both after that experience. But that first year, there were some weeks I went to class every day with a hangover." He huffed a chuckle out. "Dad was so mad. I spent the entire summer between freshman and sophomore year working my ass off for him. And it wasn't any of the fun stuff. He had me out in the heat doing the worst jobs he could find. I think every rotten job that he heard about, he took on a low bid so that I had something to do. He never said anything, but I got the message."

"I love him. What did your mom say?"

"Not much. But one night when I came in complaining about all of the work, she told me that I could make the next summer much easier if I made better choices throughout the school year. It was all up to me. Then she handed me a glass of ice water and told me to go upstairs and take a shower. That's when it finally hit me."

"They're pretty terrific parents. And I love your mom's parents. How come I haven't met them before tonight?"

"They travel all over the world. You should see their house. It's filled with things from everywhere. Grammy is kind of a hoarder. She likes to think of it as her collections, but you can't believe what they have in that house. Granddad worked as a broker in Asia for years, so they have some of the coolest things."

"Did I hear her say they were leaving for the UK tomorrow?"

"Yeah. I think so. They have friends in Wales and spend a couple of months there in the summer and then they'll come home in late August before heading to Greece this fall. More friends.

These are a bunch of Granddad's buddies from when they all worked together."

"I had no idea, Henry. What an awesome life. That's so weird though, that you didn't travel a lot when you were young."

"Mom got yanked around a lot when she was young. She hated that life and when she married Dad, they settled."

"But she moved to Arizona rather than staying in Bellingwood. They'll be traveling back and forth a lot."

"I suppose if you look at it that way. But, you'll notice that she left this home exactly as she had created it and the home she has in Arizona is her nest too. Now she has two places to live and both of them make her happy."

"She does seem happy here."

"Honestly, Polly. I haven't seen her like this in years. I think she didn't realize how much her friends and family meant to her. She and Dad were really intent on getting out of here."

"For you, right?"

"I guess so. I thought it was because she hated the winter and Dad wanted to see another part of the country."

"I think she does hate the cold. But it's all worked out the way it was supposed to."

He wrapped his arms around her. "It did."

The sun had been up for a while and Polly turned around to check the time. "We should probably start moving before Drea and Bunny get up."

"Your friend Bunny is going to hurt this morning."

"I wasn't paying attention to her," Polly said. "She was drinking too much?"

"Yeah. Like a fish. Mark had to carry her up the stairs."

"Oh, good heavens, I hope she didn't puke all over the bed. I'll kill her." Polly moaned at the thought. At least Bunny hadn't been so offensive last night that Polly needed to get involved, but there had been at least two hundred people in the room and her antics were the least of Polly's concerns.

"If she did something stupid, we'll take care of it," Henry said and tucked Polly back into the crook his body made. "You should relax. They're leaving later this morning and we'll have the whole afternoon to get ready for our trip tomorrow."

She rubbed his forearm. "You're really looking forward to this, aren't you?"

"I am, but I've been thinking. Since Joss and Nate aren't going, maybe we should take my truck instead. It's going to be miserably hot without air conditioning."

Polly turned over and lay on her back, resting her head on his arm. "Really? That would be a lot more comfortable."

"Sure. It makes sense. Without Nate, I'm a little nervous about taking my baby out on the road for such a long trip. If something happens, I can fix a few things, but I can't fix it all."

"So ..." she said with a grin. "Could we take Obiwan with us if we drive the truck? It's not like we're going to go anywhere that he isn't allowed and he's a good dog."

Henry frowned. "But if we want to go into a nice restaurant, we can't leave him in the truck. It's too hot."

"We don't have to go to nice restaurants. We can do takeout."

"Are you sure?"

"I tell you what. Let's think about it today. If it seems like something we could do, he'd love it. He loves being with us."

"And you'd have part of your world with you. Don't get your heart too set on it, okay? It would be a lot easier without him."

"When have we ever done easy?" She grinned up at him and then leaned forward and kissed his lips. "Now I'm going to get up. You can sleep with these animals as long as you like."

Obiwan jumped off the bed when he realized she was moving and ran to the bedroom door, his tail wagging.

"I know, I know," she said. "You're desperate. Let me get dressed."

Henry sat up and swung his leg over a cat, then sat on the edge of the bed. "I'll put food down for the animals and start coffee. What do you want to make for breakfast?"

"If Bunny is really hung over, she won't want much more than toast. Drea never eats a lot at breakfast. I ate so much last night, I'm still full."

He pushed his belly out and patted it. "Me too," he laughed. "Sylvie is a great cook."

"You nut." Polly laughed and pulled jeans and a t-shirt on, then slid into a pair of old tennies. "I'll be back."

Obiwan followed her through the living room into the old apartment and down the back steps. When they got outside, the sun was doing its best to hold off the clouds that were beginning to build. The forecast had promised rain and it looked like that promise was about to be fulfilled.

"Let's go, bud. I know we won't melt, but I'd just as soon not get soaked." Polly followed the dog to the tree line and then they walked down toward the pasture. The horses weren't out yet.

Obiwan sniffed the fence and looked for his equine friends, but was distracted by something moving through the brush. He took off after it and Polly wandered on. When she heard splashing, she called him back and made her way to the edge of the creek.

He was running through the water chasing a rabbit.

"Obiwan," she snapped. "Come here. You're a filthy mess."

He stopped for just a second, then continued after the rabbit.

"Obiwan!" Her voice got louder and more demanding. "Come."

He was doing everything possible to resist her command, but they'd spent more two years working together and he was programmed to obey. He slowed down, turned and looked at her, pleading for release, but she repeated the command to come and he slunk back down the creek toward her. After he clambered up the bank, she knelt in front of him, telling him what a good boy he was and stroking his head.

"Silly dog," she muttered. "You're a mess, and all for a rabbit you wouldn't eat anyway."

They walked back to Sycamore House and he waited while she grabbed an old towel from a stack she kept at the bottom of the stairs. Soon he was dry enough to go and bounded up the steps. Polly followed, carrying the towel, just in case. Drea and Henry were in the kitchen. He looked up when she entered.

"What's up with the dog?" he asked.

"A rabbit in the creek. He felt the need to give chase."

"You've got a great family here," Drea said. "I'm glad I got a chance to experience it. Ray texted me this morning asking if I approved of Henry."

"Ray's hot," Polly said. "And he likes me. So, you be good to me, hear that?" She sidled up to Henry and slid her arm around his back.

"Hot, huh. Do I need to be jealous?"

"No," Drea said. "I won't have my girlfriends hooking up with those brothers of mine. That would just be wrong."

"Ray and Jon are my knights, though. They're the ones who took care of Joey for me in Boston."

"I know," Henry said, smiling at her. "I'll never forget that week." He looked at Drea, "Your brothers made a good impression on a lot of us. They didn't have to do that."

"Oh yes they did," she said. "For several reasons. First of all, Polly is family. They wouldn't let anyone hurt her. But secondly, and most important, they had a blast. They'd never liked the creep and it gave them a chance to get all macho." She shook her head and rolled her eyes. "It's not easy living with two Italian brothers. Not easy at all."

"It's not fair." They all looked up at Bunny's voice.

"Rough night, Bunny?" Polly asked. The girl looked awful. She had terrible bedhead and her makeup was streaked across her face.

"If I pay you money will you just ship me back to Boston in a container?" Bunny whined.

"Buck up, buttercup," Drea said. "You have to get it together. You have packing to do and we're out of here in two hours."

"You hate me," the girl whined again.

"Not as much as you're going to hate flying this afternoon if you don't pull it together."

Bunny slumped across the peninsula and Polly pushed a bar stool under her bottom. She flopped onto it. "I was afraid you might give me alcohol to jump start me."

"No, but I could fry up some greasy eggs and bacon if you'd like," Henry said.

"Ohhhh." Bunny shuddered and lay her head down on her forearm. "Why did I do that to myself?"

"Because you don't have the sense God gave little green apples," Drea remarked.

"Don't be mean." Bunny stuck her tongue out at Drea and grimaced. "At least wait until we're alone in the car."

"Would you like some toast, Bunny?" Polly asked. "That might help your tummy."

"Okay. Do you have aspirin or something?"

Polly poured a glass of water and opened a bottle of aspirin she took down from a cupboard. Bunny looked up and around at the three of them.

"You're staring at me. Do I really look that bad?"

"It's pretty scary," Drea said. "You'd better get moving. I'm not waiting for you today, so you'd best get your bags packed and be ready to go on time."

Bunny stuck her tongue out again. "I'll be ready," she said sulkily. "You don't have to yell at me."

Drea chuckled. "I'm going to finish packing. I'll be back in a bit."

After she walked out, Bunny looked up at Polly. "Am I really that bad?"

"You'll feel better after you've had a shower. I promise."

Bunny took another drink of water and slid off the stool. "Don't throw that away. I'll drink more when I'm done."

She left and pretty soon, Polly heard a loud groan from the bathroom. She laughed. "She saw herself in the mirror."

"You have interesting friends, Polly," Henry said.

She nodded. "It's been an interesting life."

CHAPTER TEN

Racing around all afternoon getting things wrapped up so they could leave early the next morning had worn Polly out. Since there were plenty of leftovers from the party, Polly and Henry had invited Joss and Nate, Mark and Sal, Doug, Billy and Rachel, Sylvie and her boys, and Eliseo over for dinner. Sarah and Rebecca had joined them as well. Henry had called his parents and they came over with his sister.

Drea and Bunny had gotten out of Bellingwood in plenty of time, due in no small part to Drea's constant nagging. Bunny complained and whined the entire time she packed her bags, until Polly finally went in to help her finish. Henry had finally carried all of her things down to the car so they could leave on time. Polly worried until she got a text from Drea that they were safely on the plane and Bunny lived through it.

It had rained off and on all day, but the skies were becoming more threatening as the afternoon wore on. Polly had almost canceled dinner, but after a second phone call, Sylvie told her to quit worrying. They'd be safer at Sycamore House than anywhere else in town. Thunder rumbled and rain poured out of the sky.

Mark and Sal, Nate and Joss showed up in time to set tables up and re-heat the food. They were just sitting down to eat when her phone rang. She looked at it to see Lydia's smiling face on the screen.

"Hey, Lydia, what's up?"

"You need to get downstairs right now. The sirens are about to go off in town, but the wind is coming and they're worried about a tornado. Get downstairs. Goodbye!"

Polly hung up and everyone looked at her.

"What's wrong?" Henry asked.

"Lydia says we're supposed to go to the basement right now. Something bad is coming at us."

At that moment, the city's sirens began to sound.

Billy turned to Rachel. "You go downstairs, I'll get Billy Jack."

"I'll get those people in the addition," she said. "We'll meet you down there."

"The animals!" Polly cried. She bolted for the back door of the auditorium, just behind Billy, and ran upstairs to their apartment. Obiwan was standing at the top of the steps, wagging his tail.

"Where are the cats?" she asked and ran past him. They were both sitting on the cat tree in Henry's office, their favorite place to be when they weren't snuggled in bed with her. Polly's first thought was that she couldn't manage all three animals and then realized that Henry and Jason had followed her. She thrust Luke into Jason's arms and ran back down the steps, calling for Obiwan to join them. Henry grabbed his leash off a hook and snapped it on the dog's collar.

The kitchen had cleared out, but when she looked outside, the late afternoon light had given way to an eerie greenish glow. As she watched, she heard the distinct sound of hail hitting the windows.

"Go, Polly," Henry commanded and she went.

Jason had already run through the kitchen and was standing at the top of the basement steps, holding the door open for them, the cat tucked under his arm.

"You go on," she said. "Is everyone else downstairs?"

"I think so," he replied and went down the steps ahead of her. Both cats seemed to be too surprised to even wiggle. They were rarely out of the apartment. Obiwan and Henry followed her down and he pulled the door shut behind them.

When they got to the basement, she went into the bedroom she'd set up last summer and found Sylvie sitting beside Rebecca and Sarah on the bed.

"I've never been through a tornado before," Rebecca said. "Is it scary?"

Polly shook her head. "It's nothing to sneeze at, but we're safe down here." She handed Leia to Andrew, who was sitting on the floor in front of them. "Would you mind keeping an eye on her? If she gets away, don't worry, just help me out now."

He nodded and took the cat, then began stroking her back. Jason came into the room with Luke. "Eliseo isn't here," he said. "Mark thinks he went down to the barn."

"No!" Polly cried. "That fool." She called his cell phone.

"Hello, Polly," Eliseo answered. "Don't yell at me. I've been in worse weather and I'm going to make sure everything is okay down here."

"I *am* yelling at you. What are you thinking?"

"We'll be fine. I promise."

"You're a fool," she said to him.

"Maybe, but this is where I need to be."

He ended the call and she dropped to her knees beside Andrew and put her hand on Leia's head. "Don't let anything happen to him, please," she said quietly.

Mark and Sal came into the room. He was carrying a Coleman lantern. "I can't believe you have these, Polly."

"Jeff made me. He told me that we had to have supplies down here just in case. I suspect you'll find candles and batteries and even freeze dried food if you look hard enough. There should be four or five lawn chairs and some folding chairs."

She looked around. "Where's Billy and what about that Lois Wexler, the photographer?"

"I'm right here," Billy said, coming in the door. "It's getting kind of bad out there. The tree branches are blowing like crazy and that rain is coming down in sheets!"

He released his dog, who ran over to Obiwan. Billy and Doug planned to take Obiwan over to their apartment while Polly and Henry were gone. Sylvie and the kids would take care of the cats during the day, making sure they were fed before going home each evening. Polly felt fortunate to have so many people around to take care of her life when she couldn't be there to live it.

Polly asked one more time, "Has anyone seen our guest? Rachel, was she in her room?"

"I knocked several times and she didn't come to the door. I yelled and yelled for her. She must not be here."

"Well, there's nothing more we can do. I hope she's okay."

Henry and his dad came in with more chairs and set them up around the room.

"Well, this is a helluva way to start your honeymoon," Lonnie said. She poked her brother in the arm. "You'd better hope you can get out of here tomorrow."

"You'd better hope we don't decide that we're coming to Michigan rather than going to Arizona. We could come up and make you entertain us for a week. And we'd expect you to really take care of us. Do our laundry, make our meals and give us footrubs."

She shrugged her shoulders, "Bring it, big boy. I'd give you a vacation you'd never forget."

Polly grinned, watching the two of them. She loved seeing siblings play. That was one thing she missed. Even though she had friends she loved like crazy, there was just something about sisters and brothers and their lifelong knowledge of each other.

"How are you doing, Sarah?" she asked.

"I'm okay. It's a good week for me, so I feel fine. This is a little nerve-wracking, though."

Bill Sturtz came back in, carrying a black radio. "You were right, Polly. Your manager thought of everything. We even have a weather radio and fresh batteries were sitting beside it." He began tuning it in, messing with the antenna, trying to get a signal.

"I'm going back out into the main room to see if I can't get this to tune in."

"Be careful, Bill," his wife, Marie, said. "Don't you go upstairs."

"I won't. Stop worrying, mother."

The lights flickered once and Polly looked at Henry. He was concerned, but didn't seem too worried.

"We get two more flickers before they go out," he said.

"How do you know this stuff?" she asked.

"I don't know. It's just what I've always known."

They flickered twice more immediately and then everything went black. Cell phones lit up around the rooms as people swiped them open and Mark lit the Coleman lantern.

"I saw two battery operated lanterns in the other room. I'll be right back." He started to walk away with the lantern and then turned around, chuckling, and handed it to Sal. "Whoops. Sorry."

"What do you think about this, Sal?" Polly asked.

"I'm not sure. I mean, how much danger are we in?"

"Tornadoes can be pretty dangerous," Marie Sturtz said. "Bellingwood got hit by a big one back in 1991. There were a lot of damaged homes. It ripped through the trailer park and killed a woman."

Mark came back in with another lantern. "I left the other one with Bill out there. He's fine. It sounds like there is a tornado on the ground west of here."

"Oh god," Polly said. Then she stopped. "No. Oh, dear God, please keep this community safe."

"Amen," Marie responded and there were nods around the room.

A terrible sound resonated outside, like a train rolling down the tracks.

"What's that?" Rebecca whined a little.

"It's okay," Polly stood and walked toward the bed. Obiwan and Big Jack had both settled themselves on the floor in front of the bed. She knelt back down and put a hand on her dog. "It's going to be okay."

Bill Sturtz had come back into the room with his lantern and sat on a chair beside his wife. He took her hand in his. "This is too close," he said.

Polly shut her eyes and tried to think of anything but the damage a tornado could do to those she loved. A lot of her family was safe right here in the basement of her home, but there were too many others out there that she worried about. She looked over at Henry, tears in her eyes. He moved quickly to her side.

"You're right, Polly. It's going to be okay."

"I know. It's just that I've never been through one of these before."

"I'm scared, Mom," Rebecca said.

Before Sarah could respond, Andrew stood up and put Leia in Rebecca's lap. "Like Polly said, it's going to be okay." He sidled in between his own mom and Rebecca on the bed and reached across to pet the cat. "We're in Sycamore House. Right, Polly?"

Polly looked at Kelly and Ethan Locke, who hadn't said a word since they'd come downstairs. She hadn't had time to talk to them this afternoon and felt awful that she was no further in the search for Kelly's daughter. She planned to call Anita in the sheriff's office tomorrow to see if they couldn't do some more searching.

"You're right. This is Sycamore House. I have to believe that it's here for a reason and we're going to be safe." She sat down and crossed her legs, leaning back against Henry. "We're going to be just fine."

The sound from outside died down after a few minutes and they looked at each other, everyone breathing a sigh of relief.

"I didn't hear any terrible crashing upstairs," Bill Sturtz said. "We're probably okay here. Let me see what the radio says." He went back out to the main room and after a few minutes, came back in. "We should wait a while longer, but I think the worst has passed. We'll wait for the sirens to wind down. Henry? With me?"

Henry patted Polly on the shoulder and stood up. "We'll be back," he said. "It's hard to keep Dad from a good storm."

"Be careful," Marie said.

Polly couldn't stand it and dialed Eliseo's phone again. She got a busy signal and figured there was probably too much cell tower traffic happening, so she entered a text and hoped it would go through soon.

"Are you okay?" and she sent it.

Henry came back into the room. "I wouldn't advise any of us to get on the road yet, but I think we can go back upstairs. The wind is blowing and it's still raining, but it's not dangerous."

"What does it look like out there?" Polly asked.

"We just looked out the front door. I can't see much because of the driving rain. There are tree branches in the parking lot and it's filled with water. Come on up and see for yourself."

She looked around the room and saw that Jason was still clutching Luke. She chuckled. "I can't believe those cats didn't get away from you guys," she said.

Jason rolled his neck. "I was holding him a little tight. But he didn't scratch me or anything."

"Would you three kids mind taking the cats back up to the apartment? Here, take this lamp with you." Mark handed them one of the lamps. There were emergency lights in the main hallways of Sycamore House that should have turned on when the power went off. Hopefully that would give everyone on the main level enough light to see.

After they were all upstairs, she watched the kids take the steps up to her home, then turned to Henry. "Next purchase is a generator. What if this happened with hundreds of people in here? We need to at least have electricity."

"Not a bad idea," he acknowledged. "But it won't take long for the power to come back on."

She went into her office and looked out the window at the storm. Rain was still pelting the ground and she couldn't see beyond her own lot. What was happening in the rest of the town?

"Polly?" Henry's voice came in from the front office. "You need to see this. Come here."

She went out into the main hallway and he took her hand. "I'm sure Eliseo is okay, so don't panic."

"What? Don't tell me not to panic if something bad has happened."

He led her to the side door and out into the addition, then opened the door so she could look down at the barn. A large section of the roof had been ripped off and was nowhere to be seen. She started to run and he stopped her.

"What do you think you're doing?"

"I'm going to check on them. Mark!" she called loudly and pulled her hand out of Henry's. Before he could grab her again, she ran for the barn, caring little about the rain pouring down on her head.

"Eliseo!" she yelled as she ran. She stopped at the first gate and flung it open, then ran for the second, not bothering to shut either of them. Polly opened the main door to the alley of the barn and yelled again, "Eliseo!"

"What are you doing down here?" Eliseo came out of the donkey's stall, holding Gretel in one arm and carrying a lantern in the other. "You are absolutely soaked through. And you called me a fool."

"The roof is gone!" She couldn't stop yelling.

"Yeah. It got a little exciting in here. But we're fine. The horses were a little upset, but Tom, Huck, and I managed to keep them calm.

Mark and Henry pulled up short behind Polly and Mark started laughing. "Eliseo, you scared this woman to death. I'm sure she imagined all of you bloodied and dead down here." He looked into Demi's stall and the horse put his head out for some attention. "It probably scared you, didn't it buddy? Did you make it through unscathed?"

He opened the stall door and went in, petting Demi's shoulders and running his hand down the horse's front legs, one at a time. "You're fine. At least you had a safe place to live this year."

Nat had heard Mark's voice and was looking out at him for some attention. The veterinarian went into each of the stalls and quietly spoke to the horses, while checking each of them.

"You know they're okay, don't you, Polly?" he said, coming back into the main alley.

She dropped her head onto her chest. "I do now. Thank you."

His phone lit up. "And so it begins. I'm going to be busy tonight. Do you mind if Sal stays here for a while? I don't know how long I'll be out."

"That's fine," Polly said. "Thanks again. Tell her I'll be up. And grab some food for yourself so you don't starve."

"Will you come back up to the house?" she asked Eliseo.

"Not yet."

"Jason's going to ask. Can he come down?"

"I'd like that."

Henry took her hand and they stopped at the door, watching the rain continue to pour out of the sky. "One, two, three, go?" he asked.

She laughed. "I need to shut the gates this time. You run. I'm soaked through, it doesn't matter at this point."

"I'm never going to be able to contain you, am I?"

"It will be easier if you don't try," she said, laughing, then yelled, "Go!" and ran for the first gate.

CHAPTER ELEVEN

Polly and Henry got back up to the main house to find everyone back in the auditorium. Joss and Nate had left to check their home, but the others were gathered around tables, picking at their meals.

"We figured that since we couldn't go outside, we might as well eat," Bill said, carrying a couple of plates to his table. "But as soon as this lets up, I want to go see what happened in town."

Henry nodded and dropped into his seat, his face glum.

"What's wrong, honey?" Polly asked, sitting next to him.

"I have a bad feeling about this. We aren't going anywhere tomorrow morning."

She smiled and then quickly wiped it off her face. "I've known that for days. Something just didn't feel right about this trip."

Her phone rang. It was Aaron Merritt.

"Hey Aaron, are you guys okay?"

"We're fine, but Ken and I have a problem and need your help."

"Sure, what do you need?"

"The tornado ripped through the northwest edge of town. There are some folks without homes and quite a few others who have too much damage to stay at home tonight. The Red Cross will set up at the elementary school, but we need one more place for people to come."

"I don't have power yet, but we'll do what we can."

"No damage?"

"So far, it just looks like part of the roof blew off the barn. Everyone is okay and Sycamore House is in good shape. I won't know any more until we can get outside. How long is this rain supposed to last?"

"We're at the end of the storm. The guys are out working on the electrical lines, you'll have power back soon."

She grinned. Living in rural Iowa was amazing. They'd never gone without power longer than a few hours. Henry tried to explain what usually brought it down, but she just smiled and hoped that whoever was climbing the power poles stayed safe. That was their job and she appreciated them for it.

"People can come here now, it's just not convenient for them without power. As soon as the lights are back on, though, we'll be ready. Whatever you need from me. Are you sure you are okay?"

"We lost a big tree in the front yard, but I'll deal with that later."

"Your kids?"

"We've heard from them all. Everyone is fine."

"Have you heard from Beryl or Andy?"

"I'm on my way to Andy and Len's house right now. We can't get through to them. Beryl is fuming because her neighbor's gazebo blew into her front yard, so I guess she's probably okay."

Polly got up and walked over to one of the big windows at the front of the building. The sun was trying to peek through the clouds and the rain was beginning to abate.

"It looks like the weather is trying to get back to normal. I'm going to go so I can check out the rest of the building."

"Take care of yourself."

"And Aaron, no one has to call or anything. They can just come over. We have six rooms nearly ready at Sycamore Inn if you need them and I have a room available here. I don't know what Jeff has planned, but he can deal with all of that tomorrow."

"Thank you, Polly. You'll make this easier for me."

"I guess that's what I'm here for. I can't imagine doing anything else."

They hung up and Polly jogged over to Henry and his dad, who were getting ready to leave by the back door.

"Don't go yet, just a minute, okay?"

Henry frowned at her, "Sure. What's going on?"

"You'll see."

"Everyone?" Polly spoke loudly to get the attention of the people in her auditorium.

"I don't know what your plans are and you are certainly free to go and check on your homes and family, but that was Aaron Merritt and he says things are bad in town. The Red Cross is coming in and they'll be setting up at the elementary school. He and Ken Wallers would like us to open up for people who need a place to settle in. I've offered the extra room here and the rooms at Sycamore Inn, but I'm guessing there will be a lot going on the next couple of days as people try to get their lives cleaned up after all of this. Any time that you can give us here will be helpful."

She turned to Henry. "I just promised Aaron the use of Sycamore Inn. I suppose the first thing we should do is make sure that it wasn't damaged."

"I can head over there first. Dad's going to check the house."

"Let me come with you. I don't need to be here. Sylvie can handle this place until the electricity comes back on."

"Sure," he said.

When they arrived at the hotel, Polly was relieved that all was still in place. Plenty of debris had blown into the parking lot, but the roof remained and no glass had been broken.

"I don't know that I want to see what happened to the lodge," Henry said

"Might as well drive on back there. Get the pain over as quickly as possible."

The lodge for the winery was still under construction. It was framed and enclosed, but still just a shell. Henry drove through the parking lot, past the caretaker's house and out onto the street leading back to the winery. The homes looked fine and when they pulled into the driveway, there were quite a few cars parked in front of the lodge.

"I didn't even think about the grapevines," he said. "I'll bet the boys are in a panic."

The rain was still coming down, creating a muddy mess around the concrete driveway. He pulled in and parked, then walked around the lodge, looking it over closely. Polly waited in the truck for him until she saw J. J. Robert's car. He pulled in beside her and got out, grinning. He was a terrible flirt. It didn't matter that she was married, he never passed up an opportunity to hit on her. She rolled the car window down, hoping to cut him off before he got started.

"Have you heard anything about the vineyard yet?" she asked him.

"We've got some things down, but Wayne isn't upset. How about you guys?"

"Henry's checking the lodge. We lost part of the barn's roof, but that can be replaced. Sycamore Inn is in good shape."

"My parents said they are fine, but their neighbor's house was demolished. Everyone is safe, but they are staying with Mom and Dad until they figure out what to do next."

"That's really nice," Polly said. "They have that much room?"

"It's no big deal. There's practically an apartment in their lower level." He shook his head. "You gotta do what you gotta do. We wouldn't leave them out in the rain. And they've lived next door to each other for thirty years.

"How bad is it up there?"

"There are at least ten homes that I could count that are wrecked and I didn't bother to count the houses that had roof damage or windows blown out."

"What about downtown?"

"Totally missed it. We were lucky."

"I guess so," she said. "Some people weren't so lucky, though."

Henry got back into the truck and leaned across Polly. "I didn't see the rest of the guys. Are they down in the vineyard?"

"Yeah. I was up at my parent's house checking on them."

"I just got a call from Ben Bowen," Henry said. "He's lost everything."

Polly gasped. "Did you tell him to come over?" She liked Ben a lot and this made her heart hurt.

"I did. His wife is pretty upset. He kept assuring me that it was only stuff, but I don't think he realizes how much all of that stuff was part of their lives."

"Should we check on them?"

"No, the police won't let anyone else back on those streets tonight. Ben knows to come to Sycamore House when he gets out and to call if he needs anything."

"Okay."

J. J. started to turn away and said, "I'll talk to you guys later. I see the rest of the crew coming up. If you need anything, let us know, okay?"

"Thanks man, same goes," Henry said.

Polly left the window down, enjoying the breeze of the evening. "Let's just drive for a while," she said. "Take me past Andy and Len's house. I want to see for myself that they're okay."

Henry pulled out of the parking lot and began driving. He drove north through town and wove around some of the neighborhoods, moaning at the loss of several big, old trees. The bleachers at the ball fields had been ripped out of the ground and were gone. The shelter they used for selling concessions was in bits and pieces on the ground.

He continued to drive and they began to see the path the tornado took. Polly was thankful that it had missed the main part of town, but that didn't mean anything to the people who had lost their homes. He pointed down a gravel road to the west. "That's where J. J.'s parents live. They were lucky that their home is still standing."

Polly nodded and tried her best to take it all in. The corn was still pretty short, but she could see a large amount of debris spread across the fields. "That's going to be a huge mess to clean up."

He nodded and sighed, then turned onto a gravel road. "One of my uncles lives out here. He's an old hermit. I just want to check and make sure he's okay."

"I had no idea you even had an uncle," she said.

"We really don't talk about him much. He's not social and doesn't like people. He lives out here with his chickens. Dad used to check on him all the time, but when Loren took a shotgun to Dad's truck, that ended."

"He shot at your dad?"

"He thought my parents spent too much time worrying and insisted that he was fine all on his own. I think Dad finally decided that if Loren was going to die alone, we couldn't do anything about it. I told my parents I'd check on him tonight."

"Is he going to shoot at us?"

Henry chuckled. "Who knows?"

He pointed to a ramshackle house with out-buildings surrounding it. "That's Uncle Loren's place. It looks like he doesn't have power out here either."

"Does the house always look like that or did the storm hit it?"

"It looks worse every year. He won't let us help him fix it up. I wonder sometimes if he doesn't let it fall apart just to be spiteful."

"What's that down there?" Polly pointed down the road to something dark in the road. It was far enough away that they couldn't tell what it was and dusk was starting to settle in.

"I'll check it out first. We might be running for our lives in a few minutes," Henry said, laughing a little.

He drove on and discovered a pickup truck that had its front wheels in the ditch. "That's weird," he remarked.

"Pull over, just in case someone's hurt." Polly waited until he stopped the truck and jumped out. She approached the truck and said, "Hello! Is anyone there? Are you okay?" She turned her phone's flashlight on and pointed it at the cab of the truck.

"Henry! There's someone here! Help me!"

He ran around to the driver's side of the truck and helped to open the car door. Polly took one look at the man slumped over the steering wheel and dropped her head.

"You can check," she said to Henry, "but I'm guessing he's dead."

"Why do you say that?"

She aimed the flashlight at the man's head and Henry said, "Oh. That's why."

Blood matted the hair to the skin around a large hole. "I don't want to call Aaron," she said. "He has enough going on."

"Well, I'm not calling him. Dead bodies are your thing. My thing is keeping you out of trouble."

"At least you're here with me this time. It's partly your thing, now. Do you know who this is?"

Henry stepped forward to get a closer look and reached out for Polly, his hand flailing until he grasped her arm. "It's Uncle Loren." He backed up and walked down the road. Soon he was bent over with his hands at his knees, retching into the ditch.

"Do you need me, Henry?"

He waved her away. "No, call Aaron. I'll be fine in a minute."

Polly stepped back and walked to his truck, bringing up Aaron Merritt's phone number.

"Do you have electricity yet?" Aaron asked when he answered the phone.

"I don't know," she said. "Henry and I are out driving around."

"Did you find something we need to deal with?"

"Well ..."

"Oh, Polly, no."

"I'm sorry, Aaron."

"Is it from the storm?"

"I don't think so. He's got a hole in his head."

"We'll get someone to you as soon as we can. Where are you?"

"It's Henry's Uncle Loren. We're down the road from his place."

"Did Henry see this?"

"Yeah."

"Okay. Take care of him and we'll be right there."

"You aren't even giving me any trouble about this?"

"No," Aaron sighed. "I don't have the energy. This is going to be a long, damned night."

"I'm sorry."

"Not your problem. You find 'em, we deal with 'em."

"Thanks, Aaron."

Henry was pacing back and forth down the road. Polly walked down to join him. "How are you doing?" she asked.

"I'm fine. What did Aaron say?"

"Someone will be here soon. I'm sorry, honey."

He stopped walking. "No one liked him. He was a rotten old man. He was mean to my parents and he hated having kids around. Even when we were growing up, he said terrible things to us. Lonnie and I drove out here a couple of years ago with Christmas gifts and he didn't even open them, just flung them on the lawn and told us to go home. Said he didn't need our charity."

"How was it that he's so different than your dad?"

"I don't know if it was PTSD or what. That's probably it, but he refused to talk to anybody. He wouldn't go to the doctor and wouldn't let anyone on his land."

Henry waved his arm, motioning to the fields around them. "He owned all of this. He lived with my grandparents after he came back. I suppose Grandma and Grandpa and Loren all kind of took care of each other. After Grandpa died, Grandma stayed here until she was in bad enough shape that she had to go to a nursing home.

Henry pointed to the east. "Aunt Betty and Uncle Dick have more of the farm over there. They bought Dad's portion. He never wanted to be a farmer. But they did most of the work on Loren's portion, too, paying him rent for the fields." He chuffed out a breath. "He wouldn't let anyone in the house after Grandma was gone. No one knows what he did with all of her things."

"I can't call Dad or Aunt Betty about this. I need to tell them face to face."

"I know. Don't worry, I'll go with you." Polly had met Henry's Aunt Betty and Uncle Dick once in passing when they'd been at the house one weekend. She knew that his family had grown up around here, but had never really gotten to know much more than that. He kept warning her that his family was bigger than she knew and while she'd met some of them at the party last night, he made sure she understood those were only a small part of the group.

Henry put his arms around her and held her close. "I'm glad you're in my life."

"I love you, too."

He pushed her away from him and she looked up into his face. He was grinning. "Even if you do find my family's dead bodies."

"Stop it. It's not my fault. You're the one who drove out here."

"Yes, but if you hadn't come with me, maybe ..."

"Stop it right there. Don't you dare make me out to be the Grim Reaper. He's dead whether or not I showed up here today."

"I couldn't resist," he said, chuckling. "That was just too easy."

"Brat." She took his hand and they walked back to the truck. "So, I think this whole vacation needs to be canceled."

"I don't like it, but you're right."

"I was thinking about it and maybe we should schedule it in October before your parents leave Bellingwood for the winter. You'll be at the end of most of the big projects and you can schedule the others around our trip. Your dad will still be here to manage things when we're gone and we can be back before Halloween and all of the holidays."

"The weather would be a lot more pleasant, but some of the tourist things might be closed for the season."

"I don't care about that."

"I should know that. We'll talk more later. For now, this is going to be a really busy week."

Polly slipped her arm around his waist. "I love you."

"I love you too. Thanks for dealing with this stuff with my uncle."

Flashing lights were approaching as they arrived at Henry's truck.

"All I did was make a phone call. But I'll be here through all of this."

He hugged her. "I love you."

CHAPTER TWELVE

Later that evening, Polly and Henry pulled into the drive of his parent's home. They hadn't taken time to look at any other damage in town, since he desperately wanted to get to his Dad before the news came from somewhere else. She took his hand as they went up the steps to the front porch.

Lonnie opened the door and looked at the two of them with confusion on her face, "What are you doing here?"

"We need to talk to Mom and Dad," Henry said.

Her confusion turned to fear. "Did something happen?"

"It will be okay," he said, nodding slightly. "But yeah."

"They're in the back yard. We've been cleaning up since we got home. I just got back from checking on Mrs. Naylor. She lost a basement window, but she's fine."

"Why are you here, Henry?" Bill Sturtz asked as he came in the front room, followed closely by his wife. "We saw your truck pull in."

"We went out to check on Uncle Loren." Henry stepped forward, dropping Polly's hand. "Dad, he's been killed."

"By the storm? What happened out there?"

Marie wrapped her arm around her husband's arm, waiting for Henry to respond.

He took a deep breath. "It wasn't the storm. Someone shot him. We found him in his truck about a half mile down the road from his house."

"Oh Bill," Marie said.

"What did that damned fool get himself into?" Bill gripped the back of the rocking chair. "Does Betty know yet?"

"No, I thought you might want to go with me to tell her."

"Let your mother and me do it. You have enough other things to worry about. Who did you call, Aaron or Ken Wallers?"

Henry gave his dad a slight smile. "You haven't been around enough to know that when Polly finds someone, she calls Aaron. So, the Sheriff has this."

"You are quite the young woman," Bill said. "I suppose I'm glad that it was you who found him."

"I'm so sorry for your loss," Polly said.

"I'd always hoped he might come around and be part of the family again. I guess we won't have that chance now."

Lonnie had separated herself from the group and taken a seat on the sofa, so Polly went over to sit beside her. "Are you okay?"

The girl shrugged. "Yeah. It's strange to think about someone like him dying. I thought he'd be mean forever." She looked at her parents. "We need to get his cats and dog. And there are all of those chickens, too. I hope they're all safe after the storm."

"I forgot about those," Bill said. "We'll go over to Betty's and then check the house."

"Stu Decker was going to give you a call so you could let them into the house," Henry said. "I told him about the animals and he said he'd wait for one of us to show up."

Bill took a breath. "Okay. Let's do it this way. You and Lonnie and Polly go to the house. Marie and I will head over to Betty and Dick's to tell them what happened."

On the way back out of town, Henry half-turned to Lonnie in the back seat of his truck. "Do you remember what the name of Loren's dog was?"

"It's Duke or Prince or something like that, isn't it? And he's got a houseful of cats."

"We can put food down and make sure there's plenty of water," Henry said. "I'm not taking a bunch of cats back to our house until we know what we have going on with them."

"I'm sorry about your honeymoon," Lonnie said. "You two deserve to get out of town for a while."

Henry snickered. "Polly has been trying to talk me out of this trip for the last three weeks. If I didn't know better ..."

She interrupted him, "Don't you dare. I did not bring this tornado to Bellingwood."

"Hey!" he said. "That's not what I was going to say. I was going to accuse you of having a premonition about it."

Polly shuddered. "I don't like that idea any more than causing it. I just didn't think this was a good time to go. There are so many things happening around here."

"There are always things happening around here."

Lonnie leaned forward. "Do you think Dad is sad that Uncle Loren died?"

"I don't know," Henry said and put his hand on the back of the seat, trying to reach her. "How about you?"

"He was a crusty old bastard. I don't think anybody should die like that, but I don't feel like his death is going to change anything for me. Is that awful, Polly? I feel kind of guilty for not being more upset by this."

Polly squirmed so she could turn in her seatbelt. "When Dad died, I felt guilty that I wasn't home, but Mary told me that I couldn't do that. I'd done nothing wrong and Dad was thrilled that I was happy. She talked to me a lot about guilt. About thinking through decisions before I made them. If I was going to feel guilty, I needed to not do it and if I was going to go ahead and do something, I needed to do it with a clear conscience and not look back and feel guilty since I'd made a decision in good faith."

She chuckled. "I know. It's a little preachy. But that was a huge eye opener for me. I had made all of the right decisions for my life up to that point. In fact, I'd made most of them with Dad as my cheerleader. I couldn't feel guilty because I wasn't there when a horrible accident took his life."

"Okay?" Lonnie said. It was obvious that while she understood what Polly was saying, that didn't answer her question.

"Yeah, the point." Polly chuckled and patted Lonnie's hand. The girl wasn't that much younger, but because she was Henry's sister, Polly felt like she was so much older and wiser. "Anyway ... you've lived your life without him in it because he was a mean old man. You've made decisions about your relationship with him based on what he allowed. You did it in good faith. You can't feel guilty that he wasn't a bigger part of your life and that your life won't be scarred by his death. Guilt won't fix your relationship or make him be alive, it will just eat away at you."

"I get that. But it really makes you think about things."

"Yes it does," Polly acknowledged.

Lonnie tapped her brother's arm, "I love you, Henry. You're a really great brother."

"I love you, too. What brought that on?"

"I don't know. I just don't want something bad to happen to one of us and not have said it."

"Stop it, silly girl. Nothing bad is going to happen."

"Well, something did and Loren never told his brother and sister that he loved them. He died a mean, miserable man and was all alone."

They turned onto the gravel road and still saw flashing lights down the road.

"Should we see if Decker is still there?" Henry asked.

"Probably a good idea," Polly said.

He pulled forward and was waved over to the side by a deputy they didn't recognize.

Henry rolled his window down. "Is Deputy Decker here? I'm Henry Sturtz."

"Oh, sure. I'll get him."

The young woman jogged down the road and into the ditch. A few minutes later, Stu Decker strode back to meet them. "Hello, Henry. Polly," he said, peering in the truck.

"We're going to the house to take care of Loren's animals. Did you want to get in there for any reason?"

"If you'd open it up for us, that would be terrific."

"Dad should be coming down the road pretty soon. He's going on to my Aunt Betty's to tell her. Will you let him through?"

The deputy nodded and said, "I'm very sorry for your loss. Deputy Hudson will follow you back. Tell her if you think someone was inside the place and if it has any bearing on this. We don't yet know why he was killed."

Henry chuckled. "I don't know if we'll be able to tell you much. The last time I was in that house, my grandmother was still alive. Uncle Loren wouldn't let any of us in after she died."

"Well, maybe you'll see something out of place."

"Sure," Henry said. "We're going to take his dog and feed his cats. There might be a lot of them there."

Stu Decker laughed. "Oh, Hudson'll love that. We already accuse her of being the crazy cat lady."

He patted the side of Henry's truck as he walked away. Rather than try to turn around in the road with all of the emergency vehicles there, Henry backed down and swung into the driveway, illuminating the cluttered front yard and dilapidated house.

"I can't tell if this mess is from the storm or if it's just Uncle Loren's junk," he said, getting out of the truck. He stopped and stood in the doorway of the truck. "Let me go first and see what that dog is going to do. No sense all of us getting attacked."

Polly reached in the glove compartment and said, "Just a second." She pulled out a bag of dog treats. "Here, take these. They'll help."

"What in the world?"

"I put them everywhere. Sometimes Obiwan needs a little extra encouragement."

He opened the bag and headed for the front door, leaving the truck running and lights on. As he reached for the door handle, another vehicle pulled in beside the truck and everything lit up as Deputy Hudson turned on all she had. Henry shaded his eyes and waved, then opened the door. In just a few moments, inside lights came on and he stepped back out, a large black and tan Rottweiler standing beside him.

Hudson turned her lights down, leaving the headlights beaming and got out of the car. "Is the dog safe?" she asked.

Henry put a treat in his hand and the dog sniffed, then ate it and wagged his tail.

"I think he's fine. Probably glad to see someone."

"Does it look like anyone broke in?" she asked.

Polly and Lonnie got out of the truck and followed her.

"If they did, they didn't have to break anything. The door has probably never been locked."

"Do you remember the dog's name?" Polly asked Lonnie, who shrugged.

"Duke!" Polly said and got no response. "Prince, come here." That didn't elicit a response either. "One more," she said. "Come here, King." The dog looked at her, but didn't move.

"Henry?" she said and he just looked at her and shook his head.

"I've got nothing."

Polly bent over and looked under the dog, then said, "Duchess?" The dog glanced at the bag of treats in Henry's hand, then walked off the porch and over to Polly.

"Really?" Henry asked "Duchess?"

"She's not a boy," Polly said, laughing. "You're useless."

"Mr. Sturtz?" Deputy Hudson stepped back out onto the porch. "Can you tell me if everything looks to be in order?" Two orange tabby cats were weaving around her legs.

Henry zipped the bag shut and tossed it at Polly, who handed it to Lonnie. "You wanna do this?" she asked.

"Are you sure she's okay?"

Polly stroked the dog's neck and rubbed her ears, causing the dog's tongue to flop out as she panted. "She'll be fine. Try a treat or two and call her by name. Keep talking to her in a normal tone of voice." She'd only had Obiwan for a year and a half and was baffled to find that she was the expert.

Henry had gone inside the house and Polly wandered over to the porch and up the steps, keeping an eye on Lonnie and the dog.

She checked inside and when she looked back at Lonnie, smiled to see her squat down and accept the dog licking her face.

"She likes me!" Lonnie said excitedly.

"Just keep talking to her," Polly said. "You're doing great." She stepped in and looked around, then wondered if anything in the living room had changed since Henry's grandparents had lived there. The rug on the hard wood floor was worn and tattered, the drapes on the windows had been hung in the fifties. White sheers behind the drapes had been washed but the drapes hadn't been dry-cleaned in years. An old blue sofa and two wing chairs sat where they'd probably been placed by Loren's mother. The cushions were flat and the nap on the material was worn thin. The room was neat and tidy, not at all what she expected. Things were old, but Polly figured he'd been comfortable in a place that was very familiar to him. He kept it as his mother had kept it.

Henry and Deputy Hudson walked back into the living room.

"This is cleaner than I expected," Polly said.

"The whole house is like this. He just didn't take care of the outside," Henry replied. "It wouldn't be that difficult to bring this house back into shape."

He handed her a large envelope. "We need to get this to Dad. It's Uncle Loren's will. I was afraid he hadn't made one out. It looks like he wrote this when Grandma and Grandpa made theirs. At least he kept everything in the family."

"What about the rest of the cats?"

"We found four more upstairs," Henry said. "I've put food out in the kitchen and we'll come back in the daylight and figure out what to do with them."

"Lonnie has the dog pretty well covered. Will your parents mind if she stays there or should we offer to take her home?"

"They won't care. And if Lonnie likes the dog, they should stay together. I'm going to step outside and call Dad. He's not going to believe this."

"The house is clean," the deputy said. "We'll look through the rest of the out buildings tonight. If we find anything we'll let you know."

Henry handed her a business card. "Call either Dad or me if you need anything. Our numbers are on there. I'm sure Aunt Betty can answer questions too."

"Thank you," she said, pocketing the card, then turned toward the yard in front. "Has it always looked this way?"

Henry and Lonnie both burst out laughing. He walked over and picked up an old rusted watering can. "As long as I can remember, this was sitting on that table over there. Probably just where Grandma left it the last time she used it. Uncle Loren always put it back if it blew off. I thought he'd nailed it down. I guess not." Henry carried it over to the table and ran his hand over the spout. "Yes, it's always looked this way." He pointed to a building and said, "That's the chicken coop and over there is where Grandpa kept his tools. The bigger building was his workshop. I have no idea what Uncle Loren did with any of those buildings. I think Uncle Dick stores a tractor in the barn there, but it's been a while since I paid any attention to that."

"Okay," she nodded. "We've got it from here."

Two more vehicles pulled up and they watched a flatbed carry the pickup truck away. Henry reached out and shook her hand. "Thank you for everything tonight."

"It's not an easy thing for family to face. I'm sorry you had to see him that way."

"Me too," Henry said and took Polly's hand. They followed Lonnie back to the truck. She opened the back door and patted the seat, waiting for the dog to jump in, then climbed in.

Polly got in and grinned at the sight of Lonnie with her arm draped protectively over the huge dog's shoulders. When Lonnie sat beside Duchess, the dog looked as big as she did.

"I think you've made a friend," Polly said.

"Maybe ..." Lonnie started and then stopped.

"Maybe what?"

"Maybe this is what I can do for Uncle Loren."

Henry pulled his belt on and turned around, "Maybe that's a great idea."

CHAPTER THIRTEEN

Arriving back at Sycamore House, things were quiet. The main lights had been turned off and no one was wandering around. Polly texted Sylvie while standing in the main hallway, *"Are you okay?"*

"Everything is fine here. I'm sorry you guys can't leave tomorrow."

"No worries. It's okay. Did Ben Bowen show up with his wife?"

"Rachel put them in the downstairs room next to Sarah and Rebecca."

"Thanks. I'll be up early tomorrow when you bring the boys over."

"I'm not going to school. I have to take Andrew and Rebecca down to Indianola for their summer camp. Jason will be in the barn with Eliseo."

Polly had completely forgotten that the kids were going to be gone this week. Everyone thought it was a great idea so that Sylvie wouldn't have to worry about Andrew. Jason could take care of himself.

"Okay, thanks. I love you."

"Wait. Did Henry's uncle get killed tonight?"

"Yeah. It's weird. I'll tell you about it tomorrow?"

"Okay. Get some sleep. You'll need it. Love you too!"

Before Polly could say anything to Henry, her phone rang.

"Hey, Aaron. What can I do for you?"

"We've got a few more families that need a place to sleep tonight. Were you serious about the hotel?"

"Absolutely," she said. "I have six rooms available. Since we haven't been cleared to rent, they're empty. Henry and I will grab some sheets and toiletry stuff and be right over."

"You're a lifesaver, Polly. And even if the inspection papers haven't come through on the hotel, if I say they're ready, they are ready. How's that? The Red Cross is setting up a temporary shelter in the Elementary school, but if I can get some families into a safe place tonight, I'd like to just do that."

"No problem at all."

"Polly?" He seemed to hesitate for a moment.

"Yes?"

"Two of the families have animals. I don't think they want to be separated from them. Would you mind?"

"Why would you even ask me that, Aaron? Of course I don't mind. I wouldn't want to be separated from my pets either. If this isn't why I'm here, then I don't know any other reason."

"Thank you, sweetheart."

Polly ended the call, her eyes glistening with tears.

"What was that?" Henry asked.

"He called me sweetheart."

"Aaron did?" Henry chuckled. "Do I need to be concerned?"

She smiled through the tears, swatted his arm and said, "Brat. He's bringing some families to the hotel and I need to take linens and toiletries over. They're in a closet in the addition. Can you help me?"

"I'll meet you at the side door with the truck."

They filled the back with pillows, sheets, blankets and towels ... everything that she had been saving for opening the hotel. Two boxes filled with soaps, shampoo, and plastic wrapped cups joined the other items and they drove over to Sycamore Inn. Aaron was standing outside talking to several people when Henry pulled into the lot.

She hopped out of the truck and Aaron strode over to greet her. He looked exhausted and filthy, but she hugged him anyway. "How are you doing?" she asked.

"I'll feel better when we get some of these folks settled. They've had a horrible evening."

"I know. Thanks for letting me do this."

Aaron just smiled and shook his head. "You're a good girl, Polly."

"I'll let everyone in tonight and tomorrow Jeff can get things squared away so they all have keys to the rooms." She swiped the first room open and Henry opened the back of the truck.

"Let us help you get this organized," Aaron said.

Polly looked around the parking lot at the dazed families standing beside their cars. She wasn't sure any of them were thinking straight, much less able to function to work. "I'll take what help I can get, but if they're too upset, it's okay," she said quietly.

"Open the doors and this will work itself out. You don't have to do everything."

Aaron turned to the group gathered there, "Folks, Polly is opening the doors to the rooms, but the beds aren't made yet. She has sheets, towels and pillowcases here, though and if you need her to make up the bed, just say something." He winked at her. "They need to be able to focus on something other than their loss. This will be fine."

A young couple approached first. He was carrying a sleeping baby in a car seat and his wife held the hands of two small children whose dirty faces were tear-streaked. "Thank you so much," she said to Polly and reached out to hug her. "We can make up the room. I'm just thankful that my kids have a safe place to sleep tonight. Everything is gone." Her eyes were hollow, there was no life in them at all. Polly couldn't imagine the shock she was facing.

It took about an hour, but when everyone had unloaded the few treasures they'd been able to quickly gather, and families and pets were settled, the back of Henry's truck was empty. Polly pulled the truck door open and hauled herself up into the seat, then dropped her head into her hands. Aaron came up and put his hand on her knee.

"They'll be okay," he said. "I promise."

"This isn't enough, though. It's enough for tonight, but they have nothing left. I'm just sick."

"We all are. But you give this a couple of weeks. Things will start looking brighter. I promise. These next two weeks will be hard. We've got a lot of work ahead of us."

"How do you see this all the time and not go out of your mind?" she asked.

"I go home and hold my best friend. She reminds me that life is a circle and nothing ever stays in one place. We move forward no matter what."

"That makes sense, but it doesn't make it easier right now."

"I know you've been through a lot this evening," Aaron said and looked across the passenger seat at Henry. "I'm sorry about your uncle." He chuckled wryly. "That man was an old cuss, but he didn't deserve what happened to him. My boys ..." he winked at Polly "... and girls will figure this all out." He patted Polly's knee, "Unless, of course, you figure it out first."

"Thanks, Aaron," Henry said. "Whatever we can do to help."

Aaron nodded. "You two go home and get some sleep. Tomorrow is going to be another long day. Henry, you're going to get busier than you've ever been, I'm afraid. And Polly, I'm sending my wife over in the morning so I don't feel guilty about calling you when I need more help."

"I've got the space for whatever you need. We'll kick into full gear tomorrow."

"Have a good night, you two." Aaron pushed her door shut and walked down the sidewalk in front of the rooms, stopping and listening at each door. When he got in his car and drove away, Henry followed him out of the lot.

"What time is it?" Polly asked, her head back in her hands.

"Close to midnight," he said.

"We've crammed a lot of day into this evening."

Henry pulled into the garage, turned off the truck and reached across the console for her hand. "We have a dog upstairs who is begging to go out by now."

She shook herself. "Oh no, poor Obiwan! I'll go get him. Wanna take a walk with us?"

"Sure." He smiled at her. "A nice, peaceful walk would be a good thing tonight."

Polly opened the door leading up to her apartment. Obiwan usually heard their trucks come in and was waiting for them. Sure enough, he was at the top of the steps, panting in anticipation.

"Come on," she said. "You've been awfully good tonight."

He bounded past her and out the doors to Henry, who reached down and rubbed the dog's ears. Then Obiwan ran for the trees at the back of the property. Polly took Henry's hand and they strolled quietly over to where the dog was sniffing. The three of them walked the edge of the property, around the pasture and up around the other side of the barn. She kicked a couple of small branches out of her way as they walked and the lights on the outside of Sycamore House illuminated just how much had blown into the yard. There were twigs and branches in Eliseo's garden. She hoped that it hadn't been completely destroyed.

"We're going to have a mess to clean up tomorrow. Debris is everywhere," Henry said quietly. She jumped, not expecting to hear his voice, since they'd been walking in silence. "But I'll get up on the roof of the barn first thing and get a temporary roof built."

"It will be fine," Polly said. "I know you and Eliseo will take care of it. There are going to be a lot of people who need you, though. You just do what you have to do and take care of me when you can."

He bent over and nuzzled her ear, then said, "I'll take care of you whenever I get the chance."

She giggled. "I know you will!"

They had nearly cleared the barn, when she saw a light coming from inside. "That's odd," she said. "I wonder why he didn't turn the light off. Come here, Obiwan. Let's check."

Obiwan ran ahead of them to the door of the barn and Polly

pulled it open. "Is someone in here?" she called out.

Scuffling in Nan's stall surprised her and she crept forward. "Hello?"

Eliseo opened the door of the stall and stepped out. "It's just me." He was carrying Hansel in his arms.

"What are you doing in here?" she asked. "You should be home sleeping."

"I'm sleeping here. Well, I was asleep until you so rudely woke me up."

"Are you okay, man?" Henry asked, putting his hand on Eliseo's shoulder.

Eliseo didn't say anything, but slowly backed away from the two of them. "Do you remember me telling you that I had some rough times every once in a while? Well, storms like this tend to trigger them. It was better for me to stay with the animals tonight."

Henry took a step back to stand beside Polly and she said, "Okay, I get it. I think. Are you going to be okay?"

Eliseo nodded. "I'll be fine. I just need some open air and no one around."

"Is that why you wouldn't go to the basement with us earlier?" she asked.

Henry put his hand on her arm. "Let's leave the man alone tonight, honey. We all need to get some sleep." He began to guide her back out the door and then, turning to Eliseo. "I'm going to put plywood on the roof in the morning. If you're up to it, I'd like your help. Otherwise, do what you've gotta do."

He patted his leg for Obiwan to join them and hustled Polly out of the barn, shutting the door behind them.

"What was that?" she asked.

"He told you that he needed to not have anyone around. You wanted to jump in and discuss it. He knows how to take care of this for himself and those big horses are just the right therapy."

"Oh. Thank you. I didn't think. You're sure he'll be fine?"

"Didn't you tell me that you had a conversation with him about all of this when he started? He knows about his symptoms and has lived with himself for a long time. He's been here for a year and hasn't had a single bad episode. Let him have this one in peace. You don't have to worry, you don't have to fix him. Okay?"

"He really has done well this last year. I completely forgot about that."

"I know you did. You just accept everyone for what they give you. I love that about you."

Polly took his hand again and leaned into him as they walked around the front of the building and inside. Obiwan ran up the first few steps and waited while she pulled the main door shut. The three of them went on upstairs and into the living room. Luke and Leia came running out of the bedroom and jumped up onto the sofa acting as if they really didn't care that their humans had returned. By the time Polly dropped down beside Leia, the cat was cleaning a back foot.

"I guess I am a little tired," she said. Henry sat down beside her and she nestled into his arms. "I feel like the last few days have been all over the place. I've gone from one thing to the next without paying attention to anyone. I really miss my routine." Tears sprang to her eyes and she brushed them away.

"What's wrong, Polly?"

"This has to just be the tired talking, but I miss my friends. I didn't get to spend any time with Sylvie or Lydia or Beryl or Andy and I haven't seen Rebecca or Andrew or Jason at all." Leia shifted and Obiwan jumped up to the sofa and put his head on Polly's knee. "Your family was all here and tonight was the first time I really got to talk to Lonnie. The only good time I've had with you was once we shut our bedroom door at night. I haven't even been able to hang out with the horses and donkeys."

"Whoa," he said, laughing. Then he said. "Do you see what I did there? Whoa? Horses and donkeys? Did it make you smile at least?"

"You're a nut. Yes it did."

"These last days have been busy, but we're not leaving town tomorrow and I bet you're about to have more time than you want with all of your friends. Just think, we'll even be here when Joss and Nate bring their baby home. Now that should give you something to look forward to, right?"

She reached up and kissed him, then rested her head on his chest. "I want a big generator."

"You said that earlier."

"I want a big generator so that if the power goes out again, we can just turn it on and keep going. I didn't like that tonight."

"You really want to talk about this now?"

"I want a generator here and another one out at Sycamore Inn."

"Okay, I'll look into it."

"Good." She felt her eyes close and reached to put her hand on Obiwan's head. "It is easier."

"What's easier?" he asked.

"You."

"Polly?"

She was too exhausted to say anything.

"Polly!" Henry pushed her upright and she moaned.

"Why did you do that?"

"Because you're falling asleep on me. Let's go to bed. You are done."

"I told you I was tired."

She heaved herself up off the coach and moaned again. "It's been a long day."

"You go to bed and I'll check the house."

Polly barely had the energy to wonder why he was checking the house. He had the same app that she did and could lock the doors and shut off lights. She went into the bedroom, stripped off her clothes and crawled between the sheets. It felt wonderful.

Henry joined her in a minute and then she felt something warm and moist on her forehead. "What's this?"

"Mom used to do this for me when I was sick and exhausted." He gently wiped her face with the warm washcloth and kissed her lips. "Roll over," he ordered.

Polly rolled onto her stomach and he rubbed her shoulders and down her back with the cloth. She thought that she ought to thank him ...

CHAPTER FOURTEEN

"No more. I'm done. Please no more." Polly dropped into the chair in front of Jeff's desk late afternoon on Thursday. She was exhausted. He didn't look any better.

"What do you know?" she asked.

He grunted, "Not much. I think the groups who are staying in the classrooms and the auditorium are leaving tomorrow night. But there will be another influx Monday morning."

Several large groups of volunteers from around the state had come into Bellingwood to help with cleanup. She was impressed with their stamina. They helped unearth treasures from homes that had been destroyed, cleared mud and debris from other houses that were badly damaged, cleaned up yards and most of all, walked fields picking up things that had been deposited by the storm. Every evening they went to the elementary school for showers and then came over to Sycamore House to eat something and drop to sleep. There had never been this much continuous activity in the building, and much as she was glad to help, Polly was ready for a break. She thought that everyone in town might be ready for a short break.

Three of the families who had been staying at the hotel had already found more permanent housing and another was leaving tomorrow morning.

"What about you?" Jeff asked. "And Henry? I haven't seen him around at all this week."

"Everything he was working on has been put on hold. He's spent all week dealing with temporary construction, trying to get people's homes and farms solid enough to keep out weather. We're supposed to get more rain this weekend."

"Last year it was dry as a bone. This year we can't seem to catch a break," Jeff lamented.

"Have you seen our photographer guest around? That Lois Wexler?"

"Yes, she said this was a perfect opportunity for her to do some photojournalism. I haven't seen any of her work, but even a rank amateur should be able to get some good stuff after this storm."

"I guess she was in the right place at the right time. I've been so busy I haven't had a chance to talk to her. It's just been nuts. Every time I had a free moment, something else came up."

Polly leaned back in the chair, stretching her legs out in front of her. "I didn't want to travel this week. But I certainly didn't think this was what I'd be doing." She looked over her shoulder when she caught movement in the outer office, then sat up straight and turned to see Kelly Locke and her son standing there.

"I'm sorry to bother you again," Kelly said. "Could I please speak with you?"

"Sure, come on in." Polly had actually grown quite tired of the woman this week. She understood that Kelly was worried about her husband and daughter, but she'd pushed Polly too far several times. She sniped at her son constantly about every action he took or didn't take. She was in Jeff's office or the kitchen or wherever she could find Polly, complaining about noise or the behavior of the people who were staying there. She wasn't necessarily unpleasant, but she never seemed to be content or satisfied with the moment. She told Polly once that she knew she was a perfectionist, but when she'd informed both Jeff and Polly that she wouldn't have put so many Sycamore trees on the property because they were going to create a lot of leaves in the fall, Polly just gave up. Kelly was forever adjusting things - rearranging condiments on tables, shuffling chairs around to some pattern that Polly couldn't see. She criticized food choices and followed Rachel into the public bathrooms to instruct her on proper cleaning techniques. There would never be any pleasing Kelly Locke.

"They want to release Curt on Saturday. I told them that we didn't have a good place to go. I don't think this place is a good environment for him and we can't afford anything else."

Polly half-closed her eyes and tried not to purse her lips in anger. "What do you think should happen?" she asked.

"I don't know. I wish Jessie hadn't run away. She's the cause of all this. Her father wouldn't have been out here looking for her if she'd been at home where she belonged."

Jeff didn't miss a beat, "Doesn't your husband drive a truck? It seems to me that it was better he was here rather than out on the road somewhere. At least we were able to get him to the hospital immediately."

"Yes, but ..." Kelly started. Her son walked out of the office and dropped into a chair in front of Sarah's desk.

"Will your insurance pay for a rehabilitation facility so that he can get stronger before you have to travel back to Colorado?"

"I don't know."

"You're more than welcome to bring him here, but we can't provide any more care," Jeff said.

"Maybe your insurance will cover an ambulance to take him back to Colorado," Polly offered. "I think you should talk to him and his doctor about this."

"I can't invest any more time in Jessie. I need to be back at work on Monday. This has gone on long enough. If you find her, tell her she's on her own now."

The woman walked out of the office and Polly looked at Jeff. His face must have matched hers in shock and confusion.

"What in the heck just happened there?" he asked.

"I think she just threw her daughter away."

"People are unbelievable. The man was going to have a heart attack. Because it happened while he was in Iowa looking for his daughter, it's the girl's fault?"

"I have an idea. I can't believe I didn't think of it before." Polly jumped up and ran out of the office, catching up to Kelly Locke before she and her son entered the addition.

"Mrs. Locke?"

"Yes?"

"What was the last name of that friend of Jessie's? The one that told your husband about her boyfriend."

"That no-good trash. She won't tell you anything. I asked her repeatedly to tell me where Jessie was. I know she lied to me when she said she didn't know. I tried to get her mother to force her to tell me, but the mother isn't any better."

"Maybe she can give me a clue that she doesn't even realize she has." Polly tried to mollify the woman.

"I don't have her phone number here. It's in Jessie's phone. I left that in Colorado."

"You did what?" Polly was astounded. "Well, can you at least tell me her name? Maybe her parents' names?"

"Her name is Maggie Dunn. Her mother's name is Louise. There's no father in the house. He's probably in jail somewhere."

"Thank you. This might help me."

Kelly Locke opened the door and pushed through and her son held back. He waited until the door had closed and said, "She's just worried about Dad. She doesn't mean any of it. Anything you can do to find Jessie would be really helpful."

"Can your older brothers help at all with your dad?" Polly asked.

"They don't live close. Dave is in Oregon and Pete is in Alabama. We never see them."

"I see," she said. And she did. No wonder Curt Locke had come out here on his own to find his daughter. He wasn't ready to lose one more child to the world. "I'll do what I can."

"Can I give you my phone number? If you find her and we're gone, will you call me? Just to tell me that she's okay? And will you tell her that I miss her and want to hear from her? Even if Mom is mad, Dad and I want to be sure she's safe."

"I'll do that." He gave her his number and she entered it into her contacts.

"I'd better go before she comes looking for me. Call me, will you?"

Polly nodded and watched him take off after his mother. That poor boy had a lot on his shoulders. If he stayed close to her, he was going to end up with a great deal of responsibility.

She went back into Jeff's office. "I'm going to make a few phone calls."

"What did you find out?"

"I should have done this earlier, this week has been crazy. I'm calling Jessie's friend in Colorado if I can figure out who she is. At least now I have a name. Maybe she'll tell me something that she wouldn't tell Kelly Locke."

"You aren't a threat," he said. "At least not yet."

Polly searched the internet for Jessie's friend and landed on a phone number that had been disconnected. That was the one thing she didn't like about everyone moving to cell phones, there was no way to access those numbers easily. The next thing she did, though, was to look through Facebook. She found Jessie Locke's profile and then after a few more clicks found Maggie Dunn. All she could do was take a stab at it, so she sent a quick message to both girls and hoped for the best.

She should have tried that earlier, too. A quick search later told her that neither Kelly nor Curt Locke had profiles on Facebook, so that explained why they hadn't thought to try to reach out to their daughter in that manner. She just hoped that the girl wouldn't be too gun-shy to communicate.

"Polly?"

She turned back to the front of the office and saw her friend standing in the doorway. "Sal, what are you doing here?"

"I came by to see if you and Henry wanted to take a break tonight. Mark is going to have a free evening and maybe we could have dinner together."

"I don't know. Henry hasn't been getting home until after nine every night this week. Let me text him." Polly motioned to the chair in front of her and then sent a quick text to her husband.

"Sal and Mark are free tonight. Do you want to do dinner?"

She looked up at her friend, "I'm so sorry this week has been crazy. What a weird time for you to land in Bellingwood."

"It's actually been okay. I've been thinking a lot about things and this week is helping me make some decisions."

"Really? What kind of decisions?"

"I don't want to say too much yet. Mark and I haven't had time to talk about it."

"What exactly does that mean?" Polly couldn't let herself believe this.

"I might throw caution to the wind and move out here. Maybe it's time for me to start writing. Maybe I'll look for a job at one of the universities or colleges in the area."

"But what about your parents? Your mom will never let you come to Iowa, of all places."

"I'm in my thirties, Polly. I think Mom can let me go."

"But Mark isn't Jewish. I mean, he really isn't Jewish." Polly grimaced. "You aren't going to make him convert, are you?"

"Oh, good grief, no!" Sal started laughing. "We'll just have to figure that out as we go. It's not like this is going to carve a big hole in my life. And Mom and Dad only go to temple when they have to. I don't care what they say, we're just not very religious."

Polly's phone buzzed with a text from Henry. *"I'm busy. But go if you want. I'll see you later."*

"Henry can't go tonight. I didn't think he would."

"What about you? Do you have time for us?"

"I'd like to say yes, but I should be here to work in the kitchen. It's nuts around here in the evenings."

"I know. It was a long shot."

"So would you move in with Mark?"

"That's part of what we need to talk about. I think so. It's been a really great week so far. I've even gone out on some of his calls with him."

"In the mud and manure?"

Sal grinned across the desk at her. "Believe it or not! I like watching him take care of those big animals. He knows just what he's doing and before long, they're all fixed up and he's shaking hands with the farmer." Her face dropped. "I didn't like watching him put down a calf that had been hurt in the storm. She was a little girl's 4-H calf and that poor child cried and cried. He said there wasn't anything he could have done, but it broke my heart."

"And you still want to move here, after all of that?"

"I'm as surprised as you."

"When will this happen?"

"I don't know." Sal was shaking her head. "Like I said, we need to talk. But I tell you what, after being here through this and meeting so many different people and being able to breathe at night and not panic in the morning about getting to work, I don't want to go back at all. I just want to call my dad and have him hire a moving company to pack my apartment and ship the stuff to me."

"Wow," Polly said. "Just. Wow."

"I know! I'm really excited." She reached across the desk and Polly put her hand out to take Sal's. "Are you going to be okay with me moving to your little town?"

"Of course I will."

"But you have an amazing life here and I don't want you to think I'm horning in on it."

Polly squeezed Sal's fingers and then sat back in her chair. "You're a nut. You are one of my very best friends and even though I haven't shown it this week, I love having you around. And besides, this isn't my little town. People move in and out all the time."

"But it is your friends I'm getting to know."

"Don't be silly. We've never been like that." Polly jumped up and ran around the desk to hug Sal. "If you think you'll be happy here, I can hardly wait!"

"Oh, I'm so glad," Sal breathed a sigh of relief. "I just wanted to make sure."

"Be sure. This is going to be fun."

"It will be, won't it? We'll rock Iowa until they don't know what to do."

"Or something like that."

Sal scooted her chair back and stood. "I'd better get back to Mark's house. Are you sure you don't want to go with us tonight?"

"It sounds like you two have some things to talk about. We'll find a time before you go back to Boston."

Polly watched Sal leave and shook her head. Life never slowed down. She went back to her desk and was surprised to find that there was a message in her Facebook inbox. It was from Maggie Dunn.

"I looked you up online and I think Jessie needs your help. But you have to promise not to tell her mom where she is."

Polly responded. *"I can't make that promise, but I will do everything I can to make sure that Jessie is safe."*

"I won't tell you where she is if you are going to send that witch after her. She hates Jessie."

This conversation surprised Polly. She didn't even know the girl.

"I don't think that's true, but Jessie's dad had a heart attack last weekend and I know he'd like to know that she's safe."

"I didn't know that. Is he okay?"

"He will be fine, but he's worried about his daughter. They both are. Do you have a way to reach Jessie?"

"We talk on Facebook. She has to go to the library to do it though. We're supposed to talk at eight o'clock on Saturdays, Tuesdays and Thursdays, but I haven't heard from her since last week."

"Will you tell me where she is? Does she have a job? Is she living someplace safe?"

Polly waited ... and then waited some more.

"Maggie? Are you still there?"

"I don't think she's in a good place. But I want to talk to her before I tell you where she is."

"I understand that. If I give you my cell number, will you call me when you hear from her?"

"Yes. If she doesn't log in tonight, can I call you anyway?"

"Absolutely."

"You can't call the police or tell her mom, okay?"

"Maggie, I told you, I won't promise any of that. My only goal is to make sure that she is safe and okay. I won't make her go back home or do anything she doesn't want to do, but her family needs to know."

"Okay."

Polly gave the girl her cell phone number and sat back in her chair, then looked up and said in the way of a prayer, "Please let her log in tonight so we can find her."

She became distracted by a sudden influx of young people, coming in and moving throughout the building. Some of them waved at her. She recognized them from short conversations throughout the week. If there was one thing that kids this age were good at, it was digging in when they were needed. What a way to spend their summer break. She gave a sigh and headed for the kitchen.

CHAPTER FIFTEEN

"Shh," Polly said to whichever cat was purring loudly beside her head. She opened her eyes and saw a piece of paper on top of Henry's pillow. He'd left her a note.

"You were sound asleep. The dog's been walked. I made coffee. You're cute when you're asleep. I love you."

Last night she took supper to him about eight o'clock and he hadn't come home until after eleven thirty. He'd dropped into bed and she couldn't believe that she was the one who had slept through all of the regular morning activities.

"Good morning," she texted him. *"I love you, too. Are you going to get a break this weekend?"*

It didn't take long for him to respond. *"I hope so. There are a lot of houses that need to be protected from the rain that's coming in. It won't be long, though. I promise."*

"Okay, let me know if you need anything."

"Lunch and a kiss?"

"I'll be there."

She smiled. Even in the midst of all of this, he still made her feel important.

Neither Jessie, nor her friend, Maggie, had contacted her last night, but at least someone was communicating with the girl. Polly was going to Boone early this morning to see Curt Locke. His wife didn't go down until the middle of the afternoon and Polly wanted to talk to him about what she'd learned. At this point she didn't know what to think, but the bad feelings between Kelly and her daughter weren't going to make it easy to get the girl to safety. A side trip to the Sheriff's office in Boone might also be in order. If nothing else, Anita might be able to give her a little insight as to what was happening with Henry's Uncle Loren.

Obiwan looked up from his spot on Henry's side as she swung her legs over the side of the bed. "Yeah, you slug," she said. "You've already been out. You're going to take another nap, aren't you?" He thumped his tail and stretched his front paws out to reach her. Polly rubbed his head. "I love you, too. I'd better get going, though."

After a shower and cup of coffee, Polly headed down the back steps. It was still early, but there were plenty of people moving around the building. Rachel was in charge of the kitchen when Sylvie was gone and Polly poked her head in to see what was going on.

"Good morning," she said to Lydia and Andy. "She has you working today?"

Lydia pulled her hands out of the soapy water in the sink and dried them on a towel hanging off her apron. "Good morning, Polly. I was just coming in when your sweet husband was driving away. That boy was up and at 'em early this morning."

"He's been doing that all week. And just think, we could have been riding down into the Grand Canyon on burros."

Lydia chuckled. "I'm not sure I'd choose that for my vacation expedition, but to each his own. I haven't had an opportunity to talk to Marie this week. It seems like every time I think to call her, something else comes up. How are they handling Loren's death?"

"They're fine. No one has had much time to think about it. I'm going to Boone. I might haunt Anita for some information if she has any."

"Aaron hasn't said anything, but I haven't seen much of him this week either. You should stop over at the Methodist Church later. The ladies are serving lunch on the front lawn today."

"I promised Henry I'd feed him. That's a great idea."

"Well stop by. It's just boxed sandwiches. We'll put it in a bag for you two."

Polly hugged her, "I'll probably be there, then. Thank you."

She went out to her truck. When she turned it on and looked at the clock, she realized she had plenty of time to drive around town. After the destruction that had swooped through last Sunday evening, Polly hadn't really had time to explore things. She drove north. There were several cul de sacs that were still roped off, but debris was constantly being hauled out of town and streets were reopening every day. Henry said his main goal was to at least get temporary walls and roofs up so people could return home. It was going to take a long time for many of the residents to return to normal, but maybe when they began to redefine normal, life wouldn't be quite so frightening.

After passing a series of flattened homes and seeing families still going through rubble in an attempt to find anything that could be salvaged, Polly'd had more than she could take. Ben Bowen's wife was still a wreck. Their youngest son and his wife lived in Lehigh and wanted them to move in until they could rebuild, but Amanda refused to leave Bellingwood. Every morning she went back to their home with black garbage bags and picked through the rubble until she found something familiar. Ben was worried about her, but didn't know what to do to help. He had rented a storage unit so that everything she collected could be held until they found a place to live, and she carried bag after bag off the site. Much of it was broken glassware and china – useless - but each piece brought more tears. She'd come back to Sycamore House one night clutching a pair of candlesticks. Ben had gone out the next morning and purchased two candles for her. It was all he knew to do.

Polly's phone rang as she was driving to Boone. She didn't recognize the number.

"Good morning," she said.

"Miss Giller?" It was Maggie Dunn.

"Yes, and call me Polly. Is everything okay with Jessie?"

"She didn't log on last night. I stayed up really late and Mom told me I shouldn't call you, but I'm worried about her. She always talks to me and it's been too long."

Polly blew out a breath. "I'm going to the hospital in Boone to see her father right now. Can you tell me anything about where she has been living? Anything at all? I'm going to need something more concrete if I'm to find her."

"That Dennis guy is a real creep. I think he's done something to her."

"He told me that she left him two weeks ago and went to Waterloo to find a job."

"He's a liar. She had to get a job, but only because he made her. For a while, he didn't care what she did, but Jessie told me that he's been getting really weird lately. He's all pushy and possessive. I think she was starting to get a little scared of him. She said he does crack and then he wants her to do it too. I made her promise not to, but I don't know. He always telling her what to do. She goes to the library to get on the Internet when he works late. I don't know if his schedule changed or what, but she hasn't been on since last Thursday."

"So, she's still living with him?"

"I think so."

"Do you believe she's in danger?"

"Maybe ..." the girl's voice trailed off. That didn't give Polly a lot of confidence.

Polly hoped that her phone call last weekend hadn't gotten the poor girl into trouble with this jerk. "I need to ask some more questions around here, Maggie. I'll do what I can. Keep an eye out for her. Maybe his schedule did change and she'll find a way to get to you. Let me know as soon as you hear something."

"You have my number now, will you call me?"

"I will call you as soon as I can."

"Thank you."

Polly pulled into the parking lot at the hospital. "Keep in touch, Maggie."

She went inside, asked for Curtis Locke, and followed the volunteer's directions to his room. He was sitting up and watching television when she knocked on the door.

"Hello, Miss Giller," he said.

"Hi. And it's Polly. I mean it. May I come in?"

He nodded to the chair beside his bed and she sat down.

"It's nice to see you. I want to thank you for everything you've done for my family. Especially since I know you've been busy after the tornado. You've been very kind to all of us."

"I'm glad to help." She bit her lip and continued. "Mr. Locke, I need to ask a couple of questions about your wife's relationship with Jessie."

He dropped his head back on the pillow and let out a sigh. "Those two are like oil and water. It's my fault. I should have been there more to make it easy on Kelly. She raised those kids without me. Jessie could never find it in her to just do what her mother wanted. She's run away before, but we were always able to bring her home. This feels a little more permanent. I just hate the thought of never seeing her again."

"I've been in contact with her friend, Maggie."

His eyes lit up. "You have? Has she been helpful?"

"I reached out to her last night and she's been chatting with your daughter on a pretty regular basis, but lost contact with her last week. I think Jessie is still with that boy and there might be some trouble."

He rose up and his eyes flashed. "He'd best not hurt my girl."

Polly was certain he would set off alarms on all of the machinery he was hooked up to and nurses would rush into the room at any minute. "No. You can't do anything from here. I'm not giving up, though."

He didn't relax. "Just tell me where he lives. I don't need to be in this room any longer. I'll check myself out."

She put her hand on his, attempting to avoid the IV needle. "Really. There's nothing you can do until we find out more information. I guess, though, I need to know what you expect from Jessie. If I find her, what do I tell her?"

He sat back, confused. "What do you mean? Tell her that her mother and I want her to come home."

"What if she doesn't want to come home? She's an adult and living in her mother's home might not be what she wants."

"I don't care what she wants." His voice began to rise and then it was as if he heard himself. "I do care what she wants," he said, a little more evenly. "But she's still my little girl and I don't think she's ready to be living on her own."

"She seems to be making very adult decisions right now, even if they're wrong. I think she's asking you to treat her like an adult," Polly said. "I know it was hard for Dad to let me decide to stay in Boston after I was done with college, but when I told him what I wanted to do, he supported me."

"But you talked to him about it before you went off and did it."

"You're right. I did. I don't think Jessie's making good decisions and she needs your help with that."

He looked at Polly, his eyes sad and tired. "I haven't helped her very much. Even when she was fighting with her mother, it was easier just to let them duke it out. I wasn't around enough to feel like I was part of things and they didn't make it easy for me to come home and be part of their lives. But, that's on me. Spending all that time on the road is a hard life for a family."

"Are you going back to Colorado when they release you tomorrow?" Polly asked.

He put a hand on his forehead and shut his eyes. "Damn it, I can't believe I had a heart attack. It just makes this all so much harder to handle. Kelly isn't going to let me stay out here. We haven't even talked about how I'm going to get my car back home. This is all such a mess. She has to be at work on Monday." He took a couple of deep breaths. "I've really screwed this whole thing up."

"You have to quit taking the blame for things that happened around you, Mr. Locke. Sometimes things just get out of control."

"I don't want to leave you with this."

Polly smiled. "My husband thinks my main purpose in life is as a rescuer. I've rescued horses, donkeys, cats and sometimes I help people. I certainly don't mind doing what I can."

"Do you believe this man she's with is dangerous?"

"I don't know that, but I can assure you that if it feels like he is, I won't do anything stupid. I have too many friends in law enforcement that would make my life miserable if I got myself or anyone else in trouble."

"Then if I have to leave tomorrow with my wife, will you stay in touch with me? I don't have much money, but will do what I can to bring her home." He looked up at her. "If I leave my car with you, Jessie could drive it back home."

"You can certainly leave your car at Sycamore House. I will stay in contact, but as long as Jessie is safe, I can't make her go anywhere."

"I know that. Just have her call me. She doesn't have to call her mother. I understand that they don't like each other very much right now, but I want to talk to my baby girl." He looked as if he were going to cry. Polly wasn't sure if that was a result of what his body had been through this last week or his emotional state.

"Take care of yourself, Mr. Locke, and I'll do what I can to find your daughter." She stood to leave.

"Thank you, Polly. Your father would be proud of you."

She smiled at him and walked out into the hallway, stopping at the nurse's chair to take a breath. She'd done it again. Walked into a situation that had nothing to do with her and made promises to help someone who might not even want any help. At least Henry wasn't here to watch her do it. A flashing clock on the computer's screen saver told her there was plenty of time to stop in and see Anita at the sheriff's office.

CHAPTER SIXTEEN

Turning west on Mamie Eisenhower Avenue in Boone, Polly stretched her shoulders and scowled down at her ringing phone. "I'm busy," she said. It rang again. She certainly wasn't expecting a call from Sylvie. For these last couple of days, some big shot chef and his team were on campus and Sylvie had jumped at the chance to work beside him.

"Hi, Sylvie, is everything okay?" Polly asked.

"No it's not." Sylvie sounded annoyed. "Andrew hurt himself at camp and they've taken him to Methodist in Des Moines. I'm on my way there."

"What happened?"

"I don't know for sure, but I think he broke his arm."

"Oh no! Tell me what I can do to help. I'm in Boone right now and can be there in maybe forty-five minutes."

Sylvie exhaled a distinct sigh of relief. "I feel like such a terrible mom," she said, "But if he isn't in awful shape and it really is just a break, would you mind taking him back home?"

"Of course I don't mind. Are you okay with things at school?"

"They're taking a break and all I have to do is call and let them know what I'm doing. I really hate to miss the end of the whole thing, but I will if necessary."

Polly turned a corner to make her way back out to Story Street and head south. "You know I'll help you."

"You're a life saver," Sylvie said. "Oh Polly, I feel like a fool. I should have just told them I wouldn't be back."

"That makes no sense. You know as well as I do that Andrew is going to be proud of this cast. He doesn't need you to babysit him. You don't know what he did?"

Sylvie chuckled, "I don't know yet, but I'm sure there will be some huge story around it and he'll find a way to make it more exciting than it really was."

"You're probably right. Okay, I'll find you when I get there."

"Thanks, Polly."

This had been the craziest week. She was absolutely certain that it wasn't so long ago she'd been living a perfectly routine, everyday, humdrum life. There weren't any dead bodies or lost daughters, no tornadoes or adoptions. Everyone was living their life just like they did every day. Lydia was busy with her grandkids and other activities while Beryl cursed at her agents, clients, and galleries and spent long hours in her studio trying to finish several commissions.

It seemed to Polly like months could pass with nothing abnormal happening and then out of the blue, her world exploded and complete craziness ensued. She gave a slight giggle and looked up to the sky. "Was it just time for me to get out of my comfort zone again? You couldn't wait a year or longer before tossing my world into the blender?"

The clock on her dash informed her that there wasn't enough time to get to Des Moines and back before lunch. Poor Henry. She was a terrible wife, but she had to call and tell him that she was too busy for him.

"Hey puddin' pop." he answered.

"Yeah, that's not it either," she said, laughing. Since Polly banned the term of endearment Henry had given her because of its abuse by a crazy woman, he'd been looking for a new one. He wasn't about to be satisfied with something as simple as 'honey' or 'sweetheart.' Henry wanted it to be unique. They were mostly awful.

"I'll keep trying. So what are you bringing me for lunch?"

"Well, I was going to go to the Methodist church. Lydia told me it was a box lunch."

"That would be perfect. I know for a fact they're serving homemade ice cream, too. But it sounds like that idea is past tense."

"I'm a terrible wife, but I'm on my way to Methodist Hospital in Des Moines."

"Are you okay? What happened? And why are you terrible?"

"I'm fine. Sorry." Polly giggled. She knew exactly what she'd said and how she'd said it.

"Then what?"

"I'm meeting Sylvie. Andrew broke his arm at camp and I'm going to bring him back to Bellingwood for her."

"Oh, that poor kid. Friday night is the best night at summer camp."

"Yeah. I remember. But, there it is. Sylvie doesn't want to miss out on the end of this seminar with the fancy chef and it's no big deal for me to get down there, except that I can't feed you now. Bad wife."

Henry laughed. "I'll let you off the hook with this one. Don't worry about it. Now that I know the Methodist ladies are serving lunch *and* ice cream, we'll all take a break and head over. I wouldn't miss that for the world."

"That's not fair," she said with a pout. "I have to miss it."

"Stinks to be you."

"Thanks."

"Have you heard anything from Joss and Nate yet?"

"Not a word. I hope this works out for them. I think Nate's going to explode if they don't get this baby soon."

"Okay. Well ... "

"I know, I know. You have to get back to work. Enjoy your lunch."

"I love you ... ummm ... Polly baby."

"Yeah. That's not it either. And I love you too."

She turned the radio on after they hung up and let it distract her during the rest of the drive. She hadn't been to the hospital since last summer when Beryl's water heater had exploded and hoped she could remember the way. Her memory, with a little help from signs along the way, took her to the Emergency Room entrance, where she parked her truck and went inside.

Polly was a little surprised to see Rebecca there with a young man wearing a camp t-shirt. He didn't look like he was even out of high school, but she thought that might have something to do with the fact that she was getting older and everyone looked like a kid these days.

"What are you doing here, honey?" she asked when the little girl ran to greet her.

"I kept Andrew company on the way up. I didn't want him to be alone. He was kind of scared."

"That was pretty wonderful of you. Is his mom here?"

"Yeah. She's in there," Rebecca pointed at some doors.

The young man walked over to them and put out his hand, "I'm Roy Nelson, a counselor from camp."

"What did Andrew do?" Polly asked.

"He was climbing a tree and fell out of it," Rebecca burst in. "He said he heard his arm crack."

"You're kidding, right?" Polly looked at the young man.

"That's what he said."

Polly took the hand that Rebecca had offered and led her back to the chairs, "So was Andrew supposed to be in that tree?"

"They dared him to climb it," she said. "But he wasn't scared at all until he was lying on the ground."

"I'll bet."

Rebecca leaned into Polly and said quietly enough that the counselor couldn't hear her. "Will you take me home with you and Andrew? I don't want to be there without him."

"It's only one more night," Polly said just as quietly. "Don't you like camp?"

"The girls in my cabin were all together last year and they're stuck up. They told me they don't like me."

"Oh, I'm sorry." Polly put her arm around Rebecca's shoulders. "Are you sure about that? What about all of your things?"

Rebecca pointed to two duffel bags. "Roy packed Andrew's things and I brought mine just in case you said yes."

"Of course I'll say yes, but maybe you should talk to your mom."

"She'll let me come home. I just know she will."

Polly swiped her phone open and brought up Sarah's number, then handed it to Rebecca. "You call her. If she's ready for you to come home, then I will certainly take you."

"Thank you!" Rebecca jumped up and went to a corner of the waiting room and was soon talking animatedly into the phone. She was nodding and smiling, then ran back to Polly and jumped up on the chair beside her.

Rebecca whispered into Polly's ear. "She says I can come home with you and Andrew and that if he," she looked at Roy, who was reading a magazine, "has a problem with it, he can call her. Will you tell him or should I?"

Polly grinned at the girl. "You can start if you'd like. If you need backup, I'm right here."

Throwing her arms around Polly's neck, Rebecca kissed her cheek and said, "You're the greatest." Then she bounced down to the floor and went up to stand in front of the counselor. "Excuse me, Roy?"

"Yes, Rebecca."

"Mom says I can go home with Polly and Andrew. I have my stuff. Is that okay?"

He glanced at Polly, who nodded slightly and then he turned back to Rebecca. "If you'd like to do that, I think it would be fine. Andrew will probably be glad to have a friend with him."

"Thank you," Rebecca said, more shyly now.

He stood up and moved over to sit beside Polly. "We figured this might happen and I have a couple of things that I need to have you sign."

"Okay," she said and tried to read his body language. He wanted to say something else to her. Polly reached into her pocket and pulled out a few singles. "Rebecca?"

"Yes?"

"Would you mind getting me a Diet Dew from the vending machine?" She looked at Roy. "Do you want anything?"

"No, I'm fine. Thanks."

"Do you want something?" Polly asked Rebecca.

"Could I have a Coke?"

"How about something with no caffeine."

Rebecca's shoulders slumped and she walked to the machine.

"Thanks," he said. "We talked to her mother this morning while we waited for the ambulance. We knew she wouldn't want to stay at camp by herself, but thought it should be her decision."

"Awesome," Polly said. "Maybe next year she'll do better with this. She's had a pretty sheltered life up until these last few months."

"That's what we understand. She did pretty well as long as she could get to Andrew. She's not terribly comfortable with large groups of girls she doesn't know, but that will come."

He handed Polly a tablet and stylus and pointed to a highlighted line. "Just sign here that you are taking responsibility for her and we're good to go."

"That's pretty upscale paperwork for a summer camp," she said.

"It was my idea. I'm at Drake - Graphic Design and Computer Science."

"Seriously?"

"One more year."

"You're going to be a senior?"

"Fifth year senior. With the double major, I have another year."

"So you're, what. Twenty?"

"Twenty-two."

"You're just a kid."

He grinned at her. "That's what my mom said when I moved into an apartment last year."

"Where are you from?" she asked.

"Oelwein. Hub City, you know."

"I'm sorry, what?"

"Hub City? That's its nickname. I guess it's all about the railroad."

"No, where did you say you were from?"

"Oelwein? Why?"

"Because I'm looking for the daughter of a friend and the last we knew she was in your hometown. She ran away from home and from what I understand is with a real jerk of a guy and all of a sudden she's gone incommunicado. I was just talking to her father and wow, maybe you can help me."

"What's going on?"

Polly considered it for a moment and then told him most of the story. In the middle of the tale, Rebecca came back, handed her the bottle of pop and sat down with hers, listening raptly. It occurred to Polly that maybe the little girl didn't need to know about all of the ugliness in the world, but once she started talking, she wasn't going to stop.

She finished her story and then said, "I hate to do this, but is there anyone you know who might help me find this girl?"

He gave her a knowing smile. "You have no idea who you're talking to."

"What do you mean by that?"

"I mean, my dad's a cop."

Every time Polly turned around she was running into someone in law enforcement.

"Well, that just figures," she said, shaking her head.

"What do you mean?"

"It means that sometimes things just work out the way they're supposed to. Would you mind calling your dad and asking him about this? Here, I'm friends with the Sheriff in Boone and I've asked them to help me. We just hadn't gotten that far with it." She held up her phone. "Let me give you my information."

"I'll call Dad this afternoon. I won't be home until Sunday, but you'll probably hear from him before that."

"I just don't believe this," Polly said. "I don't believe it. It's a weird small world."

The doors opened and Sylvie came out, followed by a nurse pushing Andrew in a wheelchair.

"Polly!" he said. "They let me put a green cast on. Isn't it great?"

"Sure. Great. How are you doing?"

"The doctor said he was lucky and just needs a few weeks in a cast." Sylvie looked down at him. "Climbing trees on a dare. You are going to be the death of me."

"Mrs. Donovan?" The receptionist called Sylvie over, leaving Andrew beside Polly.

He held his arm up. "I'm going to see if Luke will hold on with his claws. Then I can lift him up. If I put a long sleeve shirt on, people will think that he's holding onto my arm."

"Uh huh," Polly said.

"So bud," Roy said. "It looks like you're going home today. I hope you had fun, even with a broken arm."

"I had a great time. Wasn't it great, Rebecca?"

She didn't say anything, just nodded her head.

"I can't wait to come back next year. Will you be there, Roy?"

"If you are, I guess I'll have to be. I need to protect the camp from the likes of you."

"Cool!" Andrew turned to Polly. "Mom said that if I was really nice, you might take me to McDonald's for lunch." He dug into a pocket and pulled out a twenty dollar bill. "I'm supposed to give you this and you're supposed to take it."

Polly laughed and took the money. "Do you think Rebecca wants McDonalds too?"

"You're coming with us?" Andrew was stricken when he looked at his friend. "You don't want to stay at camp until tomorrow? You're going to miss everything. Polly will take care of me. You shouldn't have to leave just because I got hurt. Tell her she doesn't have to go."

"It's okay, Andrew. I think she's ready to go home. And hey, I'm with her," Polly said. "It wouldn't be nearly as much fun without you there."

Rebecca stepped up to stand beside the wheelchair. "I have my stuff. I'm ready to go."

"Let's get this train a-rolling," he said. "I can walk."

The nurse who had been pushing his wheel chair laughed a little and said, "You're mine until you get to the car. Then you can do whatever they'll let you do."

Roy stood up and put his hand out to Polly again. "I will call my father."

"Thank you so much. You have no idea how much this means to me. You've lifted a huge weight off my shoulders. I had no idea how I was going to find this girl. Who knew."

Sylvie came over and kissed her son on his forehead. "You're free to go," she said. "But be careful this afternoon. I don't want to hear about any more chaos."

Andrew put his feet on the floor and tried to propel the wheelchair forward, then looked up at Polly with a puppy dog face. "Can we go to the bookstore in Boone?"

Everyone laughed and Polly said, "Not today. I need to get back to Bellingwood. We had a tornado up there, you know."

"It didn't wreck the bookstore in Boone, did it?" He gave her a sly grin.

"Whatever. I'll be right back with the truck."

Sylvie gave her a hug. "Thank you so much. I owe you."

"You owe me nothing. Now run, get back to school and learn something extraordinary to feed us."

"Got it." She kissed her son once more, shook Roy Nelson's hand, and patted Rebecca's head before running out the door.

CHAPTER SEVENTEEN

One book was all Polly took home from the bookstore, but it was a beauty. As soon as Andrew had asked about going, she knew she'd be unable to resist. The owner was prepared for her, setting the temptation of a leather bound edition of Jules Verne's *Twenty Thousand Leagues Under the Sea* on the counter when Polly walked in. It had just come in from an estate sale. Andrew and Rebecca ran over to the freshly updated kid's section and sat down to look at the newest books in several series' they loved to read. Two white cats had joined Zekey, the black lab, and one jumped up while Polly stroked the cover of the book. He rubbed against her hand and she rubbed his head before opening the book. It was perfect. There were still plenty of empty shelves to fill in her living room. This was a good start.

"Can we go up and play with Obiwan and the cats when we get back?" Andrew asked, once they were in the car and heading north.

"Sure," Polly said. "They've missed you this week."

"We had fun, though, didn't we?" Andrew looked at Rebecca, waiting for her to be as enthusiastic as he was.

"It was okay," she said.

"You had a poopy cabin. Those girls weren't very nice. I had a great cabin. Roy was awesome." He leaned forward across Rebecca. "One night he and one of the other counselors switched us in our beds while we were sleeping. We didn't even wake up!"

"He switched you?"

"Yeah. I woke up on the other side of the room!"

She laughed. "That's crazy!"

"When I got up one morning, he put plastic wrap on our doorway. I didn't run into it, but Devin did. He bounced and sat down on the floor. It was funny."

"That sounds like a lot of fun."

"Have you ever had your bed short-sheeted?" Andrew asked.

Polly nodded. "When I was in college there were a few times it happened."

"To you?"

"Once to me. It's a little surprising."

"Roy didn't come to dinner one night. They told us that he had to go into town to get something. When we went to bed after the bonfire, all of our beds were done. He watched us get into bed and then laughed at us. I'm going to remember that one and do it to Jason sometime."

"You'd better be careful. Jason might not think it's as funny as you did."

Andrew bobbed his head up and down. "He'll think it's funny."

"None of that happened in your cabin?" Polly asked Rebecca.

"No, they were too busy playing with their makeup or talking about boys." She looked at Andrew. "One of them wanted to kiss you."

"I don't think so," he said, then asked, "Which one?"

"Abbymae. She thought you were cute and told me that I didn't deserve you."

Polly reached around Rebecca's shoulders and pulled her in for a hug. "That wasn't very nice, but it wasn't about you. It sounds like she just wanted to scare you away from him."

"He's my best friend. She doesn't know anything."

"Girls are weird," Andrew said, looking down at the floor. Then he held his arm up, his mind moving to a different topic. "I need to get a marker so people can sign my cast."

"I'm sure I have something in the office you can use," Polly said.

She pulled into the garage and tried to get to Andrew before he jumped out of the truck, but he was already heading for the back door with Rebecca close behind him. "No problem, I'll get the bags," she muttered and took their duffel bags out of the back. The two had run up the steps to her apartment and she heard them laughing as they found the animals.

"Send Obiwan down," she called up and waited for her dog's nose to come around the banister. He came bounding down the steps when he saw her. This felt more normal. Kids in her house, the dog ready to go outside, and everyone preparing for a wedding rehearsal dinner tonight. By now most of the out-of-towners should be gone. She ducked into the auditorium and found Eliseo, Jeff and Rachel working. Jeff was running the vacuum while Eliseo and Rachel were setting up tables.

"Do you need help?" she called loudly, to be heard over the sound of the vacuum cleaner.

Eliseo waved her off and shook his head. Rachel just smiled, so Polly went out the back door with her dog. They wandered over to the garden at the corner of the lot. It had held up pretty well under the storm. Some plants had snapped, but several people who cared for the garden were here midweek to clean out the mess. They did such a beautiful job with this, the corner had turned into a lovely spot. Polly often saw people walking through the garden, taking a moment to sit and listen to the waterfall in the pond or just enjoy the peace and quiet it offered.

Her phone buzzed and she sat down on the park bench, letting Obiwan nose around. As she pulled the phone out of her pocket, he lay down on the warm paving in front of her and stretched out.

It was Joss.

"Hey!" Polly said. They hadn't talked much at all this week. Nate had gone back to work because one of his pharmacists had lost her home and Joss had kept herself busy at the library while they waited for the phone call that would change their life.

"Do you have a minute?" Joss asked.

"Sure, what's going on?"

Her friend began crying on the other end of the call.

"Joss, what happened?"

"We aren't getting the baby. The girl decided not to put it up for adoption at the last minute. Her grandmother is going to help her raise it."

"Oh sweetie, I'm so sorry. Can I come get you? Are you at the library?"

"No, I'm home. Nate will be here pretty soon."

"Joss, I'm just heartbroken. When did you find out?"

"Just now. I called him, then I called you. I don't want to talk to anyone else. Everyone has gotten so excited for us and they shouldn't have to get caught up in our emotional roller coaster."

"I understand that. But I want to come over and hold your hand and hug you."

"No, that's okay. Nate is going to be a wreck. He bought this silly sports bag with different balls in it so he could teach the baby all about football and soccer."

"I'm so sorry."

"This is the hardest part, Polly. I was fine with waiting, but to have my hopes yanked away at the last minute … I want to be sick."

"And you can't hate the girl for wanting to keep her baby."

"I know! But I want to be mad at someone."

Polly patted her knee and Obiwan sat up, putting his head there so she could stroke it. "I could bring my big dog over for you to cry on. He's pretty good about that." She heard a faint chuckle on the other end of the call.

"Maybe we should just get a dog and some cats."

"That's the way I like to do it. Really, though. When can I come hug you? I love you, sweetie."

"I love you too. How about I call you later? After Nate and I have talked. It won't take long. He'll come in and fall apart, then he'll go back out to his garage and beat on some metal or something."

"Just let me know. Henry will be working again this evening, I'm sure. He's trying to get as much done before it starts raining again and that's supposed to come in tonight."

"You know I feel so guilty being upset about this. There are people who have lost a lot this week and I know that I'm still going to get a baby, it's just not happening right now."

"Your stuff is your stuff and theirs is theirs. You've done what you could to help this week and it isn't wrong for you to be sad. Don't do that to yourself."

"Okay. I just wanted to call so you weren't wondering. I hear Nate's car. I'd better go."

"I love you, Joss. Give your husband a hug for me."

"Bye."

"Well, that sucks," Polly said to Obiwan, slipping her phone back into her pocket. "I was kind of looking forward to having a baby around."

He nudged her hand, looking for more affection. "No not that," she said. "I'm not having any babies, but Joss and Nate are going to be great parents and they were going to let me play and hand the baby back."

She stood up and walked back to the building, wandering in and out of the young sycamore trees lining the driveway. "Sometimes I feel like such a kid, Obiwan, and other times I feel so old. That young punk camp counselor down at the hospital made me feel old today."

Obiwan took off at a run and Polly looked up to see Henry's truck drive in.

She jogged over to meet him, "What are you doing here?"

"I came in to get some things from the shop and thought I'd see if I could get a hug."

"Man, I've missed you this week."

"Me too. Next week won't be quite so bad. I'm tired of working until after dark every night."

"Have you heard anything about your Uncle Loren?"

"Not much. Stu told Dad that there might be others."

"Other deaths?"

"Yeah. I hadn't heard anything about it."

"Around here?"

"Well, not around here." Henry smirked at her. "If it had been around here, you would have found the bodies, right?"

Polly swatted his belly. "Stop it. But what do you mean?"

"Around Iowa. It's mostly old guys who live alone in the country. I didn't know there were so many."

"I guess I didn't either. And I can't believe the newspapers aren't all over this."

"It's been happening over the last few years. Anita found the connection and Aaron's not saying anything because they think the person who did it is probably still in town."

Polly stepped back. "I'm sorry, what? They live here?"

"Yeah. I guess they move into an area and live for a few weeks, then kill an old man who doesn't have family. Apparently they're sticking around after it's done, too, because no one notices them leave. They fade in and then they fade out. The first one Anita found happened down by Hamburg, and then one up by Estherville and last winter an old man was killed in Osage."

"We have a serial killer in Bellingwood." Polly leaned on the truck. "That makes me a little woozy."

"Well, if it's any consolation, you aren't a target and if Uncle Loren was, the killer is probably already trying to find their next town."

"They've never killed more than one person in a town?"

"Not yet."

"This is just so weird. Is the person stealing from these old men?"

Henry nodded. "Yeah. That's part of it. But Aunt Betty kept an eye on the place. She didn't think anything strange was going on, but then, she didn't see everything."

"Well, he was killed on the road and she didn't see that."

"During the tornado."

"I suppose that's right. Were the others killed in their homes?"

"Yeah. I think so. You'd have to ask Anita."

"I was almost there this morning," Polly said. "So close. But now I have a couple of kids upstairs with the cats. I think Rebecca was done with camp and Andrew is pretty proud of his cast."

"At least you have company. I'd better get back to work."

"Oh Henry, Joss called."

"Are they headed to Omaha?"

"No, they're not getting the baby. The birth mom decided to keep it."

"I'm sorry. That's not what they needed to hear this week."

"I know. Would you give Nate a call sometime this evening? He's going to be in his garage, I think."

Henry pursed his lips with just a shade of disgust. "Guys don't do that."

"Tell their friends they've got their back?"

"Call to check up on them. We show up with a six-pack or something."

"So, show up with a six-pack or something."

"I'm working late tonight."

"So, your buddy is upset and because guys don't call to commiserate, you are going to let him deal with this by himself?"

"He has Joss. He doesn't need my shoulder. He wants to work it out in his head. We'll figure it out later."

"You men drive me crazy."

He pulled her into a hug. "Just because you're an upfront, face-it-down-right-now kind of girl, doesn't mean that everyone is like that."

"Yeah, yeah, yeah. Okay, you go back to work. I'm going to check on the hotel. I think everyone was supposed to be out of there by this afternoon."

"I love you, my little buttinsky." He walked away from her to his truck door and pulled it open. "Will that one work?"

"Not on your life," she said.

"I'll keep trying."

She put her hand on Obiwan's collar as Henry backed out and drove off. "Buttinsky. That one may cost him."

Polly opened the door and found Andrew and Rebecca at his desk under the back stairway.

"Look!" Andrew said, showing Polly his cast. "I asked Jeff for a marker and he gave me these." He held three up for her. "Will you sign it now?"

"Let me send the dog upstairs first." Polly opened the door and Obiwan went in, then turned around and looked at her. "Later, you goofball. Go on up." She shut the door slowly and he didn't move from the first step. Silly dog, making her feel guilty for not being around anymore than she was. She missed him too.

"Okay, where do you want me to sign it?"

"Anywhere. Look. Jeff drew a picture of me lying down in front of a tree. See how my arm is crooked?"

"Cool." Polly signed her name and drew what she thought looked like paw prints and a couple of horseshoes. "That should cover all of us, what do you think?"

He admired her work. "Jason tried to tell me I couldn't write since I was wearing a cast. But I can. It doesn't hurt. I'm not going to break it again if I write, am I?"

Jason was getting tired of his brother and did his best to not spend much time around him. Sylvie knew that the boys needed to have separate rooms so Jason could have his own space. They just weren't ready to make that change yet. Once she was finished with school, she promised Andrew and Jason that they would find a larger home to live in. Andrew was looking forward to getting his own dog, even though his mother wasn't quite ready for that commitment.

"Don't listen to your brother. Did the doctor say anything to you about writing?"

"No."

"Well, it seems like he's the one who would know."

"Okay."

Polly bent over and picked up Rebecca's duffel. "Do you want me to take this over to your room?"

"I'll do it. Mom said she's glad I'm back," Rebecca said, taking the bag out of Polly's hand. "Do you think she really missed me?"

"We all did, but I know she was a little lonely without you here."

Rebecca's lower lip started to quiver. "I should never have gone away."

Polly knelt down a little and looked her in the eye. "Your mom wants you to have as many experiences as you can have and she wants to hear all about them."

"But ... "

"No buts about it. The two of you talked about it before you went, right?"

"Yes."

"And she wanted you to go, right?"

"That's what she said."

"Your mother doesn't lie, does she?"

"No."

"Then she wanted you to go. You have to believe her and trust her. Okay?"

"Okay." Rebecca picked up a bag. "I'll be back later, Andrew. I need to put my things away."

Rebecca went through the door into the kitchen.

"She worries about her mom all the time," he said.

"I know she does. You are a good friend to her."

"She isn't drawing very much anymore. She spends all her time reading or watching television. I can't get her to play with me like she used to before ... you know."

"Rebecca and her mom have a tough year ahead of them. I suspect that Rebecca doesn't know how to deal with it all."

"She isn't going to relax until after her mom really does die, is she?"

"That's pretty insightful, Andrew. No, this is going to be part of what she has to deal with every day. She loves her mom so much that she can't stand the idea of her not being here, but she's always worried that it is going to happen when they least expect it."

"You're pretty cool, Polly."

"Why do you say that?"

"Because you talk real about this stuff."

Polly ruffled his hair as she stood back up. "It isn't easy stuff to talk about it, but we can't ignore it."

"Does Rebecca talk to you?"

"Not very often."

"She should. I'll tell her to."

"You know where to find me. Now, are you going to be fine down here? Do you need anything?"

"I'm good. I just can't carry a glass in my hand. This cast makes it all weird."

Polly hugged him. "I love you, Andrew Donovan."

"What's that for?" he asked, backing away when she was done.

"You're wonderful. Tell anyone if you need something."

She opened the door to her apartment and found Obiwan lying down on the first step. "You silly dog. Did you hear my voice out there and think I was coming to you? Let's go." He raced up the steps and waited at the top, his tail wagging.

CHAPTER EIGHTEEN

By the time Polly was ready to head over to Sycamore Inn, Andrew and Rebecca were settled in on her sofa, watching movies. Hopefully everyone had cleared out. There had been a scurry as they looked for apartments and homes to rent, but the community came together and made it happen. Ben and his wife were still at Sycamore House, but they hadn't really even looked yet for another place to live. If Amanda needed more time to deal with her loss, then Polly could offer it to them.

When she pulled into the hotel's parking lot, she was thankful to find it empty. She knocked on the door to Room 1 and opened it. They had pretty much cleaned up after themselves. The linens were all in a pile on the bed and trash had been sacked up and placed just inside the door. People had different ways of leaving these rooms. For the most part it wasn't too bad to clean up after them. She hauled the linens to the bed of her truck and then tossed the bag of trash in after it.

She dutifully knocked on the door to Room 4 and when there was no answer, swiped it open and took a breath. This was what she'd been waiting for and sure enough, here it was. There was trash everywhere. Chocolate and unidentifiable food was smeared across the beautiful wooden desk, the dresser drawers were all standing open, and towels were draped on every surface imaginable. The room stank like something had died and the bed linens were soiled beyond belief. Polly put her hands up to her head, backed up and out of the room and took a deep breath. It wasn't like she hadn't come prepared, so she went back to the truck and took out trash bags, a fresh pair of rubber gloves, and cleaning supplies. At least she'd get in some good hard work today.

Her phone rang while she was bent over, scrubbing the inside of the refrigerator. She'd found the source of the stench tossed behind the fridge and it was now gone from the room in a very full bag of garbage.

"Hello?" she said.

"Is this Polly Giller?" came a strong male voice.

"Yes it is. How can I help you?" Polly sat back on her haunches.

"Hi, Miss Giller. I'm Dean Nelson, Roy's dad. You met him this morning at the hospital in Des Moines?"

"Oh yes. Thank you for calling."

"He gave me the information you had on this girl, Jessie Locke."

"Yes. Can you help?"

"I spoke with my boss and come to find out he worked with your friend, Aaron Merritt, before moving to Oelwein. So, he made a quick call and this got turned into an official request."

"Whoa. I didn't mean to do that."

"It's okay. It allows me some latitude."

Polly chuckled. "I can't believe Aaron didn't call to tell me I'd done something wrong. But, I suppose he's been a little busy."

"You all did get hammered last weekend," he agreed.

"Tell me what I need to do to help you."

"I made a call to Dennis Smith's place of work and he is scheduled to be there tomorrow from ten until three. I'll drop by his house while he's gone and hopefully I'll be able to talk to your friend and find out what's going on. If she needs our help, we'll be sure to offer it. If she isn't interested, then I will have to walk away."

"But you can tell me if she's there or not. Maybe I can talk to her?"

"I can make that happen."

"Thank you so much. As long as she's safe, I'm not concerned with where she lives, but her family and friends are worried about her."

"I will contact you tomorrow."

"Thank you again. Your son seems like a really good kid. The young boy who broke his arm at camp just thinks the world of him."

She could almost hear the man smiling. "He is a good kid. He's made us proud. It's hard to believe that in one more year he'll be on his own in the world." He hesitated and then said, "I will speak with you tomorrow. Have a good evening."

Polly dug back into the refrigerator and when she was satisfied it was clean, stripped the bed, trying not to think about what was on those sheets. She was pretty sure that housekeeping in a large motel would never be her calling. She shuddered to think about it. This place was big enough. People could mess seventeen rooms up in a hurry.

She pulled her phone back out and quickly texted Jeff Lyndsay. *"Just in case I don't say it enough, I appreciate you."*

"What brought this on?" came the reply.

"I'm cleaning out one of the hotel rooms and this is not a job I could ever do full-time. I am glad you are working to find people that will do it and still smile at the end of the day."

"Heh, I'm a rockstar," he typed back.

"The only one I'll ever know," she sent.

She was going to have to bring the vacuum back tomorrow, but for now, she could walk away and not feel as if there was an unfinished mess in her world. Polly pulled into her garage when her phone rang again.

"Seriously?" she said out loud. "I feel like I'm getting nowhere today."

She let the call go to voice mail as she dropped the trash bags on the floor of the garage and pulled the laundry into the back room. All she wanted to do was get the first load into the washing machine and take a shower. She hadn't felt so utterly filthy in a long time. Dirty was one thing, but this was more than she could bear. After starting a load, Polly ran upstairs. Andrew and Rebecca were watching television when she went through.

"I'm taking a shower. That last room I cleaned was awful. Do you guys need anything?"

"We're cool," Andrew said, not even looking up. Polly glanced at Rebecca and got a smile.

"Are you glad to be home, Rebecca?" she asked.

Rebecca bent over and nuzzled Obiwan's neck. "I am. It's better here."

Polly looked at her phone when she sat down on her bed to untie her boots. Joss had called. Polly's heart sank. She knew that her friend needed her, but the moment she made that call, sadness was going to fill her life again. She took a deep breath and made the call anyway.

"Hi Polly," Joss said. "Nate finally went out to the garage. He's pretty destroyed."

"Would you like to meet me somewhere or can I come over?"

"No, really, that's okay. I'm just going to put popcorn in the microwave and open a bottle of wine."

"I could come do that with you. I'd even bring ice cream sandwiches for later."

"Maybe I should do this one by myself. I'm not much good to anyone and if I want to get all ugly and snorty with my crying, I don't have to be embarrassed."

"If you're sure."

"Yeah. Tomorrow will be better. Both Nate and I know this isn't the end. We just have to manage through it tonight."

"I love you, sweetie."

"I love you too."

Polly climbed in the shower and realized that tears were trickling down her face. She shut her eyes and felt the water pelt her back. It wasn't fair. They had been waiting so long. Nothing seemed fair this week. She hunched down and wrapped her arms around her bent knees. This week just plain sucked. The worst of it was that Henry was gone all the time and she hadn't had a chance to talk to him. He came home every night completely exhausted and left before she got up in the morning.

"I could use a little rain here, God," she said. "Make him stop working and come home. Just for an evening. You can have him back tomorrow. And while you're at it, all of these other things that are going on around here? Anything you want to fix would be fine with me."

She stood back up and rubbed shampoo into her hair, scratching her scalp with her nails. Good heavens, that felt wonderful.

She heard a sound behind her and turned around to see a shadow. Before a word was spoken, she screamed!

"Polly, it's just me. It's okay."

Polly peeked out of the shower door. Henry was looking a little chagrined.

"What are you doing here?"

"I'll be right back. I just want to tell the kids that everything is okay. That was a horrifying screech you just made." He jogged out of the room and by the time he came back, Polly had rinsed off and was wrapping a towel around herself.

"Well, that's not any fun," he said, pointing at the towel.

"Uh huh. Cute. Now what are you doing here?"

"Those big black clouds? We slammed plywood onto the roof of Binney's barn and called it a night. I've buttoned up as much of Bellingwood as I could before this rain came in and I'm spending the rest of the day with you. How does that sound?"

Polly threw herself into his arms and her eyes got wet again. She looked upward and mouthed, "Thank you," then said out loud. "It sounds absolutely perfect. What do you want to do?"

"How's our little gimp boy set for tonight? I'd like to go out to Uncle Loren's and poke around. I haven't been in his house for years. There are things out there that our family talked about, but we didn't know if he'd just destroyed them or gotten rid of them. Then maybe we could have dinner all by ourselves."

She hugged him tight and said, "Anything you want to do is great. Just so I'm with you. I've missed you so much."

"I've missed you too. Even when we weren't married, I saw you more than I have this week."

"I'm calling Sarah and see if she'll keep an eye on Rebecca and Andrew tonight. Jason is doing something with Doug and Billy. Other than that, I'm free."

"Did you talk to Joss?"

"Yes. Did you talk to Nate?"

He squeezed her. "No. I told you. We'll work it out. It's fine. You go deal with your world and I'm going to take a shower and get all gussied up for you."

"Really gussied?"

"No, just clean gussied."

Polly turned to leave the bathroom and he grabbed the towel from her. "Hey!" she said.

"I'z jes checkin' to see what I been missin'."

She grinned and looked over her shoulder at him while swinging her hips as she walked away.

"Polly!" he yelled, just as she thumped into the doorsill.

"Yeah. I stink at this," she laughed. Before she knew it, she was laughing so hard she dropped to the floor, holding her belly, snorting until tears ran down her face.

Henry stood over her, laughing a little bit, but he bent down and rubbed her shoulder. "Are you going to be okay?"

"I'm fine. Wow, I'm a dork," she said, still laughing. "It's a good thing you love me. Because I don't do sexy vamp very well."

"You're sexy enough without vamping me. And for some reason, even laughing until snot runs out of your nose is still pretty sexy."

He held his hand out to help her stand up again. "Are you going to be okay now?"

She let out a sigh and said, "I guess. I'm a little embarrassed, but that was too funny."

"Go get dressed and I'd advise you to watch where you're going." He patted her bottom as she walked through the door and into the bedroom.

When he came in to find her, Polly was sitting between Rebecca and Andrew with a book in her lap.

"What are you reading?" he asked.

"*A Wrinkle in Time*. I can't believe Andrew's never read it before. This is Rebecca's first time too."

"It made me dream of being in space," Henry said. "Can you guys finish this without her? I want to take Polly away tonight."

"Are you going to start your honeymoon now?" Rebecca asked.

Polly put the book in her hands and stood up. "No, we're just going out to his Uncle Loren's house and look around."

"Cool! I want to see that sometime," Andrew said. "I'll bet there's a lot of interesting stuff in there. You should take pictures."

"I'll do that. You guys head down to Rebecca's mom when she calls, okay?"

Andrew scooted closer to Rebecca. "We're going to read for a while, though. This is cool. I like having people read out loud to me."

"It never gets old," Henry said to Polly as they headed down the back steps. "You're a good reader, too. I like listening to your voice."

"You're just saying that because you have to."

"Not really. So, did you get everything taken care of for tonight?"

"Jason is going to take Obiwan out later, Rachel has food to feed the hordes, the kids are staying with Sarah until Sylvie gets here and I think that's it."

"You're amazing." He kissed her on the cheek and held the truck door open for her.

"I was pretty motivated."

Henry pulled into his Uncle Loren's driveway. Nothing had really changed. The yard was still littered with junk, but at least Polly knew that when she went inside, it would be relatively clean.

"What happened with the cats and chickens this week?"

"Aunt Betty has been over to take care of the chickens. Mom spent the week looking for homes for the cats. I think she got all of them dealt with. Two of them just became shop kitties. Since Dad is out there all the time, they'll be happy and safe. When I was over this morning, they'd already found a home in an old toybox of mine. Dad's such a sucker." He opened the front door and flipped the light on and gestured for Polly to go in first.

"So, what did your uncle's will say?" Polly asked. Wow. They hadn't had time to talk about anything this week.

"He left everything to Dad and Aunt Betty. They'll figure it out. It's not like anyone is in a hurry to sell, so this will probably be here until they're dead and gone and all of us kids will have to deal with it."

"That's not a good idea, Henry." Polly placed her hand on his arm.

"Don't worry. I know and so does Dad. It will get handled."

He led her through the living room, into an immense dining room and then into the kitchen. It was a small room, with ancient appliances. Old yellow curtains hung from the window over the sink and on the window of a back door.

"When Grandma was still alive, this was the place to be," Henry said. "I'd sit there in front of the cupboard and watch her cook and bake, helping whenever she had something for me to do. Dad would always bring me out when she was canning, so I could run everything down to the cellar and stack it on her shelves." He looked out the back window. "She had a huge garden out here and over on that side, there were even a couple of rows of grape vines. She made the best jelly."

Henry sat down and looked around, then jumped up. "This cookie jar was always full." He took the lid off. "As she got older, the cookies were more store bought than homemade, but I could always count on getting a cookie when I was here."

He pointed to a worn corner on the table. "I remember her teaching me how to use her old grinder right there. She made carrot salad all the time. It was just ground up carrots and mayonnaise, but whenever we ate here, that was on the menu. I ground more carrots for her ..."

Another door was standing open and Polly looked through it to see a wooden staircase leading up. "What's up here?" she asked.

"The bedrooms. Let's go." He followed her up the steps and pointed ahead. "That's the bathroom. She had a clawfoot tub in there. I don't think she ever put a shower in. Especially once she quit using these rooms all the time. We kids liked the tub. It was fun and different."

"This front room was Loren's, but the other two were for us kids whenever we visited. The back bedroom was Dad's when he was a boy, so that's where I liked to sleep. She had a white chenille bedspread on the bed with blue and pink flowers. I used to run my fingers through the patterns at night."

Polly had never seen him reminisce like this and followed him to the back room.

"Wow. Loren didn't change a thing. Look at this, Polly."

Sure enough, the bedspread was still on the bed, the pillows tucked in and everything neatly arranged. There was a linen runner on the dresser and a little chair sitting beside the bed.

"That's kind of weird. He never wanted anyone to visit, but he kept it ready, just in case."

"I wonder if he slept up here in his old bedroom or moved downstairs into Grandma and Grandpa's room."

The front bedroom was immaculate and when they checked, the dresser was empty. They went back downstairs and through the kitchen into an office utility room. Just off that room was another bathroom with a shower and then the master bedroom. This was where Loren must have been staying.

"Look, though," Henry said. "His clothes are all out here by the washer and dryer in this little chest of drawers. I wonder if he left Grandma's things in place."

"Do you think he slept on the couch or in here on the bed?"

"Oh Polly, do you think that he just existed out there?"

"There is a pile of sheets and blankets beside the couch and a couple of pillows there. I'll bet he didn't use anything else."

"That's so sad." Henry opened the door of a wardrobe standing at the end of the room. "Look at this. Here's his uniform, still in the plastic from the dry cleaners. And here are his boots, polished to a shine."

"This is really a wonderful house. It would be too bad if it just sat here empty. If someone fixed up the outside, it would be awesome for a family."

"Don't even think it. I'll never have time for this."

"I know. But still." Polly sat down in a chair at a secretary. "Have you guys looked through this stuff yet?"

"Not really. We haven't had time."

She pulled the top down, creating a desktop. There were papers and receipts shoved in every nook and cranny of the top. "Umm, wow. Do you guys even know what kind of money he had?" Polly started drawing out old savings records. She flipped one open. "Henry, the last deposit date on here is in May and there's forty-two thousand dollars in the account."

He huffed a chuckle and shook his head. "That doesn't surprise me. Aunt Betty was paying him rent to farm the land. He didn't have anything to spend it on, so he socked it away. At least he put it in the bank. Honestly, I wouldn't have been surprised to find it stuffed in mattresses and buried in the back yard in coffee cans."

"Do you suppose that's what the killer was looking for?"

"Money? Maybe."

"If they thought he was hoarding money and didn't find any, all of that time they spent in Bellingwood would be wasted. What if they're not done yet?"

"Oh come on, Polly. They wouldn't stick around after killing someone."

"They would if they didn't get anything from your uncle. There are other old men living by themselves around here. Old men that don't have the Sturtz OCD tendency. No one would look at the outside of this house and think Loren was organized. His truck was old and beat up and you said he was a mess."

Henry was nodding as she spoke. "But what can we do about that?"

"I want to call Stu Decker tomorrow."

"It's Saturday. What if he isn't working?"

"Then I'll call and find out who is working. It wouldn't hurt for Aaron to think about some of the old guys who live in Bellingwood. If this person doesn't leave right away because they don't want to draw attention to themselves, maybe they aren't planning to leave until they get what they want or need."

"You have a crazy vivid imagination. Sometimes you freak me out when you think like a criminal."

"I don't think like a criminal. I'm not that creative, but if nothing's missing, then this other is a possibility. Am I right?"

"I suppose."

"And you'd be destroyed if something happened to someone else."

"You *are* right about that."

"Hello!" and a knock came from a doorsill in the living room.

"Aunt Betty?" Henry called out. "Is that you?"

"Hi Henry," she said, coming into the room with them. "We saw lights on and thought we ought to check it out. With everything that's happened, I didn't want to take any chances."

"Is Uncle Dick with you?"

She glanced over her shoulder and Polly stood up when Dick walked in carrying a shotgun.

"I guess so," Henry laughed.

"I recognized your truck when we pulled in, so I felt safe enough."

"Polly and I were just looking around. Now that I can get in here again, I wanted to remember this place before it all changed again," Henry said.

"Can you believe that old Loren kept everything the same?" she asked.

"Even the bedspreads upstairs."

"I haven't done anything with those yet because I suspect that the first time they go into a washing machine, they'll fall apart."

Betty and Dick Mercer were only a couple of years older than Bill and Marie Sturtz. Loren had been the oldest of the three. Betty was comfortable in her jeans and boots, while Dick, a red-cheeked, pale Norwegian, looked most at home in a pair of bib overalls. Both had infectious grins.

"We should have called," Henry said. "I didn't mean to interrupt dinner."

"That's okay. It's just sandwiches, but I didn't want to make a mess down my front," Betty said, laughing as she gestured to the flowery apron she wore. "I don't always wear my aprons when I go out, but Dad here thought we should get moving and didn't give me time to even take it off. Would you two like to join us?"

Henry glanced at Polly and she shrugged. "Another time, Aunt Betty. Polly and I have a date tonight."

"And you started it out here?" Dick stepped forward. "Son, this is why it took you so long to find the right woman."

"At least I found her. If I'd let this one slip away, I might have turned into Uncle Loren."

Betty drew the back of her hand up to her forehead dramatically and said, "Heaven forfend! Your poor mother would have signed you up for dating websites before she let that happen."

"We'll let you two enjoy the rest of your date. Come on, Mother. Leave them alone." Dick put his hand on his wife's shoulder. "Maybe *we* should have a date tonight."

"Oh you." Betty swatted his hand away. "It's nice to see you both. Come out some time when it's not so busy. We'd like to get to know you better, Polly." She turned and pushed her husband backward, then crossed in front of him and walked to the front door. Dick winked at Henry and Polly and then followed after her.

"They're really something," Polly said when she heard the door close.

"She can be tough as nails when she needs to be. Uncle Dick is a pushover, so she handles the business end of things. No one in three counties wants to face Betty Mercer when she's negotiating for a new piece of equipment. And that woman knows when to sell corn - it's like a sixth sense or something for her."

"I like them. We should have them over sometime."

"That's a good idea. Are you ready to head into town and get dinner?"

"Anytime," she said. "I just want to be with you."

"Then let's get going. It's prime rib at Davey's tonight. That sounds really good." He let her go out the door first and turned the lights off.

"You haven't said anything about a funeral," Polly said when they got to the truck. "Are you going to do that?"

"I don't think so. Loren didn't know anyone in town and it seems silly to make a big production out of his death. Mom and Dad said something about scattering his ashes later this summer. If Betty and Dick's kids can be there and Lonnie can come, we'll have a family memorial."

"Okay. I was just wondering. You know Lydia is going to ask, too."

"She probably already has. I'll make sure with Mom, though."

Polly reached out and put her hand on his arm while he drove down the gravel road. "Thanks for bringing me out here tonight. It was fun to see you like this."

"I just needed to get in there one more time. I think I can let it all go now."

CHAPTER NINETEEN

Even though rain was pouring down, this was the first morning in what felt like a year, that things seemed normal. Henry hadn't gotten up before dawn to work and there were no extra people in the building. Polly was in the kitchen scrambling eggs, watching lightning flash across the sky. She wouldn't mind it if no one called or knocked on their door or needed anything all day long.

Sylvie's car drove by, heading for the barn. Polly smiled when she realized that her friend was in the passenger seat. Jason had turned fourteen and the first thing he'd begged for was his driving permit. How in the world could time be passing so quickly? He was heading to Boone this fall for his freshman year in high school. It was good that Andrew had Rebecca, otherwise he would desperately miss his older brother.

Henry came into the room, smelling fresh from a shower. "What's up for you today?" he asked.

"I don't know. I feel like hiding up here with you. Will that work?" She pulled two plates out and set them on the counter.

"Uh. I. Uh."

Polly poked him in the ribs with her elbow. "I'm kidding. I

want to spend some time in the barn and whether she wants me there or not, I'm scooping Joss up for lunch. Andrew and Rebecca will probably be around and who knows after that. What about you?"

"Ben and I were going to head over to his place. I think he just wants someone there to listen while he works out his plans."

"I'm sorry, and I know he's a friend of yours, but that wife of his is zippety ki yi yay in the head. I know they lost their house, but so did a bunch of other people in town and she is acting like her life is over. All of her life."

"Some people don't handle tragedy like you do, Polly."

"I know. You're right. But still."

"You have such a pragmatic outlook on life. It's kind of incredible and sometimes a little intimidating."

"Really?" Polly filled their plates with eggs and bacon and slices of buttered toast. "Do you want jelly this morning?"

"No, this is fine." He took a plate and a cup of coffee over to the peninsula. "And yes, really. You know that tomorrow will bring something new and if today sucks, all you have to do is wait. A lot of people get stuck in the suck and don't have faith that tomorrow is coming. Amanda can only think about what she's lost and doesn't see that she'll get a new home without all of the problems the old house had. She doesn't know that it will be fun to look for new furniture. She's still thinking about how comfortable that twenty year old chair was. She doesn't do change like you do."

"I suppose. Ben's a saint, then."

"He's a good guy." Henry chuckled. "But you gotta know that some of those guys think the same thing about me." He laughed a little maliciously.

"That you're a saint for living with me? But I'm fun!" Polly tossed a dish towel at his head.

"Yes you are, but you're also opinionated and nearly always right. You don't back down from anything once you get a good head of steam going."

"Damned straight," she said. "A girl's gotta go through life with a little bit of confidence. Right?"

He nodded his head up and down with eyes wide open. "Absolutely, sweetie pie, absolutely."

"Yeah. That one doesn't work either."

"Man, I'm never going to find the right words, am I?"

"It's kind of cute."

"That's me. Cute. Let's not tell the guys that, okay?"

When they were finished, Polly and Obiwan headed down to the barn. The dog wandered through the pasture, but decided rain wasn't what he wanted to play in, so came inside immediately.

"Good morning!" she called.

"Hi Polly," Jason said, coming out of Nat's stall. "What are you doing down here today?"

"I missed everyone, so I thought I'd come help. Is that okay?"

He just smiled at her.

"I saw you driving with your mom this morning. How does that feel?"

"It's great. But I can't believe I have to wait another two years to drive by myself."

"I can't believe you're already driving. It took six months before I was allowed on the road."

Jason nodded back toward the feed room. "Eliseo helped me. He takes me over to the school parking lot so I can practice."

"Good morning, Polly." Eliseo came out of the feed room, followed by two donkeys. They picked up speed when they saw Polly and soon she was surrounded by big floppy ears and wet, smelly donkeys.

"They don't much like being cooped up," he said. "And a little rain won't hurt anyone. Jason, do you want to let the horses out? It's not coming down hard enough to stop them from playing. There's no reason for any of them to be inside."

"Sure," Jason said. He walked through Demi's stall to open up an outside door and then led everyone out to the pasture.

"I guess I'm a little late to be helping," Polly said. "Sorry."

"It's no problem. I got started early this morning and Jason helped me finish up." He picked up a broom and began sweeping phantom dirt from the floor of the alley.

"Is everything okay?" she asked.

Eliseo stopped, put his hand on the top of the broom and looked at her. "I think so. I feel restless for some reason."

"Restless how? You aren't leaving me, are you? Do you need more money, more free time? You can't go." Polly's heart clenched inside her. Eliseo was the only reason she was able to have these animals in her life. Without him, she couldn't handle this.

"Oh no, no, no," he said. "For the first time in my life, I feel like I'm missing something important."

"What do you mean by that?"

He swept his arm around the barn. "This is the best thing that's ever happened to me and yes, I feel part of it. You've given me a lot of freedom, but it's still all yours. I have nothing that is truly mine."

"What do you think you want?" Polly swallowed. She didn't know what else to say.

He sat down on the bench across the alley. "This is a terrible time to be thinking about it, especially while there are so many folks in town trying to find a safe place to live. But I'm ready to find my own house. Maybe a house with a little land. I could get a dog and have room to breathe at night. If I want to sleep under the stars, no one will come out of their homes and find me, then call the police because they think I've gone off the deep end. I've been in that little house for a year and I'm tired of renting and neighbors and noise. I want something that is my own."

"Wow." She breathed an audible sigh of relief. "That's a big deal. Did you ever imagine settling in Iowa?"

"Not on your life." He chuckled, a grin lifting his cheeks. "The winters are terrible here. I've never been so cold as I was this last year. The bugs in the summer are enough to make a sane person fly off the handle. That's one of the reasons the horses like the rainy days, no flies to bother them. I need to get another set of fly sheets next week for them. Those help. The flies are awful."

Polly nodded. "They look kind of funny all dressed up out here. My horses are all fancy and stuff."

"It really helps them, though."

"What kind of house are you looking for?" she asked.

"I don't know. Something bigger than what I have."

"That is a pretty small little house. You've done great work putting it back together."

"We've gone over the year mark and I certainly don't mind paying full rent for the place, but I'd like to start building a home."

"I'm really excited you plan to stick around," Polly said. "You should talk to Henry. After everything that has been going on this week, he's going to know more about the real estate in town than anyone. And, he can tell you who the good agents are."

"I'll talk to him. This isn't anything I'm in a hurry to do, but when I start looking, I don't want you to be surprised."

"Say something to Jeff, too. That man knows everyone."

"Do you think he'll ever move to Bellingwood?"

Polly laughed. "No. I doubt it. He's a city boy at heart. Fortunately, Ames is less than a half hour drive. Can you imagine? Living in Ames and commuting to Bellingwood? What a hoot. Most of the time it's the other way around."

"I guess he has his own life to lead."

"Yeah. I guess."

The donkeys had wandered back outside and Obiwan was sitting on the floor in front of her.

"So ...," she began.

"Are you going to ask about me sleeping here last Sunday?"

"Well, maybe."

He chuckled. "You don't let much go, do you, Polly?"

"I think it's one of my failings."

"I'm fine. The idea of being in the basement with all of you and wondering if the place was going to come toppling down on my head was more than I could handle. Being out here with the animals, even though they were upset, was a much better place to be. And then, I just fell into one of my slumps. I couldn't move. I couldn't do anything."

"And Nan helped?"

He gave her a weak smile. "Would you believe they all helped? Even the cats. When the worst of it was over, I opened the stalls so the donkeys could move in and out and before I knew it, Tom and Huck pushed me into Nan's stall and Tom lay down with me until I could breathe again. Nan stood over us until the next morning. Hansel and Gretel were both in there, too. I had my own therapy session."

Polly felt tears come to her eyes. Dang, she had to quit crying at everything all the time. "You can never leave us," she said.

"No, I don't think I can. I've never gone this long without an episode and I've never come out of one so quickly."

"Wow, I just don't think any of us get that."

"I hope you never do."

"Is it flashbacks?"

"Yes," he said. "I have those all the time and most of the time I breathe through them, but sometimes I get stuck in them."

Polly and Eliseo's relationship had grown over the last year, but he'd never really confided in her about these things.

"I was talking to a man who had been in Viet Nam," she said. "He told me that he came back all messed up. Is it the same thing?"

"Those poor guys didn't have anyone around to tell them what they were dealing with. They were expected to drop back into civilian life and deal with it. The army was barely ready to admit that PTSD was a real thing when I got out. And I hate to say it, but at least I had physical scars that made what happened to me real. Some of my buddies were completely screwed up from the things they saw and experienced, but because they looked normal on the outside, no one believed they were falling apart. So what if they got drunk all the time. And if they freaked out and beat on their wives or became immobilized by all of their emotions, it was their problem and they had to just deal with it."

Jason slipped in and sat down beside Polly on the bench. "Do you wish you hadn't gone into the army?" he asked Eliseo.

"No Jason, I don't. If I hadn't gone through all of that, I wouldn't be here. I wouldn't know you and Polly and your mom and Andrew. I wouldn't have these big old animals in my life and I wouldn't be living in Iowa. Our lives are made up of the choices and decisions we make and to look back and regret any of them is to miss out on what they teach us."

"You've certainly learned a lot," Polly said.

"And now," he said, standing up. "I think it's time for another driving lesson. Are you ready?"

Jason said to Polly, "We're going to try gravel today."

"Don't worry," Eliseo assured her. "We're just going down the road. I want him to feel the difference under the tires."

"Sylvie has it easy with you teaching her son to drive," Polly said, smiling.

"He's a good kid."

"Well, I didn't help much with the animals, but it was good to talk to you this morning," she said to him and then turned to Jason. "Have fun. I'm not ready for you to grow up."

"Not you too," he complained.

"What do you mean?"

"Mom is always talking about how I'm growing up too fast. She drives me crazy."

"Got it," Polly said. "I'll be good. Just stop growing up right now, okay?"

Jason rolled his eyes.

Polly took Obiwan back to Sycamore House. He was wet and his paws were muddy, so they went up the back steps. "You animals are pretty important," she said to him as she dried his paws. "I can't imagine living without you, but just think about what everyone down at the barn did for Eliseo. Why can't there be more of that for people?" Obiwan shook himself and she giggled as his feet slid on the floor. Then he reached up and licked her face. Polly spluttered, "Thanks for that."

After she showered and dressed, she called Joss. The girl wasn't allowed to sit around and mope any longer. Even if it was a dreary and wet day.

"Good morning," Joss said. "I didn't expect to hear from you."

"What are you doing today?"

"I dunno. I could get some work done at the library. Nate's working."

"How was your night?"

"It was fine. We sat around and watched stupid television until we were both too tired to stay awake. I'm trying to be upbeat about this."

"You've spent the last several months being upbeat. It's okay if you want to get pissy, you know."

"Nah, it's fine. I'll get over it."

"I'm picking you up and we're going to do something today. How's that?"

"I don't feel like it, are you mad at me?"

"Nope, not mad at you at all, but I'm showing up at your house in a half hour. Will that be enough time for you to take a shower and get dressed?"

"You're kind of mean."

"Yes I am. And then we're taking your car and going somewhere. Because Sal has been stuck in Bellingwood all week long, helping Mark and acting like a good girlfriend. We're going to go get a little crazy. Shop and eat out and act like girls."

"A half hour?"

"If you need a little more time, that's fine, but you don't get to sit around and mope today. I miss my friends."

"Fine then. A half hour. Bye, you tyrant."

Polly chuckled when she hung up the phone and then called Sal.

"Hey girlfriend, why are you bothering me on a Saturday?" Sal asked.

"Are you hanging out with your man today?"

"No," Sal grumped. "He left early this morning and said he'd be back later. I don't know when later is."

"Are you up and dressed and ready to go?"

Sal's voice brightened. "Are we going somewhere?"

"I don't know where, but yes. I'm meeting Joss at her house and then we're going to come get you. We need to shop and be girly girls."

"Oh thank god!" Sal exclaimed. "I couldn't take one more day of not knowing what to do with myself. You've been so busy I didn't want to bother you and the last thing I wanted was to get all busy with your stuff."

"You brat. Gather your wallet and comfy shoes, because I need some retail therapy."

"I'll see you later and thank you!"

Polly sat down on her sofa and felt better than she had in days. Normal. Yes, normal was what she wanted.

She called Henry.

"Hey, I'm going out with Joss and Sal and I don't know when we're coming back. Do you need anything?"

"Nope, I'm good. Where are you going?"

"I have no idea. And hey, I had a long conversation with Eliseo this morning."

"Oh Polly, you didn't. Can't you leave the poor man alone?"

"Hey! I didn't start it. He did. He wants to buy a house and I told him to talk to you, that you know all about the houses in town."

"Okay. I'll talk to him. There's probably not a lot available right now. What's he looking for?"

"A big house with some land where he has a little freedom to ..." Polly stopped herself and then said, "Henry, he's looking for your Uncle Loren's place!"

"We're not ready to sell it yet. There is a lot of work that has to be done first. And I don't know what Dad and Aunt Betty are planning to do with it."

"Don't be silly. He just did all of that work on the house he's renting now. What if you let him live there rent free for a year while he fixes it up and then negotiate a fair purchase price on it?"

Henry didn't say anything.

"Are you still there?" she asked.

"I was just thinking about what you said. Sorry. It's not a bad idea. Let me talk to him and see if he's at all interested and then I'll talk to Dad to see what he has to say."

"I bet Eliseo wouldn't mind keeping the chickens either."

Henry laughed a little. "You just aren't happy unless you're fixing someone, are you?"

"If I have a good idea, it's a good idea. Now don't be mean to me."

"I love you more than I can say, but you are a buttinsky if there ever was one."

"You're walking into trouble, big boy. Better be careful."

"Nah, nah, nah. You don't scare me. Your bark is pretty bad, but your bite is all mine."

She burbled out a laugh. "You're terrible. It's just an idea. You do with it what you want."

"Yeah. Whatever. If I don't do something proactive with it, you'll just keep bothering me. I'll talk to him."

"I love you, Henry."

"Have fun today. I love you, too."

CHAPTER TWENTY

Polly and Joss pulled up in front of Mark Ogden's home and Sal came running out.

"This is fun!" she exclaimed. "Where are we going first?"

"No idea. Who's up for what today?" Polly said.

Joss chuckled. "This is your party. You tell us."

"Let's see. You're from Indiana and you're from Boston." Polly pointed at each of them. "And I don't shop. This could be bad. Let's head to Ames. If we can't find enough to get us in trouble, we'll go down to Des Moines. If we can't achieve it there, I don't know what comes next."

"Downtown Ames it is," Joss said and turned onto the highway.

"Sooooo," Sal said, scooting up in her seat and leaning over Polly's shoulder. "The two of you have made this little town your home and I know for certain that Polly was used to a bigger city than this. What about you, Joss? Are you a small town girl or is this your first time?"

"We've lived here for five years, so I feel like a native, but I did grow up in a much larger town than this."

"How did you live when you first got here? There's not enough to do. What if you don't have everything you need to make dinner or breakfast the next morning? No one is open after seven at night. And there isn't a good coffee shop in fifteen miles."

"You learn to plan," Polly said. "And you learn to make your own coffee."

Sal pushed Polly's shoulder, "You know I'm no good at that."

"Are you moving to Bellingwood?" Joss asked.

"We're talking about it," Sal replied.

"You talked to Mark about it? How did that go?" Polly turned so she could see Sal's face.

Sal gave her a smooth smile, her eyes twinkling with happiness. "He told me that if I wanted to move out here, he'd support me for as long as it took to find my feet. He's the one, Polly. I can't believe I found the one in the middle of Iowa."

The seatbelt around her shoulders was the only thing stopping Polly from grabbing her friend into a hug. "I can't believe you're moving to Iowa! Your parents are going to kill you."

"Yeah. I think I'm just not going to tell them. They won't miss me for a couple of weeks and then I'll be too far away to hear Mom scream."

"When is this going to happen?"

Sal shrugged as if it were no big deal, "I'm calling to quit my job on Monday. If they want to be done with me right away, that's fine. I'd really love to not go back to Boston for a while. Call a moving company and have them pack my stuff and send it out."

"You don't want to face your family that bad?"

"You're right. I don't. I will sooner or later, but things just seem too good right now."

"Are you going to get married?"

"Now you stop that," Sal said, wrinkling her nose and pursing her lips. "No. We talked about it and decided we don't know each other well enough to make that kind of decision. And that's just not who I am. It's been a while since I've been in a long term relationship and the last thing I'm going to do is rush into a life commitment in the middle of nowhere." She threw up her arms to stop Polly's protest. "I know, I know. It's not nowhere, but I don't have a security net built out here. If things fell apart between us ... well, it's not going to. I get that, but ..." She stopped talking and looked at Polly. "Sorry. I'm babbling. I have all of these things going on in my head. Things I need to say to my parents and I feel like I have to explain what I'm doing and I don't want anyone to make me feel guilty for my own decisions."

"No guilt here," Polly said. "Do you want her to feel guilty, Joss?"

"No guilt from me," Joss replied. "Okay, maybe a little guilt. Every girl in town is going to be heartbroken that the hot, young vet is settling down. After that, though, no guilt."

"See, yeah. That. I made Henry wait forever. It felt like everyone was pushing us to get married. You do whatever you want with Mark as long as you don't make him move away." Polly gave Sal the evil eye. "If you try to make him move, I will end you."

"No, if I commit to Mark, I know I'm committing to Bellingwood. I get that." Sal sat back and let out a huff of air. "See, now I'm getting all terrified. I shouldn't have opened my mouth. It was more fun when all I thought about spending time with Mark and starting a new life."

"Go back to that part," Joss said. "Focus on the good stuff. It's the only way to get through the absolute terror that lands in the pit of your stomach. Trust me, I know."

"I suppose you do. You're waiting for a baby, aren't you?" Sal sat up again and touched Joss' shoulder.

"Yeah." Joss opened her mouth to say something else, then closed it again. She stopped at a stop sign, waiting for traffic to pass so she could turn onto Highway 30 and head into Ames. "We're still waiting. It feels like we'll end up waiting until the two of us are too old to keep up with the poor child." She slammed the palm of her hand on the steering wheel, then said, "Sorry. I'm sorry."

She turned to Sal, "I'm sorry. I didn't mean that." Joss turned back to the road and pulled out and made the turn. "We lost the baby yesterday and are back to waiting again. We'd spent all week getting excited and then it got yanked out from under us."

"I didn't know," Sal said. "I didn't mean to open that wound up again. I apologize. That was so insensitive of me."

"No, it's good to say it out loud. I know in my head that it's not over and there will be a baby for us when the time is right, but it felt like my world dropped out from under me yesterday."

"I get that. Did they give you any idea about how long you'd have to wait?"

"No, we just got the notification that this one was off the table. We'll find out more on Monday, I hope."

Polly watched her two friends connect. If Sal had at least one more friend when she moved to Bellingwood, it would make it that much easier on her.

"Shall we go downtown? There are some sweet shops and restaurants there," Joss said.

"That sounds great. Something a little different than the chain stores at the mall."

"I don't feel like walking around a mall anyway," Sal said. "I can go into those shops no matter where I am in the country. Show me what the Midwest has to offer."

Joss drove around until she found a parking space and the three sat in the car trying to get their bearings. The rain had let up to a light drizzle.

"This looks nice," Sal said. "I could spend time here. But seriously, I need a coffee shop!"

Polly grinned and pointed down the street. "I think we might find a couple for you. Shall we start walking?"

They wandered in and out of stores and finally reached a shop that offered much more than just coffee. Sal opened the door and waved the aroma out at Polly and Joss. "Smell that! This might become my new home," she said. "There's chocolate in here, too."

"Then let's get you some caffeine and chocolate." Polly took Joss by the arm. "We need to keep the East Coast girl happy or she gets really loud."

They found a place to sit and Polly relaxed. "What do you

think, Sal? Could you live near a town like this?"

"This is where the university is, right? The other Iowa university?"

Polly remarked to Joss. "Sal was at the University of Iowa last summer for a seminar."

Joss nodded in understanding.

"There's one more state university," Polly continued. "The University of Northern Iowa."

"You people take your education seriously out here. It's like there's a college in every town," Sal said.

"Pretty much," Polly said. "We're just that good." She felt her phone buzz and when she looked at the number, realized it was from Roy Nelson's father.

"Do you guys mind? I really want to take this."

"Go." Sal waved her off and Joss smiled as Polly stood and went outside.

"Hello?" she said.

"Is this Polly Giller?"

"Yes. Hi. What have you found out?"

"Are you serious about helping this young girl?" Dean Nelson asked her. "Because if you are, she really needs you. She's with me and I'm taking her to the station."

"What's going on?"

"He had her chained to the bed. She could reach the bathroom and the bed, but that was as far as she could go. She still seems healthy, but that wasn't going to last long."

"Oh no!" Polly cried. "Can I just come over and get her?"

"We'll need to ask her some questions. Dennis Smith will be arrested in the next few minutes."

"This is awful. Does she know that I'm coming for her?"

"I'll explain it again to her, but right now she's on the edge. I don't think she believed she was ever going to be free again. I'm glad you sent us to look for her."

"I'm shocked. How did you even find her?"

"Well, no one answered the door, but it didn't feel right, so we walked around back. One of my buddies looked in a window and saw her sitting on the bed. He tapped on the window and when she jumped up, he saw the chain and handcuffs. That was enough for us to go in."

"I'm in Ames with friends right now, but I'll get there as soon as possible. Do I need to bring anything? Does she need clothes?"

"She might appreciate something a little nicer to wear. She's just in shorts and a tank top."

"Can I speak to her? Ask her what size?"

"She's just a bitty thing. She actually looks about the size of my daughter and I know she wears size six."

Polly couldn't help herself and she chuckled. "Okay, are you talking as a dad who doesn't know much about girl's sizes or can I trust you on this?"

"I think you can trust me on this. My wife hates shopping more than anything and I've done most of it for our kids."

"You're really something, Mr. Nelson. I'll pick up a few things and be there as soon as I can."

"She's lucky to have you in her life right now. I look forward to meeting you."

Polly leaned on the corner of the building and took a deep breath. This rescuing thing was never going to end. She opened the door and went back inside. Sal and Joss were laughing at something and both stopped when she approached the table.

"What was that?" Joss asked.

"It's probably the end of the story with Curtis Locke and his daughter."

"Is everything okay?"

"I think it is now. That was the policeman from Oelwein I talked to yesterday. He went to check on her this morning as soon as her boyfriend left the house and found her chained to a bed."

"What?" Sal's gasp and Joss's outburst garnered a little attention from the room, but people soon went back to what they were doing.

"She could get to the bathroom, but nowhere else in the house. I don't know how long it's been like this, but I'm afraid that my phone call last weekend precipitated his behavior." Polly shook her head quickly. "Much as it frightens me that I was the cause, I can't focus on that. Office Nelson is going to ask her some questions and then I can take her with me, but I need to head over to Oelwein. We can either go back to Bellingwood and I'll take my own truck, or ..."

Joss and Sal both stood up, "Or we'll go with you. There's plenty of room for one more girl and we're just the chicks to make sure that she knows she is safe," Sal said, looking at Joss for approval. Joss smiled and nodded in agreement.

"She needs some clothes first, though," Polly said. "She's only got shorts and a tank. After what she's been through, I suspect something a little more substantial would help her integrity."

"All of these adorable shops right here. We should be able to find plenty for the girl. Let's go." Sal marched out of the coffee shop and turned right. They went into a clothing store two doors down and fifteen minutes later, they walked out, each carrying shopping bags.

"That was dangerous," Sal said, laughing. "I should never be sent on a mission that involves shopping for clothes."

They got back to the car and Joss asked, "So, where are we going? I need to program the GPS before I pull out."

A couple of quick internet searches and they had it programmed and were on the road, heading to eastern Iowa.

"We should make some phone calls to let our guys know what we're doing," Polly said.

"Hah. Mark doesn't care. When I texted to tell him I was going out with you, I think he was relieved to not be responsible for me."

"I'll let Nate know what's happening when I get there. He's working all day today at the pharmacy," Joss said.

Polly gave them each a thin smile. "I feel a little silly calling Henry, then."

"You shouldn't," Joss replied. "It's cute to watch you two be all couple-y. It won't last forever, so you might as well make it worth your time now. Call him. Are you going to call the girl's parents?"

"I don't think so. I'll let her do that." Polly hesitated over her phone's screen. "I feel kind of guilty, though. It was her father who asked me to do this."

"If you think the right thing to do is let her make the call, that's the right thing to do. Call your husband and don't worry about it."

"Okay." Polly swiped the phone to call Henry and waited while it rang.

"Hello, Polldoll," he said.

"Nope. That doesn't work either."

"Rats. What's up?"

"I'm with Joss and Sal and we're heading to Oelwein."

"Of course you are. What are you going over there for?" Polly waited for him to put it together. "Oh yeah," he said. "You're on another rescue mission. Did you find the girl?"

"We did. She was chained to a bed, Henry."

"What?" His voice changed from playful to furious. "Who the ... what that ... I hope they've caught him."

"The jackass was at work like nothing was out of the ordinary. Henry, I can't believe this stuff happens in Iowa."

"I tell you, Polly, people always amaze me with how depraved they can be."

"When I watched those girls come out of that house in Ohio on the news, I thought it was something that happened far away from me. This is too close."

"Honey, there are terrible things that happen in Bellingwood every day, too."

"Don't tell me that. It's my idyllic little utopia and I want to keep it that way. At least in my head."

"Even with all the dead bodies you find? You know better than anyone that people will do horrible things to each other."

"I know. You're right. But I like to put on my rose-colored glasses as often as possible, okay?"

"You're one lucky girl, Polly. You've managed to surround yourself with really great people, but those are only a small portion of the folks who live there. You know that, right?"

"I guess I just hope that maybe I can be a good influence on the world."

"That's why I love you. Now go rescue yourself a girl and bring her home. I know you'll take care of her as long as she needs you and you know I'll be there to help you."

"Thank you. I was a little worried you would give me trouble."

"I'm learning. Sometimes you're a force to be reckoned with, but it's always for the good. Call me if you need anything."

They hung up and Polly started thinking about things Jessie would need if the girl consented to stay with her.

"I'll be with you in a minute," she said to Joss and Sal. "I need to make another couple of phone calls."

Her first call was to Jeff Lyndsay. She was surprised when Sarah Heater answered.

"Hi Sarah, this is Polly. What are you doing with Jeff's phone?"

"He got caught in a meeting with people from the city. Something about the storm damage, so he asked me to man the phones. What can I do for you?"

"Did Kelly Locke leave this morning?"

"She sure did. It was pretty early. Like about eight o'clock. She told me they were releasing her husband and she wanted to get on the road as soon as possible. Rachel has already cleaned out their room. She stopped in to see if we were going to charge her for the room or food, but Jeff said that you were taking care of it."

"Okay. That's fine. Is Rachel still around?"

"Sure. She's in the kitchen with Sylvie. They're doing inventory after this week while getting things ready for tonight. Do you need something?"

"Can you direct me to the kitchen phone, then? I need to ask Rachel for a favor."

"Sure. I'd be glad to. And Polly?"

"Yes, Sarah."

"Thank you so much for taking care of my girl yesterday. I didn't realize the week was going to be so difficult for her. I'm glad she went and I hope she goes again, but you were wonderful."

"I didn't do anything, but you know that I adore her."

"I do know that. Thank you. Now, just a second."

"Sycamore House Kitchen, this is Rachel, how may I help you?"

"Wow. That's so stinking professional. It almost sounds like a real place," Polly said.

"Hi Polly. Sylvie says we're going to get busier so we have to sound like that all the time."

"Sylvie's the boss!"

"Do you want to talk to her?"

"No, I need to ask if you have time to run up to my apartment and change a bed."

"Sure, which one?"

"Let's do the front room. I'm bringing a girl back from Oelwein who has been in a terrible situation and I want to just open the door and let her go in."

"Absolutely. No problem. Rebecca and Andrew are upstairs with the animals. I'll ask them to help."

"Good luck with that," Polly said. "But thank you."

"I'm glad to do it."

Polly hung up and set the phone in her lap. She knew Henry was right. There were plenty of people everywhere who weren't as wonderful as her friends, but wow, she'd gotten lucky.

"It isn't luck," Sal said from the back seat.

"What. Did I say that out loud?"

"Yep," Joss smiled at her. "And Sal's right. It isn't about luck. You make people want to do the right thing. You treat your employees like friends and your friends are more like the good part of your family. None of us want to ever hurt you because we'd be hurting ourselves. You give and you give and you don't expect anything from anyone."

"And you love us like crazy, too."

"Well you two can just stop all that nonsense right now," Polly said, wiping at her eyes. "Right now."

CHAPTER TWENTY-ONE

"Unlock the doors, please?" Polly chuckled as she reminded Joss again that the back seat was child-proofed. She patted Joss on the shoulder and said, "Thank you for driving today. I'm glad you two were along." Polly gathered up the shopping bags and stepped out of the car.

"It's just in here," she said to Jessie, and waited for her to come around Joss's car. Polly opened the door from the garage into the back hallway. "Now there's a big, loving dog up at the top of the steps. He's going to be glad to see you. Very glad."

The girl nodded. She hadn't said anything on the drive back to Bellingwood. Polly had taken a pair of loose pants and a top into the police station and when Jessie came out of the bathroom without the clothes she'd worn in. She hoped they were gone forever.

Sal and Joss had sat up front and chattered about inane things during the trip. It nearly killed Polly to not reach across the back seat and gather the petite young woman into her, but Jessie crossed her arms and dropped her head, essentially closing out the rest of the world.

"There are also a couple of kids upstairs. Andrew and Rebecca. You can ignore them if you like. I'll show you to your room and the bathroom. Are you ready?"

Jessie nodded and Polly opened the door leading up to her home. Sure enough, Obiwan was at the top of the steps, wagging his tail.

"His name is Obiwan."

That was the first time Jessie reacted. "Like Star Wars?"

"Yeah. Like Star Wars. The cats are Luke and Leia. I have an obsession."

"That's funny."

"People think I'm a little odd. I just got an R2D2 robot as a wedding gift from a bunch of my friends."

"Really?"

"Yeah. If I'm a little odd, my friends aren't much better."

Obiwan waited for them to reach the top step and then began sniffing Jessie's leg. She reached down and stroked his head. "I've never had a dog. Mom told us they'd shed all over the house."

"Oh, he sheds like crazy, but it's worth it. I just have to change the vacuum bag more often."

They made it past Henry's office and into the media room, Polly's old living room. Rebecca and Andrew were at her dining room table.

"Rebecca. Andrew. This is Jessie Locke. She's going to be staying with me for a couple of days."

The kids looked up from whatever it was they were drawing.

"What are you working on?" Polly asked.

"She's showing me how to draw dragons," Andrew said. "I want mine to have horns. She says they don't have horns."

"Well, don't hurt each other." Polly said. She turned to Jessie. "Do you want anything to drink or eat?"

"Not right now."

"I'll be back after a while, kids."

"Okay."

Polly led her across the big living room and opened the door to the front bedroom.

"Wow. This is huge," Jessie said.

"This is an old schoolhouse. It was a classroom. I'll put your bags in here and then let me show you to the bathroom."

Jessie followed her to the second spa bathroom and her mouth fell open again. "You live here?"

"Well, yeah. I used to live in that apartment where the kids were at. The office was my old bedroom. But when I got married, we took over the whole floor. We have guest rooms for rent in an addition on the other side of the building. There are a lot of things that happen here at Sycamore House. Andrew's mother is our chef and he's here today because there will be a wedding reception tonight." Polly tapped her foot on the floor. "Right below us. That's the auditorium where everything happens. If you want to see the whole place, I'll show you around, but I thought you might want to take a bath or a shower first."

"Why are you doing this for me?"

"Because your father asked me to find you and I'm certainly not going to find you and then let you get lost again."

A little bit of fire returned to Jessie's eyes. "I'm not moving back home."

Polly hesitantly reached out to touch her forearm. When the girl didn't pull away, she left her fingers there. "You certainly don't have to. If you want to stay in Iowa, I'll help you find a good job and a place to live."

"But why? You don't know me."

"I don't have to know *you*. Your dad and my dad went to college together a long time ago. So, someone knew someone once upon a time. And besides, it's the right thing to do. You've been through enough. I can't fix what happened to you, but I don't have to let it get any worse."

"I don't know what I'm going to say to my parents. I don't want to call them."

"They're really worried about you and so is Maggie. You're going to need to get hold of her too."

Jessie's eyes lit up. "Did you talk to her?"

"A couple of times. She helped me find you."

"I'm glad. Can I call her tonight?"

"You sure can. Will you call your parents?"

"I'll call Dad. At least I know he'll be glad that I'm okay."

Polly wasn't sure what to do with that. Kelly Locke would be devastated to know that her daughter had been harmed, but at some level, Polly was certain the woman figured that Jessie had brought the trouble down on herself. Calling Curtis was the thing to do.

"Why don't we get the call to your dad done first? That way the hardest thing is over and you can move forward."

"I don't have a phone."

"I know. You can use mine."

"Will you stay with me?"

"Of course. Let's go into your bedroom and shut the door so no one bothers you."

They did so and Polly sat down at the desk while Jessie sat on the bed. Polly brought up her father's number and handed the phone across to the young girl.

Jessie waited a moment and then said, "Daddy?"

That was all it took before tears came out of her eyes and she began to sob.

"I'm okay. I'm with Polly at her house."

Polly caught Jessie's eye, pointed to herself and then to the door. Once the ice was broken, she didn't need to be there. The girl nodded and Polly slipped out, shutting the door. She sat down on the sofa and waited, not knowing how long the call would take. Obiwan curled up beside her and she relaxed while rubbing his head. It took about fifteen minutes before Jessie re-emerged. Her eyes were red-rimmed and her face was blotchy from tears.

"Thank you."

"You're welcome. What do you think, now that the first step is behind you?"

"I'm better. They aren't going to make me go home. I told him that I still didn't want to do that and he agreed with me. Mom is pissed, but she's always pissed, so that doesn't matter."

Polly wasn't surprised that Kelly had managed to turn a happy moment into an opportunity to be annoyed, but at least the call was over.

"Did he say anything about his car?"

"He said that since he couldn't drive for a while because of the heart attack, I can keep it here and we'll discuss it later."

"That's terrific," Polly said, smiling. "The keys are downstairs."

"I have to get a job. Mom said she'd mail my phone, but they're going to cut me off in two months."

"Then we'll have to get right on it. But not today. Today you are going to rest and find some sanity after this last week. Do you want to take a shower or have the grand tour?"

"I want a shower. I want to get rid of the smell."

"There should be another couple of outfits in those bags. We weren't sure of your size. Would you believe Officer Nelson told us what it was? He does all the shopping for his kids because his wife hates to do it."

"He said that you sent him to find me."

"Well, he did his job. All I had to do was give him a little bit of information."

"I have to go back over there, don't I?"

"Yes, I'm sure you do. But don't worry. Whenever you have to go, there will be someone with you."

Jessie stood up and slowly walked toward the bedroom. "I'm really tired. Would it be okay if I went to sleep after I cleaned up?"

"I don't care what you do today," Polly said. "Sal picked out a night gown for you and Joss bought pajamas. Whatever you're comfortable wearing, just drop into bed and if I don't see you when it's time for supper, I'll knock on your door."

"I can't believe you saved me."

"Someday when you least expect it, you're going to be in a position to do something for a person who desperately needs it and you're just going to take care of them because you can't imagine doing anything else. Then you'll believe it."

The girl started for the bathroom and then stopped. "I don't have any shampoo or anything."

"Everything you need is in there. But if it isn't, let me know."

Polly leaned back on the couch and smiled. This was the stuff that filled her heart.

"Polly?" Rebecca was standing in the doorway.

"Yes, honey."

"Can we get some brownies? I'm kind of hungry."

"Well, sure." Polly hauled herself up off the couch and patted Obiwan's head as she walked past him. "Maybe some milk, too?"

"Andrew was just going to get it, but I thought we should ask."

"It's okay. I trust you two, but thanks for asking. How are the dragons coming?"

Rebecca ran to the table and picked up a piece of paper. "This is Rikka. She's the queen of the land."

Andrew piped up and showed her his blue dragon. "This is the Blue Knight. He's king of the sky and his name is Startron."

"Well, you two have done a great job. Are you writing a story about these two?"

"Rebecca thinks I should write a love story. That's stupid."

"I don't think you meant to use that word, did you?" Polly asked him.

"But it is."

"Andrew?" Polly's voice warned him.

"Okay. It's not stupid. But I don't want to write about love."

"Then just say that." Polly put a plate of brownies out on the table and set down two glasses of milk.

"Polly!" She heard Jason's voice from the front door and ran out. He rarely came upstairs since summer had arrived. If there was an opportunity for him to do something in the barn with the horses or donkeys, he chose that every time."

"Is everything okay?"

"Yeah. Eliseo sent me up to ask if you wanted to ride tomorrow morning? Rachel too."

"I'd love to," she said. "Would you like a brownie?"

"Would I!" He dashed past her into the other room and when she arrived, he had poured himself a glass of milk and sat down at the table beside his brother.

"What 'cha drawing?" he asked, tugging at the sheet of paper.

"It's nothing," Andrew said and quickly flipped it upside down.

"Hey! That looks cool. I didn't know you could draw."

Andrew shyly turned the paper back over and said, "Rebecca was showing me. You think it's cool?"

"Yeah. It's a dragon. I can even tell what it is. Good job." He slugged down the rest of the glass of milk and took another brownie off the plate, then looked up at Polly. "Can I take a couple of these to Eliseo?"

"Sure," she said, in shock. This Jason she could deal with as easily as she could the young boy who had counted on her to make sure things were safe last year. "Take as many as you like. Are you coming back up for supper?"

"Okay. What time?"

"Well, why don't we say six thirty. We have a guest with us tonight, too. It's a girl."

"Do I know her?"

"Not yet. Her dad had the heart attack last week."

"Oh," he said abruptly. "Okay. I'll see you later."

He scooted out the door and was gone before she could say anything more.

"He liked my dragon," Andrew said. "Should I frame this and put it on my wall?"

"You probably should. Finish your brownies. I need to call Henry."

"Polly?" Rebecca said.

"Yes honey."

"Is that girl going to stay here?"

"For a while."

"Did she get hurt?"

"Why do you ask?"

"She has red marks on her wrists."

"Someone did hurt her. But she's going to be okay now."

"Because you brought her here?"

"Well, that's part of it, yes."

"You like bringing people here, don't you."

Polly smiled. "I really do. I love Sycamore House so much and I want everyone to love it like I do."

"Mom said you want lots of people to live here. Jeff should live here too."

"Wouldn't that be fun?" Polly asked. "But I think he likes living in Ames."

"He's really funny. He told me that when I grow up I should be a ballerina." Rebecca stood up on her tip toes and tried to spin around, dropping clumsily back into her chair. "Do I look like a ballerina? I want to be an artist like your friend Beryl."

"You should be whatever you want."

"I told him that I liked pink but I don't like to wear it. It's too girly."

"Your room at your house was pink."

"I like it, but I don't want to wear it," Rebecca repeated, as if Polly should fully understand.

"Got it. Don't want to wear it."

Andrew watched the exchange and went back to drawing.

"Miss Giller?" Jessie poked her head in.

"Hi Jessie. We've been having brownies. Would you like one?"

"Polly made them yesterday. They have nuts in them," Rebecca said. "We even have milk." She walked over to the older girl and reached for her hand. "Come on."

Jessie glanced at Polly, "Okay. Just one."

Andrew jumped up to get the milk out of the refrigerator. He was figuring out how to work with that cast. Polly watched him start to use the fingers on the arm that was broken and then shift to his other hand. "Can we have some more?" he asked.

"Why not? Polly asked. Another brownie wouldn't hurt them and Jessie wouldn't have to eat alone. "I'm going to call Henry and make a plan for dinner."

Polly left Jessie in two very young sets of capable hands and went into the office and sat down at Henry's desk. Luke leapt from his perch to the desk top and nudged her hand while she made the call.

"Hi Polly. Do we have another house guest?"

"Yeah. She's in the front bedroom. It took a while, but she's started to open up a little bit. She called her dad and took a shower. Now Rebecca and Andrew have insisted that she eat a brownie with them."

"What do you think?"

"I think that the poor girl has no idea what's coming next and I want to be a buffer between now and then."

"Of course you do. Just tell me what I'm supposed to do to help."

It really didn't take much for Henry to get on board these days. Either he figured that life would be easier if he played along or he really was beginning to understand her passion for taking care of people.

"Will you be here for dinner tonight?"

"I think so. Ben and I spent time looking at his lot. I've sent him back with some house plans. Maybe if Amanda starts thinking about the future, she'll feel better."

"That's a good idea. Jason and the kids will be here with us for supper."

"Should I pick anything up?"

"Well ..."

"You want ice cream sandwiches, don't you?"

"Would you?"

"Of course I will. See you later."

He was such a good guy. They were never going to be able to run around the house without being fully dressed now. Someone was always there, but Henry never complained. Polly scratched Luke's head, turning to watch the kids at the dining room table.

Jessie Locke was quite small. She was only a few inches taller than Rebecca and her reddish, brown hair hung to her shoulders. A good cut would give it some life and bounce back, but right now, it was straggly and straight. The size six clothing that Polly and her friends had purchased was still a little large on the girl and the pants needed to be rolled up in order to stay above the tops of her feet. The red marks and bruising around her wrists would fade, but there had been a bad cut across the top of her forearm. It should probably have been stitched, but was healing and would leave a large scar. Polly grew infuriated at the thought of that.

The girl reached up to push her hair back and Polly watched her jerk her hand back. What in the world?

"Okay, kids," Polly said, walking back out of the office. "I'm sure that Jessie would like to take a nap. We're eating dinner at six thirty and we should give her a couple of hours of peace and quiet."

"It's okay, Miss Giller," Jessie said. "I actually feel better right now."

The platter of brownies was empty and the gallon of milk was nearly gone. Chocolate always helped.

"Then why don't you kids show her some of the video games we have or start a movie or something. Andrew, maybe you could introduce her to the cats."

"Come on," Andrew said. "You're gonna love these cats. They're named Luke and Leia from Star Wars. Do you know about Star Wars? It's Polly's favorite movie. We watch it all the time. Do you want to watch it? Polly, can we turn the movie on?"

"You know I never mind a little Star Wars. Turn it on and then take her into the office to meet the cats."

Jessie walked over to the bookshelves. "Did you read all of these?"

"These are the books Rebecca and I like to read," Andrew said, pointing to three of the shelves in the middle of the case. "These others are boring."

"Hey," Polly protested. "They're not boring. You'll like them someday. And Jessie, if you want to read any book on any shelf, help yourself."

Andrew tried to draw her into the office, but she stopped and pulled out the first Harry Potter book. "I've never read this. All my friends did, but Mom said it was silly and I didn't need to fill my head with silly things."

Polly bit her lip and waited.

"That's not silly," Andrew said quite loudly. "It's a great book. You have to read it. Have you seen the movies? Polly has those too." He started babbling again and Polly cleared the dining room table. Just try to be sad or depressed around an excitable eleven year old. This one had a new audience and a lot of things to tell her. They would get along just fine.

CHAPTER TWENTY-TWO

"Someone's out there. What's that noise?" Henry asked softly as he tapped Polly's arm in bed.

"It's the television in the other room. What time is it?"

He turned over and swiped a phone on. "It's 4:30."

"It has to be Jessie. Let me check on her." Polly pulled her feet out from around a sleeping dog and put her robe on. Light and sound was coming from her old apartment. Maybe she was just going to call it the media room. It didn't feel like her old apartment any longer. It felt like something new and different.

Polly found Jessie curled up at the end of the sofa, wrapped in a blanket and holding a pillow in front of her.

"Jessie?" she asked quietly, hoping not to scare the poor girl to death. It didn't work, Jessie jumped.

"I'm sorry. Did I wake you up? I was having nightmares."

"It's okay. I'm glad you found your way over here. Do you want to talk about it?"

"Not really."

That made sense to Polly. "What about a brownie?" When in doubt, feed the frightened girl.

"I don't need anything."

"Well, I might need a brownie. Would you eat one if I brought it to you?"

Jessie smiled and nodded, then turned the sound down on the television.

"What are you watching?"

"Just some infomercial. There's nothing interesting on."

Polly put a few brownies on a plate, poured two glasses of milk and, balancing the plate on top of one of them, went back to the media room. Jessie took the plate and one of the glasses from her.

"Thank you," she said.

"Are you interested in this infomercial?"

Jessie shook her head. "Not really. It was just noise so I didn't have to think about anything."

"You have a lot to think about." Polly flipped through her hard drive and found the original Star Wars movie and started it. "If you're going to watch silly noise, this is my favorite thing. It always calms me down." She took a brownie from the plate and tucked herself into the opposite end of the sofa, her feet underneath her.

They watched in silence for a while and finally Jessie put her glass back on the table and asked, "Do you think it's weird that my mom left me out here?"

Nothing like starting with the easy stuff. Polly felt more comfortable dealing with a girl who needed to recuperate from an abusive jerk than one whose mother had left her behind.

She breathed deeply. "I think your mom has a lot to deal with, worrying about your dad's health."

"I suppose. You know when I told her I was leaving, she told me that I had to go without any of my things except the clothes I was wearing. They paid for everything and owned it. If I wanted to go with Dennis, I couldn't have any of my own stuff." Jessie started to cry. "She made me leave my guitar. I couldn't even bring Durango. I've never been without him."

"Who's Durango?" Polly asked, scooting a little closer.

Through her sobs, Jessie smiled. "He's a purple stuffed horse

Dad gave me when I had my tonsils out. Told me that if I ever got scared I should imagine riding away from it on Durango."

"I'm sorry," Polly said. What in the hell kind of mother pulled this crap? She stopped herself from saying anything. Kelly Locke had her own stuff to worry about, but why in the world would she be so cold to her own daughter?

"She hates me, doesn't she?"

"I can't imagine she hates you. She's angry and has said some things she doesn't know how to take back," Polly said.

"My older brothers never come home. They're married and Denny's wife is going to have a baby. I'm never going to see them again." The girl's tears continued to flow. "I'm never going to see my daddy either and Ethan is stuck at home by himself with her."

"I think he'll be fine," Polly said. She couldn't stand it any longer and moved in to gather Jessie into her arms. At her touch, the tears came harder and the sobs grew louder. Polly glanced at the television, feeling incredible sorrow as Luke Skywalker stood over his aunt and uncle's lost farm on the screen. He had to make a new life too, and if Polly was going to be an Obiwan for another young person who had to start fresh, she could do it. At least now she had a large number of friends around who would help.

Jessie cried and cried and then began to relax in Polly's arms until Polly realized that she had fallen asleep. She looked around and saw Henry standing in the doorway. "Help me," she mouthed at him.

He grinned at her and shook his head in the negative, then crossed his arms.

Polly tried to be angry with him and give him a nasty glare, but when that didn't work, she slowly slid out from under Jessie, replacing her body with a couple of pillows. Jessie sighed in her sleep and stretched out on the sofa. Polly covered her with a blanket, then walked over, took Henry's arm and led him back through the main room and into their bedroom.

"You're a brat."

"What exactly did you want me to do?" he asked with a chuckle. "You handled it."

"She's going to be here for a while. You know that, don't you?"

"I figured as much. But I hope *you* know she's probably going to need some professional help. That girl's been through a lot."

"Not the least of which was her mother kicking her out of the house with nothing at all and then leaving town before she was found."

"Pretty devastating to her self-esteem. Who does that?"

"A woman who doesn't have much of her own. Did you notice how she was always trying to transform the space around her? I thought it was a tad OCD, but it makes me wonder if she is just so unsure of herself that she has to be in control of everything."

"Okay, what are we going to do with a girl on the couch this morning?"

"She'll sleep for a while. I'm taking Obiwan down to the barn. Everyone will be there and we're going for a ride today. You can do what you'd like."

"Then I'll go to Mom and Dad's house for breakfast. Lonnie is leaving for Ann Arbor today. With the dog."

"Jessie and I will go to the diner for breakfast after I'm back. We'll all meet up later. Tell Lonnie goodbye for me, though."

Polly pulled on jeans and a t-shirt. Obiwan recognized her clothing and jumped down from the bed, wagging his whole body. She scrawled a quick note on a piece of paper and put it on the table in front of Jessie, then took the dog outside and down to the barn. Eliseo's car was parked in front of the barn and she heard noise as she opened the door.

As early as she was, Polly was the last to arrive.

"I can't believe I'm late!" she exclaimed, heading back to the tack room for Demi's saddle. "I've been up since four thirty."

"No worries," Eliseo said. "Everyone was excited to get going." They hadn't been out together for several weeks.

"Where are we headed today?" she asked.

"Since we're all here early, we'll take a longer ride. Ralph Bedford's place is a few miles down the road and I told him we would stop by. He wants to show me an old plow he has."

"That sounds great." Polly cinched the saddle and then Eliseo gave her a hand while she climbed up. He tossed her helmet to her and after checking everyone else, they headed out.

Jason and Rachel went on ahead with Obiwan running back and forth. Polly knew he'd settle down and walk with them once the excitement wore off. He loved these rides.

"Did Henry talk to you yesterday?" she asked Eliseo as they rode.

"About his uncle's house?"

"Yeah. What do you think?"

"I think you are determined to find me a place to live. You just never quit, do you?"

"Hey, you don't have to take it. I was just thinking ..." she paused and looked over at him. Sometimes it was difficult to tell whether or not he was teasing her. He had turned his head away so she couldn't see his lips.

"Thinking what?" he asked.

"Nothing. I was thinking nothing. If you don't want to do it, then it's none of my business."

He finally turned to look at her, his eyes sparkling with laughter. That was Polly's favorite thing about Eliseo. He had the most expressive eyes and when they lit up, they were gorgeous. "I didn't say that. I'm meeting his aunt and uncle to look at the house today."

"I'm kind of worried about you living out there, though," she said.

"What worries you?"

"Well, there's a lot of land around the house and you might want to have your own garden and your own animals. Then what would I do? I need you here."

"I'd like to have a dog of my own," he mused. "And when I want more horses, you and I will talk before I make any decisions. Why don't you not worry about it until something actually happens?"

"You know me better than that. Right?" she said. They watched Jason and Rachel walking their horses back and forth across the road, laughing at something.

"How's he doing?" she asked.

"Jason?"

"Yeah. He's changed so much this summer. I worry about him. He'll be in high school this fall and he's gotten a lot less tolerant of Andrew's antics. He doesn't play as much as he used to."

"He's trying to grow up. It has to be difficult being the oldest male in the family."

"Does he ever say anything to you about that?"

Eliseo had grown quiet and Polly turned her head to look at him. He was watching the two younger riders.

"Eliseo?" she asked.

"He talked about his dad once. I'm very glad that man isn't around here any longer and I'm very glad that I didn't know him when he was."

"That bad?"

"That bad. Jason remembers his mother getting beat up. He only saw it a couple of times before she kicked the man out, but it made an impression."

"I don't think Sylvie realizes that he remembers so much of that time. She knows that he had more exposure than Andrew, but she believes she kept it from him."

"Nope. His dad threatened him one night, too."

Polly gripped the horn of the saddle as she felt the air rush out of her lungs. "He what?"

"He came home drunk one night and woke Jason up. Told him that if he ever took his mother's side again, he'd beat the hell out of him and make sure that Jason could never talk again. He was just a little boy, Polly."

"Oh, Eliseo. And he's never told his mother that?"

"I don't think so. He made me promise not to say anything and I figure that as long as they're safe, there's no reason to bring it up. Jason is okay."

"I'm always so shocked at how awful people can be to each other. Especially to their own children." Polly thought back to the young girl on her couch. It was going to take a lot for Jessie to get past her mother's rejection, not to mention the abuse and humiliation she'd faced at the hands of the psychopath who chained her in his house.

"Yeah. Just about the time you think you've heard it all, something else comes up that is really close to home. Speaking of kids and abuse, how's that young girl you've rescued."

Polly looked at his face and his eyes were twinkling again. "I'm just not going to get a break, am I?" she asked.

"It's a good thing you're doing. Henry's never going to have a quiet household, but it's a good thing."

"Yeah. Just wait until I start moving them into your house."

"I figure I'm lucky to be one of your early rescues," he said, laughing.

"That's not fair. I didn't feel like I was rescuing you."

"Well, whatever you felt, it's what you did and you need to quit reacting like it's a bad thing. You saved my life."

"You saved yourself. And I hope that Jessie will figure out how to save herself. All I can do is give her a safe place to live until she decides what's next."

"Did your Dad do this?"

Polly thought for a moment. "No, not this, exactly. But our table was always open for people who needed a meal and people did show up. Dad loved making toys at Christmas for kids who needed them and I've found a few thank you notes from people he'd helped."

"At least you come by it honestly." He looked up and called out, "Jason? Rachel? It's the next lane on the left."

Jason gave a wave and they headed into the lane.

"You've really enjoyed spending time with Ralph, haven't you?" Polly said.

"He's such a great old guy. He's even taught me a few things about these horses." Eliseo leaned forward and patted Nan's neck. "They love working and he showed me how to make it fun."

Eliseo urged Nan forward and caught up to Jason and Rachel, then went ahead of them to the barn. He swung off the horse and led her forward and called out, "Good morning, Ralph. We've got the whole crew here."

When there was no answer, he turned around and shrugged. He handed the lead to Jason and said, "Let me knock on the door. I'll be right back."

They waited as he knocked. There was no answer.

"Ralph?" he called again. "Are you here? Wake up! You've got company."

After a few minutes, he walked back over to the group. Polly swung off Demi's back and jumped to the ground. "Nothing?" she asked.

"He should be here. We talked about this yesterday afternoon. I'm going to check the barn. Jason, you and Rachel stay here with the horses."

Polly handed Demi's reins to Rachel and followed Eliseo. "I'm going this way," she said. "Come on, Obiwan. You're with me."

Ralph Bedford's old Chevy pickup truck was parked on the other side of the house. Polly and Obiwan walked toward it and when the dog picked up speed, sniffing at the ground, Polly had a sinking feeling. She started running and pulled up short when she got to the truck. On the ground between the truck and the house lay the old man. But he was still alive. He wasn't conscious, but she saw his chest rise and fall.

He'd been shot twice in the torso that she could tell. How he was still alive, she had no idea.

"Eliseo!" she yelled. "Bring a blanket and something to stop bleeding. He's been shot!"

Polly knelt down on her haunches and brushed her hand over Ralph Bedford's forehead. It was cold and clammy. She opened her phone and made a call that she knew would bring help.

"Oh Polly, not again."

"Aaron. I'm down at Ralph Bedford's place. He's been shot, but he's still alive. We need someone here right now."

"I'll call you back."

Aaron hung up and Polly looked around for Eliseo. He was right there in front of her and looked into her eyes. "Go back to the kids. I've got this. Don't let them come over here."

"But ..."

"You've done what you needed to do, now go. Walk away from this. I'm going to take care of him until they get here."

Polly hesitated.

"Go!" he snapped and his voice startled her enough that she jumped back to her feet and turned around, then ran toward Jason, Rachel and the horses.

Jason had gotten down from Nat when she turned the corner.

"No, Jason. Stay here. Leave them room."

"What's going on?" he asked.

"Someone shot Ralph Bedford."

Rachel let out a little whimper and Jason tried to hand the reins he was holding to Polly. "I can help," he said.

"No. You can stay here. Eliseo wants us to stay here. He's got it. I think he's seen more of this than any of us."

"He's not dead? Because you've seen a lot of that," Jason said.

"No, he's still alive. I called Aaron."

Jason was nearly as tall as Polly and when he stood in front of her, she had to look across at him, rather than down. "Do you think the same person that killed Henry's uncle shot Ralph?"

"I have no idea," she said. "But if they didn't, then we have a lot bigger issue in town, don't you think?"

"I think this is scary," Rachel said. "Why would they hurt a nice old guy like him?"

Polly's phone buzzed before she had to come up with an answer to Rachel's question.

"Hi Aaron."

"Stu Decker is on the way and Sarah should be there pretty soon with the ambulance. What are you doing at Ralph's this early in the morning?"

"We're here on the horses. Eliseo talked to him yesterday. We were coming over to look at a plow or something. Personally, I think Eliseo just wanted to check on the old guy. He's kind of taken a liking to him."

"I'm glad you did. Can I ask why you found the guy and not Eliseo?"

"Shut up," she said.

"That's what I thought. You are drawn to these things. It's like it's your super power."

"You're not funny and Stu is driving into the lane right now, so I'm hanging up on you."

Polly did just that and waited until Aaron's deputy got out of his car.

"Well, we meet again," Stu said. Your reputation is going to grow and grow."

"You all think you're hilarious." Polly pointed to the side of the house. "Eliseo is over there with him."

"Sarah is just around the corner. Send her over, okay?"

He was just out of sight when the ambulance pulled in. Polly pointed across the lawn and they drove as far as they could, stopping in front of the old pickup truck. Polly's favorite EMT, Sarah, and her newest young protégé jumped out and she ran around the truck, while he opened the back of the vehicle and began pulling bags out.

"Do you think he's still alive?" Rachel asked.

"I hope so. They'll let us know." Polly took Demi's reins from Rachel and walked away with him. She just wanted to breathe and she wanted the strength of a big animal beside her while she tried to regain her sanity. She stroked his shoulder and smiled when he nuzzled the back of her head. Then she saw a large stump and led Demi to it, using it to give her height to easily slip her foot into the stirrup so she could swing onto his back again.

They waited a while longer and then Aaron's SUV pulled in behind Stu Decker's. Polly waved to him. He acknowledged her and strode across the lawn to the action.

Several minutes later, Eliseo emerged, wiping his hands on something and talking to Aaron. They walked over to Polly.

"Is he alive?" she asked.

"They're getting him stabilized for a trip in the ambulance, but Eliseo kept him alive until help arrived," Aaron said.

Eliseo shook his head. "I managed to remember a few things about emergency medicine from my days in Iraq. I'm sorry I snapped at you, Polly, but you were starting to go."

"What do you mean? I was fine."

"Polly, I'd asked you three times if you were okay and you never responded."

"I what?"

"You just sat there, staring off into space. It wasn't until I snapped that you came back to me."

She ducked her head. "I'm so sorry. I might have an extreme aversion to blood."

"You can deal with death, but you can't deal with blood?" Aaron shook his head in disbelief. "You are quite a character."

"At least this one wasn't dead," she said.

"And at least there was someone here who could take care of it when you couldn't."

"You're right. I'd like to think I'd manage if I was alone, but ... " she looked at Eliseo. "Three times?"

"You worried me."

"I'm really sorry."

"It's okay. I managed to get you moving and did what I could for Ralph."

A gurney came into view and they loaded it into the ambulance, then Sarah ran around to the front and got in. They waited until she had driven away and Stu joined them.

"I'll get the team in," he said to Aaron. "They won't like working on a Sunday morning."

"Yeah. Neither do I," Aaron growled. "Lydia just put my breakfast on the table." He turned to Polly and Eliseo. "You might as well get out before everyone arrives. I'm sorry your morning ride was disrupted."

"Let's hope that we were here in time," Eliseo said. He swung up onto Nan's back and moved her forward, then waited for Jason to re-mount Nat.

Henry was never going to believe this one. Polly decided to wait until later to tell him. He could enjoy breakfast without having to announce to his family that his wife had done it again.

CHAPTER TWENTY-THREE

"Hi there." Jessie was up and dressed and curled up on the sofa with one cat on her lap and the other in her arms.

"I see you've made a couple of friends," Polly said.

"They're great. I got your note. Thanks."

"How about some breakfast downtown? I just need a shower."

"You don't have to do that. I can eat toast or something."

"Ohhh no," Polly said. "My husband is having an awesome breakfast at his mother's house. We're not getting stuck with toast. I'm taking you to the best breakfast joint around."

"You two are weird," Jessie said.

"You've got that right. We're very weird, but why do you say so?"

"You really like each other. Like all the time. And everybody knows it. They just expect you to be nice to each other."

"I suppose. I rarely spend time with people I don't like and there's no way I'd want to be married to someone unless we had fun together and respected each other."

"It's just weird."

"I hope it's not as weird as you think," Polly said.

"My parents never act like they're happy. Dad is always gone and Mom is always mad. If she isn't mad, she's telling someone what to do or telling us why we're doing things wrong."

This was going to be difficult. Polly wasn't sure if she was going to say the right things, but off she went.

"Sometimes people don't know how to be happy. They've had a lot of things break in their past and never get fixed. Did you ever talk to your mom about her life before she married your dad?"

"She didn't want to talk about it."

"Did you ever meet your grandparents?"

"I think I met my dad's parents when I was really little, but then they were gone."

"Any aunts and uncles or cousins?"

"No. Mom was an orphan. At least that's what she said."

"Did she talk about being adopted?"

"No."

"Did she talk about being a foster child?"

"Yeah. I guess."

"Do you think that her not having a family of her own might have something to do with all of this?"

"But shouldn't she be nicer to us so that we'd stick around and she could have a family?"

"That makes sense to you and me, but when a person hurts inside, they do things that don't make sense."

"I don't want to hate her, but I really got tired of the way she treated me."

"Hating her won't do you any good. Maybe someday you can see life from her perspective and that will help you understand her, though. It won't change things, but it will help you."

"What do you think broke in Dennis to make him chain me up?"

"I've got nothing on that one, Jessie. I hope he can explain himself to a good lawyer. That's what I hope. Now let me take a shower and we'll go get breakfast."

Polly went into her room and shut the door. With all the people that had been in and out lately, the animals were getting more used to closed doors, but that didn't mean that ... yep, there it was. Scratching at the door.

"Hello there," she said to Luke, who walked in as if he'd been waiting hours for her to allow him access. "It's not going to do me any good to shut this door is it?" He pranced over to the cat tree in front of a window and jumped up on it, ignoring the conversation. "Fine then."

She sat down on the bed and kicked off her boots, then took out her phone. Henry didn't need to hear this from someone else.

"Good morning. Are you heading out for breakfast?" he asked when he answered the phone.

"I'm about to take a shower, but I wanted you to hear this from me first."

"No." he said.

"Well, not quite."

"What does that mean?"

"We went down to Ralph Bedford's house and he'd been shot. He wasn't dead and they're taking him to the hospital right now. It had to have happened just before we got there."

"And you didn't see anyone driving away?"

"Nope."

"Are you okay?"

"I guess. I don't know what else to be."

"Freaked out? Shook up? A wreck?"

"I might have freaked out a little, but I didn't know it. Eliseo says I zoned out."

"What does that mean? Are you okay?"

"Yeah. I think it was the blood. He asked me three times how I was doing and said I never responded. He finally yelled at me and snapped me out of it. I couldn't figure out why he told me to go away, but apparently I'm not good with blood."

"We've known that. I didn't realize it was that bad, though."

"Don't ever cut a limb off with one of your saws. I'll be useless."

He chuckled a little, but not very long. "Got it. Dad has always insisted on safety precautions and I don't work without them."

"That's probably good."

"Did they say whether or not they think the person who did this is the same one who killed Uncle Loren?"

"No one said anything, but Aaron called Stu Decker in. That was his case, right?"

"Yeah. Maybe they do think that."

"It kind of freaks me out that old men who live alone are a target. How horrible."

"I guess I'm lucky you married me."

"That's awful, Henry. You aren't old enough yet, though. Oh, by the way, I talked to Eliseo about the house. He's looking forward to meeting your aunt. I think he likes the idea."

"Much as I hate to admit it - you had a good idea. We'll see what happens. I know he was good friends with Ralph. How's he taking this?"

"Well, he saved the man's life since I couldn't do anything to help him. We rode the horses back and everyone was pretty quiet. Then he told us all to go ahead and leave. He didn't even want any help dealing with their saddles and tack. Rachel and I just came up to the main building and left Jason with him."

"Can you even imagine what's going through his head right now?"

"I'm just glad he's got those big old beasts to take care of his heart."

"You go take your shower and head for the diner. We're getting Lonnie and Duchess packed up right now."

"Give her a hug for me."

"You mean Lonnie, right?"

"If you'll hug them both, I'm fine with that."

~ ~ ~

Joe's Diner was busy when Polly and Jessie walked in, but Lucy waved from the back and pointed to a table for two.

"I promise," Polly said. "You're going to love this."

Jessie took Polly's arm and stepped in to whisper. "I can't pay for breakfast. I don't even have a job yet."

"Don't worry. I wouldn't have asked you to come with me if I expected you to pay. Give life some time. You'll get a job and find a place of your own and before you know it, you'll be inviting me out for breakfast. Today, let's just enjoy it."

Polly waved and smiled at people she recognized as they made their way to the table. She was stopped by someone tugging at her arm. She turned around and smiled down at Helen Randall.

"Good morning, Helen."

"I hear you've been at it again," the woman said, smiling knowingly.

"I don't know what you heard, but he was alive the last I knew."

Jessie's eyes grew big.

"Well, it's a good thing you found him when you did is what I heard," Helen's husband, Frank, said. "They had to work on him all the way to the hospital and nearly lost him twice."

"I didn't know any of that," Polly said.

A man she recognized from one of Henry's crews leaned over and said, "I heard she nearly passed out from the blood."

"Where are you guys getting all of this crazy information?" Polly said, laughing. "Now let me get some breakfast."

She pushed away from them and led Jessie to the table. Before they even sat down, Lucy put glasses of water and a carafe of coffee on the table.

"What do you think you'd like this morning?" Lucy asked.

"Jessie might need a minute to look at the menu, but if Joe is making up any of that garbage plate, I'll have it."

"What's that?" Jessie asked.

"This morning it's sausage, ham and bacon with green peppers, onions and mushrooms all fried up with potatoes and eggs on top. Do you want gravy on it too?" Lucy asked Polly.

"Of course I do."

"What about something to drink, sweetie?" Lucy asked Jessie.

"A Coke, please? And I'll have the same thing as Polly. That sounds good."

"Great choice. I'll be back with your Coke." Lucy hadn't even put the menus on the table. Polly still watched in amazement as she negotiated the tables and took care of folks as she moved past them. There were two other waitresses working the room this morning and they were good, but no one was as smooth as Lucy.

"Everybody knows you here," Jessie said.

"The funny thing is that I didn't think that would ever happen. I've lived in town for two years and it's only been the last few months that I don't feel like I'm searching for names every time I see someone."

"What was that about you finding someone alive? Were they serious?"

"I'm sorry - I didn't tell you about that yet. When we were out riding horses this morning, we found a man who'd been shot. I called the Sheriff and he got the emergency vehicles there right away, so hopefully the man will live through this."

Jessie's eyes had grown huge again. "You're the one who found him?"

Polly pursed her lips. "I hate to tell you this, but it's kind of my thing. If you spend any time at all with me, you will hear people tease me about the fact that I find dead bodies."

Jessie sat back in her chair, "No shit?" She clapped her hand over her mouth. "I'm sorry."

"No, that's fine," Polly said, laughing. "Sometimes that's how I feel too. But yes, if someone is killed in a three county area, it's going to happen right where I'm scheduled to be. Everyone in town thinks it's funny. I think it's a little creepy, but that doesn't change the way it works. Luckily, Sheriff Merritt and I are friends so he doesn't believe I'm a mass murderer."

"Aren't people scared to be around you?"

"That's just not funny at all, missy," Polly said. "Some folks might be. But that's too bad for them. I'm a lot of fun. And since I found Mr. Bedford alive this morning, maybe that will help my reputation."

Lucy brought Jessie's Coke. "You did it again, didn't you?"

"He's alive. I think," Polly said. "I haven't heard any different. So this time I didn't do it."

"He's such a sweet old guy. He comes in all the time with your farm hand."

"Did he ever come in here with anyone else?" Polly asked.

Lucy shook her head. "Not really. I met his granddaughter last week. Nice girl. I guess she was in from Texas."

"His granddaughter?"

"Yeah. Short little thing. Just about this girl's height. She spoke with an accent and everything. Wore cowboy boots and had a flashy red cowboy hat. Said she was up doing a rodeo in Nebraska and came over to see her grandpa."

"She told you all that?"

"Yeah. He'd gone back out to his truck to get a map or something. We just got to talking. She seemed really nice."

Polly nodded. She was going to have to ask Eliseo about this. A flashy girl in a getup like that would garner some attention in town. She'd already begun to wonder if the person committing these murders was female. The targets were too easy. Some of these old men were pretty lonely and a little feminine attention could go a long way. It would surprise Henry to find out that his uncle had gotten messed up with a little chickie, but everyone had a chink in their armor somewhere.

"Don't you think?" Polly looked across the table. Jessie had asked her something, but she'd missed the conversation.

"What?"

"I was just talking about how this would be a great job. I could wait tables in a place like this."

"Sure you could. There's another restaurant in town and a pizza place down the block. We can check those out, too," Polly said. "How long until you turn twenty-one?"

"A little over a year." Jessie frowned. "I was going to party with Maggie on my twenty-first birthday. We knew just what bars we were going to hit. Now I can't do that."

"You never know what's going to happen tomorrow. You might be back in Colorado."

"No," Jessie smacked the table in front of her, making the silverware jump. "I'm not going back there."

"Okay," Polly said. "That's off the table." She slid a glance to the silverware. "Literally."

"Sorry. I'm just so afraid someone is going to make me go back. I didn't even know I wanted to live in Iowa. I just knew I had to be someplace else."

"No one is going to make you do anything you don't want to do. It's up to you to figure out what's next."

Lucy put two plates down in front of them and dropped the receipt in front of Polly's plate. "Wave if you need me," she said.

"Thanks." Polly smiled up at her and then said to Jessie, "Dig in. You'll love it. The name sounds awful, but it's the best breakfast food around."

"Hi Polly."

She looked up to see Doug Randall make his way to her table. "Hey Doug. I just saw your parents."

"Yeah. They're going to late church today. Rachel said you were coming up here for breakfast and she also told me you found old Mr. Bedford and he was shot." He looked pointedly at their table and then realized he didn't recognize the person sitting with her. "I'm sorry. I didn't know you were here with someone."

"No. It's fine. If you can find a chair and get Lucy's attention, you can sit with us."

"Thanks. Rachel and Billy are going to some deal for Caleb at church and then to her mom's house for lunch. I didn't want to sit at home alone. I thought I'd catch Mom and Dad, but they were already gone." He looked around and then asked a group at another table to take one of their chairs.

"Doug, this is Jessie Locke. Her dad and my dad were college friends."

"Wow. She's a lot younger than you."

Polly swatted his shoulder. "Thanks. I thought you were my friend. Jessie, this brat lives in the apartment over my garage. Most of the time he's a really good guy."

Jessie put her hand out to shake Doug's. "Hi," she said shyly.

"Jessie's going to be staying with us for a while."

"Cool," he said.

Lucy put a plate down in front of him, "I figured you wanted your regular?"

"Awesome. Thanks!"

"And your mom paid already. She said you'd be in."

"Aren't moms great?" he asked, reaching across the table for the jelly container. "So Polly, when are you going on your honeymoon?" He turned back to Jessie. "She couldn't go because the tornado messed up the town. We've been really busy this week. And Jerry says next week isn't going to be much better. I'll be really glad to get back to regular work. He asked if we'd donate some time to getting people back up and running. No big deal for me, but if we hadn't taken today off I was going to fall over sound asleep in someone's basement."

He stopped talking and looked back at Polly. "So?"

"So what?"

"When are you going on your honeymoon?"

"Probably not until October."

"That's a long time." He looked at Jessie. "She got married a couple of months ago. They didn't tell anybody about it. Just got married. But that was after some wicked psycho chick got all jealous of her and kidnapped little Rebecca. Have you met Rebecca? She's just about the cutest thing ever. Her mom isn't probably going to live very long because she has cancer. Everyone thinks that Polly will adopt Rebecca after Sarah dies, but Polly isn't talking about that either. Wow, if you're going to live with Henry and Polly you have a lot of history to catch up on. But she rocks."

"Shut up and eat, Doug. You're wearing us out," Polly said.

He took a bite of his eggs and reached for the coffee pot, "Is there enough in there for me to share?" he asked, then realized he didn't have a mug. "I'll be right back." He took off for the counter.

"Does he always talk that much?" Jessie asked.

"I didn't think so. This is new," Polly replied.

Doug slid back into his seat and poured coffee. "Do you need some while I'm pouring?" Polly pushed her mug closer to him and he refilled it.

"Where are you from, Jessie?"

"Colorado."

"I was there once when I was in high school. It was the middle of the summer and not nearly as hot as it gets out here."

"It depends where you live."

"I suppose. We were up at Rocky Mountain National Park and then we were in Denver. I got to go to a Rockies game even though I'm a Cubs fan. Everyone around here is a Cubs fan, I think. Do you like baseball, Jessie?"

"I suppose."

"Billy and I play on a team. You should come out and see us."

She nodded.

"How come you never watch us play, Polly?"

"I don't know. Honestly, I didn't even know you had a team in Bellingwood."

"Seriously? How could you not know?"

"I got nothing."

"Are you playing in the summer band again this year?"

"Doug, are you on something?"

He put his fork down on his plate and stopped moving. "No. Why?"

"You have been dinging off the wall since you sat down."

"I had a couple of energy drinks this morning," he said, laughing. "Am I really that bad?" He turned back to Jessie. She nodded.

"Sorry. I have a lot to get done today before we start working again tomorrow. I told Dad I'd come help with the garden and I have to get laundry done. I'm totally out of ..." he paused. "Well, they aren't purple, but I'm out of them."

Polly rolled her eyes and said, "That's a story for another time."

He whispered at Jessie. "I saw her panties once. They were purple with pink bows. It was, like, the first time I met her. She threw them down the stairs at me."

"Stop it," Polly said. "You're awful."

"Well it's the truth. And then they had that party where everyone wore purple. It's your color now."

"Uh huh. Are you about done?"

In the middle of all his talking, Doug had managed to plow through his breakfast. He looked down at his plate. "Whaddya know. I'm done. I suppose I should go back home and get my laundry. Maybe Mom will do it for me while I help Dad in the garden. It was nice to meet you, Jessie. Maybe I'll see you around."

He slid out of his chair and trotted to the front door. When he got there, he turned around and gave them a little wave and then he was gone.

"So he's not always like that?" Jessie asked.

"Nope. I need a nap now, though. Just. Wow."

They walked out of the restaurant together and when Polly got in the truck, Jessie said, "Do you think I could use your phone again this morning? I want to call Dad and see how he's doing."

"Sure. I'd like to ask him a couple of questions, too."

"Okay, like what?"

"I think it would be nice if you could have some of your clothes and things. We can buy new for you if we have to, but there's no reason for that, don't you think?"

"Mom's not going to like it."

"Maybe she will have had some time to re-think her position. Let's hope for the best."

CHAPTER TWENTY-FOUR

Every one of her animals was waiting at the top of the stairs when Polly opened the door to go up.

"We're running the gauntlet this morning."

"I like how they are happy to see us."

"They always are," Polly said, picking Luke up as she crested the top step. "This one will trip you if you aren't careful.

Henry was in the living room and she dropped Luke on the couch beside him.

"How was breakfast?" he asked.

Jessie gave him a shy smile. "It was pretty good. They called it a garbage plate though. I wasn't too sure."

"Polly likes that. When she drags you back for a pork tenderloin, just follow. They're terrific."

Polly handed Jessie her phone, after swiping it open and bringing up Curt Locke's number. "You can go in your room if you want some privacy. I'd like a chance to ask him a couple of questions before you hang up, though."

"Thank you." Jessie took the phone and had it at her ear before she'd cleared the threshold of the bedroom.

The door closed and Polly slid over the back of the sofa, landing beside Henry. "I love doing that. Mary would have had my head. But these are ours and I get to play on them as hard as I want to."

"You're just a big kid sometimes, aren't you?"

Polly ignored him. "Lonnie's on her way back to Michigan?"

"I think she's happy to have Uncle Loren's dog as a companion. Her roommates are excited about the dog, too. It just wasn't something we grew up with."

"That's weird," Polly said. She turned to him. "You have to ask your aunt if she ever saw a girl over at Loren's place."

Henry tilted his head at her. "A girl? What are you getting into now, Polly?"

"Lucy told me that she met Ralph Bedford's granddaughter last week. I'm going to ask Eliseo if he met her, but I was just wondering."

"I can certainly ask Aunt Betty. But don't you think you should talk to Stu Decker about this?"

"Yeah ..." Polly dipped her chin, a little embarrassed. "I really don't mean to get involved in all of this, but people talk about things and I put them together into a convoluted but connected story. It's probably nothing."

"It wouldn't hurt to ask questions," He nodded toward Jessie's room. "How's she doing this morning?"

"She's trying to come to grips with the fact that her mother essentially tossed her out of the house. How do you explain that parents are just as messed up as the rest of us, to a girl who was chained up for over a week?"

Henry visibly shuddered. "I guess she's doing pretty well then, if she can even smile at all."

A rap at the front door got their attention and Polly jumped up to answer it. She pulled the door open and looked down at a grinning Rebecca and Andrew.

"What are you two up to this morning?"

"It's not morning," Andrew scolded. "It's afternoon. Mom dropped us off after church. We brought lunch over for Sarah and

Rebecca and I asked if I could stay. Can I stay?"

Polly chuckled. "Of course you can."

"Look at my cast," he said, holding up his arms. "Everyone signed it at church." He twisted and turned it and then pointed to a small image. "That's a penguin. Doctor Mason said I was cool."

"You're very cool," Polly agreed. "What are you planning to do today?"

Andrew peered up at her, looking around her. He took her right hand in his and squinted while looking at her fingers.

She pulled her hand away. "What are you doing?"

"Rebecca and I think we should conduct experiments on you."

"What do you mean by that?" Polly planted both hands on her hips and tried to scowl at him, but all she could do was smile.

"They were talking about you at church. How you found Mr. Bedford this morning. Somebody asked if you'd been bitten by something radioactive. That it's like your superpower. Mom said it was because you drank special water every day."

"They're laughing at me, Henry," Polly said. "I told you this town was going to think I was nuts. And now that you're married to me, you are going to be laughed at, too."

"I can take it." Henry stood up and came over to the door and physically pulled Polly back a step into the living room. "Are you going to let them in?"

"I don't know," she said. "They want to do experiments on me."

"How about we don't do experiments until Polly has taken a break."

Polly wrinkled her forehead at him. "I don't need a break."

"You've been awake since four thirty and you haven't stopped moving. I'm going to insist. Kids, if you want to hit the video games, be my guest, but Polly is going to take a nap."

Rebecca and Andrew ran into the media room and soon, the sounds of racing cars filled the apartment.

"I don't need a nap."

"Polly, I love you, but you've been taking care of everyone for days. We were supposed to be on our honeymoon this last week. Not only have you been cleaning up after folks down at the hotel and traipsing all over the city helping after the tornado, you've accepted the responsibility for a young woman and this morning you were involved in the rescue of Ralph Bedford. You can slow down a bit."

"Polly?" Jessie's voice came from her bedroom doorway.

"Yes, Jessie. What is it?"

"Did you want to talk to my dad?"

"Oh! Yes. Thank you. Is everything okay?"

The girl brushed a tear away from her cheek. "I guess so. Here he is."

Polly took the phone and placing it to her ear, said, "Curt?"

"Yes, Polly."

She walked into the bedroom and sat down at her desk. "How are you feeling today?"

"I feel like I was hit by a Mac truck. These last couple of days have been exhausting, but I'm home and Kelly insists that I rest and obey doctor's orders."

"I'm glad you're home and safe. Curt, what kind of plans do you and Kelly have for this mess with your daughter?"

"We're talking about a couple of very stubborn women. Jessie insists that she isn't coming back to Colorado and Kelly is just mad enough to let her stay out there."

"Even after all her daughter has been through? You have to be kidding me!"

"I know it doesn't seem right to you, Polly, but my wife hasn't had an easy life and now that I can't work, it isn't going to get any easier on her."

"Your daughter was chained up by a man in his house. You're telling me that your wife is okay with staying mad at her? What kind of sickness is that?"

Henry had come into the room and put his hand on Polly's shoulder. When she looked up, he shook his head.

"She feels like Jessie has made her own decisions and if she is going to insist that she's an adult, she has to live with the consequences."

"That's just crap and you know it."

"Miss Giller, there isn't much I can do about any of this right now. My wife is hurt and angry. She's scared that I'm going to die and she doesn't know what to do to help our daughter. I'm glad that you are there to make sure she is safe."

"I'm so angry, I don't have words to express my fury."

"I understand, but as I said, there's nothing I can do. If I could send you money, I would, but I don't have anything extra. If I could be there I would, but you know that I can't. All I can do is talk to my girl when she wants to and tell her that I love her."

Polly wanted to spit into the phone. She wanted to bang it over his wife's head. She wanted to do a lot of violence, but instead, she held it together.

"How can I get hold of some of Jessie's things? Curt, she doesn't even own any clothes. Your wife," and Polly practically spat the word at him, "wouldn't let her bring anything with her."

"Well, that's where you're wrong ..." he began.

"No, I'm not wrong. She has nothing."

"The only thing I can give to her is that car. I talked to Kelly and told her that we weren't going to take it back. I'll send the title out to Jessie and it will be her car. We'll figure things out on this end. It's not much, but maybe it will help her get around."

"Okay. That's a start."

"If you open the trunk, you'll find most of her things. Her brother and I packed up her room. Her clothes and some of the things she loved are in there. I wasn't going to say anything if she wanted to come home."

"Curt," Polly said, breathing out. "That's wonderful."

"I know it isn't enough, but it's what I can do right now. Maybe when Kelly calms down some and isn't quite so worried about me and our finances, she will feel a little pity for our girl and we can mend some fences."

"What about her phone?"

"I'll ask Ethan to send it to you in the next couple of days. Polly, don't hate Kelly for this."

"It's not my place to hate, Curt, but I am shocked and infuriated at her decision to abandon her daughter."

"I'm sorry."

"Will you be here when she has to testify against the man who hurt her?"

"I don't know, Polly. I will do my best. But please, make sure she knows how much I love her and tell her to call me whenever she wants to talk."

Polly wasn't sure how to express his love and his absence at the same time, but maybe Jessie understood all of that. She'd lived in his home for nearly twenty years.

"I'll do what I can," she said with a sigh.

"Your father would be proud of you."

"Good-bye, Curt."

Polly put the phone down on her desk and pinched the bridge of her nose, trying to stop herself from crying. She wasn't sure if it was sorrow or anger. Probably a little bit of both.

"How are you doing?" Henry asked.

"I'm so mad. I just don't understand it. How could that woman be so callous? And how can he just let her do that?"

"You probably made it easy for her to choose. She doesn't have to worry about Jessie, assured that you're here to deal with it."

"But she left town without knowing whether her daughter was safe or not and when she found out what that girl had been through ..." Polly turned on him. "What mother doesn't rush to her daughter's side after something like that?"

"I don't have a good answer for that, Polly. I wish I did."

Polly stood up and let him draw her in close. "I'm so glad you're here to take care of me and I'm glad you had normal parents and I don't have to worry about you."

"Not even a little?" he asked with a smile in his voice.

"Okay, a little." She stepped back. "At least her dad came through for her with some of her things. They're in the trunk of the car he left here. That will help. And he says that she can keep the car. I guess that's something. I probably need to tell her that bit of good news."

Henry drew her back in for a lingering kiss. "You go take care of your waif and then come back up here and let me force you into a nap. You've had a long day so far and we're only halfway through."

"Tomorrow is going to be a better day, right?"

"I sure hope so." He gently pushed her to the door. "Get going and come back."

Polly went out and when she didn't see Jessie in the living room, went on through to the media room. She found the girl watching as Rebecca and Andrew were playing some game. Jessie was holding Leia, stroking the cat's back absentmindedly. Leia's eyes were closed and her tail twitched every once in a while.

"Jessie, could I see you out here, please?"

Putting the cat down on the sofa beside Rebecca, Jessie met Polly in the living room.

"I have a little good news for you. Your father is going to send the title for the car and let you keep it. He's also sending your phone."

"That's really nice," Jessie said. "I'm surprised Mom let him do anything for me. She's really pissed at me for leaving."

"I know she is. Hopefully she'll get over it."

"She didn't even want to talk about what happened to me. Dad let me tell him, but Mom said she didn't want to hear about it."

"I'm sorry, Jessie."

"Oh well. I guess I brought it all on myself and I probably deserve it."

"No, that's not true and I don't want you to ever think that." Polly said, drawing the girl to the living room sofa. "No one deserves to be treated like that man treated you and to be completely honest, no one deserves to be treated like your mother is treating you."

"Then what did I do to make all of this happen?" Jessie began to cry and Polly pulled her close and let her sob. Rebecca and Andrew looked out the door at them and Rebecca tentatively approached them, sending Andrew back to the media room with a little wave.

"Jessie?" she asked. "Are you okay?"

"She's had a pretty rough couple of days," Polly said.

Rebecca sat down on the other side of Jessie and rubbed her back. "My mom says that when I'm sad, I should think of the prettiest thing I've ever seen and tell God thank you."

"What's the prettiest thing you've seen, Rebecca?" Polly asked.

"I saw two rainbows one day. Mom told me they were a sign from God that things would get better. And she was right because the next day we moved to Bellingwood."

Jessie sat up and smiled down at Rebecca. "Thank you."

"What's the prettiest thing you've ever seen?" Rebecca asked her.

Jessie took hold of Polly's hand and looked up at her. "It had to be yesterday when I saw Polly come in to the police station for me. I didn't know what I was going to do."

Polly hugged her again.

"Polly showed up at my house when I didn't know what to do either. She made my mom go to the hospital and then brought me here to stay."

"Okay girls, that's enough of that," Polly said through tears that threatened to overwhelm her. She was getting tired of crying all the time. "I have one more piece of good news, Jessie."

"What?"

"Your dad and brother packed some of your things in the trunk of that car. I think your clothes are there and I'm not sure what else. He didn't tell me."

Jessie jumped up, her face brightening. "Let's go see!"

"The keys are in the office downstairs. Let's ask Andrew and Henry to help." She was glad to give the girl something to look forward to after the wrenching pain she must have been going through the last couple of days. That Jessie was functioning at all was a surprise to Polly.

"I'll get Andrew," Rebecca said, jumping up and running into the media room.

"Henry?" Polly called. He came out of the bedroom. "Would you help us bring some of Jessie's things up from her car?"

He nodded and went back into the room, coming out a moment later with his shoes on. Polly watched him cross the room and still couldn't believe that he was living in the same house that she was and that he was so comfortable here. With all of the chaos that surrounded her, he was normal and stable.

They went downstairs to the office and Polly took the keys that Curt Locke had given her from the top drawer of her desk and handed them to Jessie. The parade made its way to the front parking lot and an old red car parked at the end. Jessie opened the trunk and a sound of joy escaped her as she reached in and grabbed a beat up rag doll.

"Milady!" she cried. "He sent Milady!" A stuffed black cat and a brown stuffed bear ended up in her arms. "They're all here. I never thought I'd see them again."

Polly smiled. No matter how old you get, some vestiges of childhood will always be important.

Jessie rummaged around in the trunk and finally pulled out a stuffed purple horse. "This is Durango. I don't ever want to leave him behind again."

Henry lifted out two plastic garbage bags filled with clothes and Rebecca grabbed a grocery bag filled with bottles and jars. "Is this your makeup?" Rebecca asked.

Jessie nodded.

"Can you show me how to wear it sometime?"

Jessie looked at Polly, who just smiled.

"Sure. When I find everything and if your mom says it's okay, we'll do that."

"I can carry something." Andrew looked into the trunk and lifted out a paper bag that had been taped shut. "What's in here?" He held it up to Jessie and said, "It's kind of heavy."

Jessie slid her fingers under the tape and ripped the top a little. "It's my CDs. I haven't listened to these in forever since I got my phone. But I don't have a CD player."

"There's one in Polly's media room. I know how to use it," he announced. "I'll show you."

"That would be great," Jessie said and looked back at the empty trunk. "I guess that's all he sent. That's okay. This is better than nothing."

"Is there something you're missing?" Polly asked.

"It's okay. There's nothing important."

"What is it?"

"I kind of hoped to see my guitar and my journals. I guess Mom got her hands on those. She probably threw them all away by now. Dad probably didn't even know they were there. And I had some earrings and bracelets that he gave me. None of that is here either."

Polly pushed the trunk lid down. "I'm sorry. We'll get you a couple of empty journals tomorrow. I know that doesn't replace what you had, but at least you can start again."

Jessie nodded. "I guess." Then she looked at Rebecca and Andrew, who were following Henry into the building. "She would tell me to think of something pretty. I should be thankful that I got my clothes and my animals back."

"You can be sad when you need to be sad. I think you've earned a few days of that." She saw Eliseo and Jason coming up from the barn. "Can you find your way back upstairs? I need to talk to Eliseo for a few minutes."

Jessie looked at the two coming toward them and then glanced away, "Sure. Thank you." She turned and went to the front door while Polly walked to meet them.

"Is she staying here for a while?" Jason asked.

"Yes she is."

"You take everyone in, don't you?" he said.

"I guess that was the purpose of Sycamore House. But it does seem to work out that way. What are you two doing?"

"We're going down to Boone to see Mr. Bedford," Jason announced. "I have to ask Mom if it's okay."

"Go on in, Jason," Eliseo said. "Let me know what she says."

Jason took off and Polly said, "Did you know Mr. Bedford had a granddaughter? Lucy said they had lunch together at the Diner last week."

Eliseo shook his head. "He never said anything to me about her. But then we hadn't seen much of each other this last week. It's been pretty busy around town."

"Have you heard how he's doing?"

"They might still have him in surgery. He was pretty messed up. I'm sorry you had to deal with that this morning."

"It feels like it was a week ago," she said. "I'm just glad we were there. And it should be me apologizing for wigging out on you. I've never done that before."

He chuckled. "You were pretty funny. I really think I could have tipped you over. The weird thing is, you were fine until I got there. Then it's like you quit focusing on everything."

"It was a lot of blood."

"You're right, it was."

Jason came running back outside. "Mom says they took him to Ames and that he might not live."

Eliseo shut his eyes. When he opened them back up, he said. "Then we're going to Ames. We'll be back to bring the horses in this evening, Polly. Don't worry about them."

"Just call if you need me to do anything," she said.

"Are you coming with me, Jason?"

"Mom said I could. Can I drive?"

"Maybe I'll let you drive on the way back." Eliseo shot a smile at Polly. "It's going to be difficult to keep this one contained. He's ready to go."

"Good luck with that."

She watched them go back down to Eliseo's car and drive off. Things really needed to slow down again. She was ready for normal, even if it only lasted a few days.

CHAPTER TWENTY-FIVE

"Down he goes!"

Polly woke from her nap to the sound of kids yelling. She went out to the living room see what was happening. Henry looked up and said, "I'm sorry. We tried to stay quiet as long as possible and it got out of control."

"What's going on out here?"

Jessie was in one of the overstuffed chairs with both cats on her lap. Andrew and Rebecca were flopped on the floor playing Battleship.

"You're playing Battleship and you didn't wake me up?" she asked. "That's not fair."

"Henry's playing the winner of this game. Jessie said she didn't want to today. But that's okay" Rebecca backed up, taking her board with her and sat in front of Jessie's chair, leaning back on her legs. The older girl had definitely found an ally.

"I told them we could play as long as they stayed quiet." Henry stood up and walked over to Polly. "That was most of the fun - watching them try to laugh with no sound."

"Thank you for letting me sleep, guys. Now I have to figure out what to do for the rest of the evening," Polly said.

"Mom is downstairs cooking something for some class. She's making supper for everyone."

"I'm going to run down and talk to her. You can be as loud as you want now. I'll be right back." Polly gave Henry a quick hug. "Do I need to take the dog out?"

"Nah. Don't worry about it. We'll get him later. He's fine." He kissed her on the forehead and went back to the Twister mat. "Are you two ready for some more?"

Polly left by the front door and went down to the main kitchen. Whatever Sylvie was making, it smelled wonderful.

"Hey there," she said, walking in.

"Just a sec. I nearly have it." Sylvie didn't look up.

"I have an idea and you're going to think I'm crazy."

"What's that?" Sylvie still didn't look up from the stovetop. She was watching the pan intently.

"I want to go out tonight. I want to call Joss and Sal and go out with my girlfriends. I don't want to think about dead people or laundry or kids or people being in trouble. I just want to spend time with you. When you finish here, what do you think? We could go for pizza and then head over to the Alehouse."

"Uh huh." Sylvie pulled the sauce pan off the burner and poured the chocolate into molds sitting beside the stove. "There. Those should be perfect." She set the pan down and looked up at Polly. "Sorry about that. The chocolate was almost finished. I'm taking these with me tomorrow morning."

"Okay. Got it. So, do you want to go out tonight? We've never done anything like this and I think it's time."

Sylvie laughed. "I haven't had a girl's night in years. It sounds awesome. But what about the kids?"

"Well, Henry will be here and Jessie is upstairs. Rebecca has fallen in love with her and I suspect that spending time with those two little ones is good for her soul. Jason can either hang out with them or Eliseo or I can call Doug and Billy. Is this a yes?"

"Why not?" Sylvie shrugged. "It would be good for me to think about something other than work or school. I'd love it."

"Great. I'll call Sal and Joss and make sure Henry is going to be here. It's a date."

"Tell them that dinner will be ready if they want to eat here in the kitchen. Ben and Amanda will still be eating with them. I've already talked to her and told Sarah."

"Thanks. They'll be down." Polly went up the back way, taking a load of laundry with her. When she got back upstairs, the noise hadn't lessened. This time, Henry was playing against Andrew. She couldn't believe how lucky she was to have found a man that enjoyed playing with the kids she loved. Polly dropped the laundry on her bed and went into the living room and sat on the edge of the sofa. When the action broke, she interrupted. "Henry, would you mind if I went out with Sal, Joss and Sylvie tonight?"

He leaned back and said, "That sounds great. We can take care of everything here. Are you okay with that, Jessie?"

The girl nodded. "I guess."

"I was hoping you could hang out with Andrew and Rebecca," Polly said to her. "Sylvie will have dinner ready downstairs and you can meet Rebecca's mom. I don't know when Jason and Eliseo are going to be back from the hospital in Ames."

"Don't worry about a thing. There are more than enough kids around to keep all of us adults in line," Henry said. "Go have fun."

Polly bent over and kissed him on the cheek, then picked up a red peg and placed it in Andrew's board. "That's his patrol boat."

"Hey! That's not fair," Henry cried.

"Ah ha!" Andrew said. "G-7."

"You got me."

Polly went into her bedroom and shut the door, then called Sal and Joss. Neither had plans for the evening. Sal told Polly that Mark was still exhausted and wouldn't mind going to bed early. He had another long week ahead. Joss and Nate were still mourning the loss of hope for a child, but Nate was in the garage working on a car. She was more than ready to get out.

They were meeting at Pizzazz downtown, the pizza place owned by Mark Ogden's brother-in-law. Polly was surprised at how busy it was on a Sunday evening. In fact, the entire business area was buzzing with people who were walking around or sitting in their cars chatting.

"Is it always like this?" Polly asked Sylvie. They'd decided to walk since it was such a beautiful evening and really only three blocks from Sycamore House.

"You never come uptown in the evenings?"

"Not on Sundays. I usually put the horses to bed, make dinner and crash for the next week."

"Well, you need to get out more often. Yes, it's usually like this. Especially in the summer when it's nice."

Sal was waiting for them just outside the front door. "I made Mark call his brother-in-law. He's holding a table for us."

Polly poked Sylvie. "It's good to know people, isn't it?"

Joss came around the corner, "I should have just walked," she said. "I parked down at the medical building."

"How are you doing, honey?" Sylvie asked, hugging her.

"We're doing fine. It was disappointing, but something will happen. I'm starting to believe again. Nate's still angry, but he'll get over it. Some grease under his fingernails, an expensive tool he desperately needs to buy for the shop, and he'll settle down."

"Let's get the party started," Sal said, louder than Polly expected. A few people looked up at them and she just waved back.

The owner of the restaurant, Dylan Foster, showed them to an empty table. "My wife tells me that Mark finally talked you into moving to Iowa," he said as he held Sal's chair for her.

"Yeah," she said. "But don't let him think he had anything to do with it. It will go to his head."

Dylan winked at the others. "It sounds like this one knows exactly how to manage my brother-in-law. Appetizers and drinks are on me tonight. I'll send Bri over to take care of you. Have fun." He patted Sal on the shoulder before heading back to the kitchen.

"Well at least someone in the family likes me," Sal said.

"Oh come on, you met them all last Christmas. That wasn't bad, was it?" Polly asked.

"No, they're really nice. Mark's mom is gorgeous."

"That must be where he got it," Sylvie said. "All the women in town just call him the hot doctor. You won't believe how mad they were that he pawned all his small animal work off on his partner. He's a nice guy, but not nearly as pretty to look at."

"We're going to have to find you a man one of these days," Polly said. "You have until your classes are finished and then I'm going to be relentless."

"I won't have time for that. And how would I ever explain to Jason and Andrew that I'm dating again."

"Yeah. Because single moms never date," Sal said snidely. "That's a terrible reason."

"Jason is really protective of me. I think it gets worse every year he ages. And speaking of age, I'm no spring chicken. Look at us. I'm an old lady in this group."

"So that's why you like spending time with Lydia. You get to be the youngster!" Polly said, laughing.

"I was until you came along. But at least they put me in the same age group as you. Young."

"Well you can just stop calling yourself old right now. You're beautiful and you're going back to school and building a fabulous career. Any man would be lucky to get you." Joss rubbed Sylvie's forearm. "And I'm with Polly. We're going to be on a mission."

"The last man who was in my life was the biggest jackass the world has ever seen." Sylvie caught herself and looked at Polly. "I'd daresay he was worse than your Joey."

"He wasn't *my* Joey. I didn't want anything to do with him," Polly protested.

"Well, Anthony Donovan was one of the worst." Sylvie took a sip of the beer in front of her, then took another long drink and set the mug back down on the table. "He was awful."

Polly had never heard the man's first name and this was the first time Sylvie had said anything about her ex-husband. She didn't know whether to offer sympathy or stay quiet in hopes that Sylvie would continue to talk. She chose to stay quiet. After her conversation with Eliseo earlier this morning, she had no idea what to say.

"But that's not what we're out here to talk about tonight. This is supposed to be fun and those years were definitely not fun."

"How long did you stay with him?" Sal asked.

"Much too long. Jason was getting old enough to know that his dad was hurting me. I don't even know if Andrew remembers him, though." Sylvie took another drink and then reached for a tortilla chip and dipped it in the queso dip. "One day I saw my fear reflected in Jason's eyes and that's when I knew it was time to deal with it. My boys weren't going to grow up afraid for their mom and they weren't going to learn how to hurt others."

"What did you do?"

"The next time he beat the hell out of me I called the Sheriff. Aaron Merritt was the one who showed up. He took one look at me, saw that there were two little boys in the house and got us out of there. I moved in with my mom for a while and then got my own place. Anthony went to jail. I don't know what Aaron said to him but he never came back to Bellingwood. I divorced him while he was in jail, packed his stuff and gave it to Aaron. He's called a couple of times over the years, but I never saw the man again."

"Do the boys ever ask about him?" Joss asked.

Sylvie gave her a weak smile. "Jason hates him. I don't know how to fix that because the man was evil. He didn't just beat me up when he was drunk, he beat on me whenever he felt like it."

"Why did you stay?" Sal asked.

"I don't know. I had no job and two little boys that needed me." Sylvie rested her head in her left hand, then looked up at them. "My dad knocked my mom around some. It wasn't as bad as what Anthony did to me, but he always made her believe that she'd done something to deserve it. When we first got married, things were fine. He got mad, but he never really hurt me. He wasn't even really too bad when Jason was born, but after Andrew came, it was like we were all too much for him. And I knew that I pissed him off. I was taking care of two little boys and ..."

Sylvie had been speaking with her eyes on the table. She looked up and around at the three sitting with her. "I almost made the same excuses that I made back then. I don't care that I pissed him off. It took me a long time to figure out that it wasn't my fault. Neighbors had called the police several times before Aaron finally showed up and made me deal with it."

Polly put her hand on Sylvie's knee. "I'm sorry you had to go through that."

"I am too," Sylvie said, "But I learned how to take care of myself and I wouldn't trade that for anything. I wish Jason had never known that kind of fear, but I can't change what was."

"Jason already keeps an eye on people to make sure they are taken care of. He's going to grow into a terrific young man. He's got a lot of compassion," Polly said.

"Yeah, but I'm going to end up killing him before he gets to be that terrific young man," Sylvie said, laughing. "Oh, he's got some serious attitude. If Eliseo wasn't around to make him straighten up, I'd be punishing him every day."

"I'm never having children," Sal moaned.

"Yeah, like that'll happen. How could you not bring those gorgeous babies into the world," Sylvie replied. She looked at Joss and Polly. "Can you imagine how pretty those babies would be? With Mark and Sal's good looks?"

Sal rolled her eyes. "Whatever. I'd be a crazy mother. They wouldn't have a chance."

All of a sudden, everyone turned to Joss and Sal said, "Oh, I'm sorry dear. See! I'm a horrible person. I'm not even sensitive to my friends."

Joss chuckled. "I'm fine. Stop worrying about me. We'll get our baby and then I'll make you all sick to your stomachs when you have to listen to my ooey, gooey baby talk."

"Hey, isn't that your guest?" Sal asked, trying to nonchalantly nod at a woman a few tables away.

"Where?" Polly asked.

"Well, don't stare. Over there under the flickering sconce. Maybe you can't see her from your angle."

Polly tried to stealthily stand up and spy on the table Sal was pointing to. It looked like it might be Lois Wexler, but she couldn't be sure. "Who's she with?" Polly asked.

Sal gave her a 'how should I know' look and both Joss and Sylvie had their backs to the rest of the room so they weren't able to see what was happening.

"I didn't know she had any friends in town." Polly craned her neck in order to see what was happening at that table, but she couldn't get a good enough angle to see faces.

"Oh sweetie, you're pathetic." Sal got up and strode across the room, causing every person to turn and watch her. Sal was tall, but tonight she was wearing heels that gave her extra height. The girl drew attention and walked with the confidence of someone who was completely comfortable with that. She smiled in greeting as she approached Lois Wexler, bent over and said something to her and then waved to Polly, who gave a little wave back.

"She has no fear," Polly said with a sigh. "I've always envied that in her."

"This coming from you?" Sylvie said. "Every time I think about running away from something that scares me, I think about you moving out here and opening Sycamore House."

"Yeah, but I've been able to do most of this because I have people around me."

"You didn't when you started."

"Well yeah. I did. When I met Henry, I knew that he would take care of everything for me."

"Is that when you fell in love with him?" Joss asked.

Polly snorted with laughter. "Uh. No. He says he fell in love with me right away, but it took me a long time. And it took me even longer to admit it. But, really, Sylvie. If it weren't for you and Jeff and Eliseo, I wouldn't have the courage to do half the things I do around here."

"But you are always so straightforward when you deal with people," Sylvie protested.

"Uh huh. Because I just can't imagine they're so stupid as to keep going down such an insane path. When it doesn't make any sense to me, I have a terrible habit of saying things I shouldn't. And it's not like you don't deal with stupid people and put them in their place."

"You went into the police station in Oelwein to get Jessie with no fear," Joss said.

"Because you and Sal were right there and I had no other choice. If I hadn't, that poor girl would have had nowhere to go."

Sal slid into her seat. "See. That wasn't so hard."

"Who was she with?"

"Oh, it's just the sweetest thing. She's taking her granddad out for pizza."

"Her what?" Polly gasped.

"It's this cute little old guy. He seemed so happy to be spending time with her."

Polly bent down and lowered her voice, "Lucy said that Ralph Bedford was with his granddaughter at the diner last week. I didn't know he had one." Polly stopped. "What if she's the murderer?"

"You don't suppose, though ..." Joss said.

"How can I not suppose? What if the murderer has been staying at Sycamore House all this time?"

Sylvie whispered, "But I thought she was supposed to be traveling from town to town in Iowa. Why would she have come in on a plane?"

"I didn't see her come in an on airplane. I just saw her at the car rental place," Sal interjected. "Wouldn't Bunny just pass out if she thought she'd sat in the back seat of that car with a murderer?" She started to laugh. "I can see it now. She'll be calling all of her former beaus, asking them to come protect her. A murderer knows what she looks like!"

"Stop it," Polly said. "Poor Bunny's not here to defend herself. But I have to do something about this."

"You have no proof that it's her," Sylvie said.

"So I'm supposed to let this poor old guy die tonight because I have no proof? That's not right!"

"Does it make sense, though," Joss said quietly, "that she killed Henry's Uncle Loren? He never comes into town. When would she have met him? Especially if she'd only gotten here on Friday."

"You're right," Polly said. "But I still don't like this." She took her phone out and looked around the table. "Are you going to laugh at me if I call Aaron?"

"Well, you'd better do something fast. They're headed out the door," Sal said.

Polly spun around in her chair, in time to see the door close behind the girl.

"Damn. I don't even know who that man was." She got up and tried to weave through the crowd in the restaurant, but it seemed to have grown since they came in. She kept having to stop and wait while people got up from their seats or tried to sit down. Who in the world would expect a pizza place in Bellingwood, Iowa, to be this busy? By the time she got to the front door, they were nowhere to be seen.

Polly went outside and dialed Aaron's phone anyway.

"Polly? What's up?"

"Well at least you didn't accuse me of finding a body," she said.

"I figure one per day is plenty, even for you."

"Have you checked on Lois Wexler, the photographer who has been staying at Sycamore House?"

"I don't think so. Why?"

"Okay, just hear me out and then tell me whether or not I'm nuts."

"You're usually not nuts. Go ahead."

"I don't know how Loren Sturtz fits into this, but Lucy told me that Ralph Bedford was at the diner last week with a girl who said she was his granddaughter. Her description matches Lois Wexler. I just saw her at Pizzazz. I'm here with Sal and Sylvie and Joss. Sal went over to say hello to her because they gave her a ride up to my place last Friday."

Polly could almost hear him putting the pieces together in his mind.

"When did she make the reservation at Sycamore House?" he asked.

"I don't know that. You'd have to ask Sarah or Jeff."

"Okay, anyway ..."

"Anyway. Sal came back and said she was having pizza with a

little old guy and the girl said he was her grandfather. He didn't deny it. Now why would Lois Wexler come to Bellingwood and stay at Sycamore House if she was here to spend time with her grandfather?"

"Do you know who the man was?"

Polly still felt like a newcomer to Bellingwood some days. People who had lived there all of their lives knew everyone. She was just starting to get to know enough people that she recognized the same faces over and over.

"I'm sorry. I don't."

"And Sylvie and Joss didn't recognize him?"

"They didn't get a good look at him. Aaron, if I'm right, what if she hurts this poor guy tonight?"

"I'm surprised she's picked up another one so quickly if that's really who she is. I would have thought she ..." Aaron stopped. "No, I don't know anything. Okay. I'm coming up. Lydia is just going to have to eat leftover pizza for the next few days. Maybe someone saw them together and knows who he was and we'll just do a gentle check-in on him tonight."

"So, you don't think I'm nuts?"

"Well, I didn't say that, but thanks for calling."

"Do you need us to stay here for any reason?"

"No. That's fine. Enjoy the rest of your evening. I'd like to know when she made the reservation at Sycamore House and when she plans to check out, though."

"Do you need that tonight?"

"Jeff says you won't learn how to use the system at Sycamore House. Is it a problem for you to get that information?"

"I'll ask Sarah to help," she said. "And Jeff needs to stop telling on me."

"Then yes, I'd like it tonight. Otherwise, I'll be there tomorrow morning."

"Thanks for not laughing at me about the strange connections I make. Sarah will call you later with the information you need."

"You be good tonight."

CHAPTER TWENTY-SIX

Opening the door to the living room as quietly as she could, Polly glanced back at her husband, who was sleeping peacefully. She wanted to get down to the barn and spend time with the animals before another crazy week started. He turned over, opened his eyes and peered at her.

"What are you doing up so early?"

"Going to the barn. I'll be back soon."

Henry stretched. "I should get up, too. I'm taking Ben and Amanda up to the Diner for breakfast. I think she's finally ready to start talking about building their new home. You should have seen her last night. It was like a light finally switched back on."

"I'm so glad."

"You missed all the fun last night," he said. Polly hadn't gotten back until after midnight. Sylvie had taken off earlier to get her boys home, but Joss was glad to be out and Sal announced she was establishing her independence. It had been a lot of fun.

"What did I miss?"

"Believe it or not, I think Ben is going to try to rent the house that Eliseo is living in. When Eliseo got back from the hospital, he was ready to talk to my family about buying Uncle Loren's house. I took him over to Aunt Betty's and we met my parents there. Nothing is set in stone yet, but it's going to happen.

"That's good news. He'll be happier out in the country."

"The man never stops. He just keeps working and working. I feel lazy next to him."

"Yeah. That's what you are. Lazy. I'll be back. Gotta go." She waited for Obiwan to join her, then slipped out of the door and pulled it shut only to find Jessie reading on the couch in the living room.

"What are you doing up this morning?" Polly asked.

Jessie jumped up. She was dressed in jeans and an old t-shirt. Polly was so thankful the girl's clothes had made it to Bellingwood. At least she had something of her own.

"Can I go down to see the horses with you?"

"Of course."

"I met Eliseo last night and he's really nice. He told me that if I came down with you in the morning, I could help."

"You want to help?" Polly couldn't help herself. She laughed, wondering if the girl knew what she was getting into."

"Those horses are big and they're so pretty. But Eliseo said that they weren't scary."

"Come on," Polly said, crossing to the front door. "You'll love them. Everyone does. It's hard work, but in the summer Jason is here every day and with all of us working, it goes pretty fast."

"Jason told me that Eliseo would teach me how to ride. I've never done that before."

"Eliseo is an amazing instructor. Jason had never been around a horse until last summer and you can believe how far he's come."

They got to the side door and Polly held it open while Jessie walked through.

"I talked to my little brother last night. He said Dad's going to be okay."

"But you talked to your dad yesterday, too, didn't you?"

"Yeah. But I wanted to hear it from Ethan. Dad would lie so I wouldn't worry. We're going to talk again today after Mom goes to work. Ethan has to stay home and take care of him. Mom made him quit his job before they came out last week."

"Well, I suppose someone had to, and your Mom is supporting the family right now."

"But Ethan was saving money to go to college. She told him that they were going to use his savings if Dad couldn't work."

"Sometimes there just aren't any good answers," Polly said. The last thing she wanted to do was create more division between Jessie and her mother, but this was too much. Even parents made horrible decisions sometimes.

Obiwan ran for the pasture while Polly opened the door to the barn and flipped the lights on. She was surprised they'd gotten here before Eliseo and Jason. "Is this what you expected?" she asked Jessie.

Daisy came to her feet first and Jessie stepped back from the stall when the horse's massive head came out to greet them.

"Wake up everyone," Polly called out. "We've got a guest." She poked her head into Demi's stall and wasn't surprised to find both cats curled up on top of him.

"Look at this," she said, beckoning Jessie over. "That's Hansel and Gretel. He's their favorite. Mostly because he's so easygoing." She tripped the latch and opened the door. The cats were used to people now and didn't immediately run away when someone new came into their space, but they looked up warily.

"He won't move if they're on top of him," she said. "Kneel down here and rub his nose. Let him sniff your hand. Go slowly," Polly directed, hunching down on her knees.

"It's so soft," Jessie said.

"I know. It makes me melt every time." Polly heard a noise behind her and barely stood up before Tom's head gave her a push. "Hey," she said. "No shoving!" She bent over and hugged his neck.

"We also have two donkeys down here. Tom and Huck."

Tom approached Jessie, nosing at her side.

"You're new. He's looking for a treat. That's generally how we introduce him to new people."

The cats had both stood and stretched. Gretel took off when Tom entered the stall, but Hansel tried to find a soft place to sleep on Demi's haunches again.

"Let's back out," Polly said, "so Demi has plenty of room to get up once he decides to kick the cat to the curb. "Come on, Tom. Out with ya."

"Demi's a weird name," Jessie said when they got back out into the main alley.

"Yeah. We have Daisy and Demi, Nan and Nat. Their former owner named them for characters in the book *Little Men*."

"And you have Tom and Huck and Hansel and Gretel?" Jessie asked with a smile.

"We like to read around here."

"Good morning, girls," Eliseo said coming into the barn. "Sorry I'm late."

"It's my fault," Jason said, right on Eliseo's heels. "Well, it was Mom's fault. She was late."

Eliseo nudged him, "Don't disrespect your mom, son. She's doing everything she can to give you a good life."

"Yes sir," Jason said, his shoulders drooping.

"Why don't you show Jessie here where the feed is and we'll break her in this morning," Eliseo rubbed the boy's shoulder and gave him a little push.

"It's down here." Jason picked up the pace and when he passed Jessie, stopped, and waited a moment for her to follow him.

Eliseo had stopped to greet each of the horses. When Demi heard his voice, he shook the cat off and came to his feet. "How are you doing, old man?" Eliseo asked, stepping in to scoop up the cat. "Don't you ever get tired of these little ones sleeping on top of you?"

He didn't wait for a response, but walked back out and pushed his hip at the donkey who was trying to get close.

"You really love it down here, don't you?" Polly said.

"I wake up every morning grateful for the chance to come in and spend time with these animals."

"Are you sure about taking on another student?"

His lips pulled up into the half smile she'd gotten accustomed to seeing. "As long as they're ready to work hard, I'll never turn one away."

Polly spoke low and quiet, "You know she's got some hurts, don't you?"

"I think we all do. Some of them are just more obvious than others." He touched his own cheek. "Mine are obvious. Hers might not be, but if you look at her eyes, you see how fresh they are. She'll be safe with us."

"Thank you," Polly said. "Henry tells me you are serious about his uncle's house."

"That's beautiful land out there and his aunt and uncle are good people. They'd make mighty fine neighbors."

"Oh, good heavens, Eliseo. Now you're even starting to talk like an Iowan."

His chest shook as he laughed. "You bet'cha. I'm just fittin' in."

"How was Ralph doing yesterday when you saw him?"

"I think he's going to be okay. There was a lot of damage and he hasn't come awake yet. They said something about keeping him in a coma so his body can cope with everything."

"I guess that means he can't tell us what happened."

"He's a good old guy. Who would hurt him like that?"

Polly put her hand on his forearm. "So you're sure he never said anything about a granddaughter?"

"Nothing." Eliseo couldn't really furrow his brow with the scar tissue covering his face, but that was his reaction. "If she'd been around, I'd have met her."

"I keep thinking about what Lucy said. That they were at the diner together and the girl said he was her grandfather."

"I had no idea."

"If Lucy's timeline was correct, he wasn't at the table when the girl said that."

"What girl was this?"

"Well, I'm wondering if it isn't Lois Wexler, our upstairs guest."

His eyes flashed at her. "Oh, come on. That can't be true. She's just a little thing."

"Well, if her prey is old men and she uses a gun, she doesn't need to have much heft to pull that off."

Eliseo sat down on a bench and leaned over to pick Hansel up. "He was busy last week. He planned to come over to do some work with the horses in the back pasture. Jason and I were clearing rocks. But he canceled both times. I just assumed it was because he was cleaning up storm debris on his own place.

Polly realized that she needed to pay better attention around here. That explained why Jason's chest and shoulders were starting to fill out. She didn't realize they were already taking the horses across the creek to the far pasture. Time was moving past her much too quickly.

He looked up at Polly. "Has the Sheriff talked to her yet?"

"I don't know. She was with another old guy last night, but I didn't know who he was. I hope she hasn't hurt him."

"Is she the one they think killed Henry's uncle?"

Polly shook her head. "I really don't know. It sounds like she finds these men in town and then latches on to them for a while. Loren never came into town. She had no way to come into contact with him. And Lois didn't have time to hook up with him. She came into Bellingwood with Sal just before the wedding party."

"Yeah. That makes sense. Ralph is all over the place. There are a bunch of those guys. They meet up at the diner every morning. Some of them eat at Davey's in the evening."

"Does Ralph have a lot of money?"

"He's in good shape. It isn't like he's overly wealthy, but he has money and there are some nice things in his home that his wife collected over the years."

"Were you in there? Did you see if everything was still in its place?"

"I haven't gone inside. I don't know if I'd even recognize that anything was missing." She watched a shudder pass through his body. "They really think there's a serial killer in Bellingwood right now?"

"I don't know, but if this is her, she's off her game. From what I understand she's never killed more than one person in a community and though she stays for a while to obscure the fact that she was the one who did it, she's never picked a second victim, she just goes silent."

"Do you think it's about the money or the murder?" Eliseo asked.

Jessie and Jason had been passing back and forth as Jason showed her how they fed the horses. When he handed the girl a muck rake, Polly grinned. Eliseo wasn't paying any attention - he was lost in his thoughts.

"Murder?" Jason asked.

"Yeah. We're just talking about what happened to Ralph yesterday," Polly replied.

"Did you see the body?" Jessie asked Jason as they went into Daisy's stall.

Polly quit listening and turned back to Eliseo. "Are you okay?"

"I am. What do you think?"

"Huh?"

"Do you think she's killing for the money or because she wants to kill."

"I have no idea. If you were to press me and I had to pull out all of my knowledge based on all of those years reading mystery books and watching police procedurals," Polly chuckled and went on, "I'd have to say that she believes it is because of the money, but in truth, she's turned into a murderer who enjoys what she does."

Eliseo grinned up at her. "Then on that basis, we'd have to assume that she is still in town because she didn't manage to kill Ralph and couldn't satisfy her need for a clean death."

"Maybe I'll talk you into joining my private investigation firm and we'll put Aaron out of business," Polly said. "Are you going back down to the hospital to see him today?"

"I don't know." He shook his head. "There's so much to do here. With him in ICU and completely out of it, there's not much I can do. I need to talk to Deputy Decker and see if I can check his house, just to make sure that it's all cleaned up and ready for him to come home." He pounded his hand down on the bench beside him, startling the cat. "He's an old man, damn it. I guess I hope he can come home at all. What a despicable thing to do."

"We should be glad he's still alive, right?"

"You're right. I know that. How's he going to take care of himself out there?"

"Now's not the time to worry about that," she said. "First we need him to wake up and be okay. He'll be in the hospital for a while."

Eliseo put the cat down on the bench and stood up. "I can't do anything sitting here getting frustrated. I'll take care of what I can and let the rest fall into place. Thanks."

"I didn't do anything."

"You didn't let me bury this in my head." This time it was Eliseo who reached out and touched her arm. "It wasn't much, but thanks."

Before she could respond he turned away. Her phone rang. "Excuse me," she said and walked to the front door. Why was Joss calling this early?

"Hello, Joss? Is everything okay?"

"Polly!" Joss squealed a little on the other end of the call.

"What?" Polly asked, laughing.

"We're on the road to Omaha!"

"Wait. What? Did the girl change her mind again?"

"No, it's another girl. She just made the decision last night and she's going to have a Cesarean this afternoon."

"But everything's okay?"

"Yes! Can you believe it?"

"I'm so excited! And I'm glad I'll be in town when you bring the baby home. I really don't think I would have been able to stand it if I was clear out in Arizona."

"Thanks for making me go out last night. I have a feeling that will be the last one of those for a very long time."

"Oh, I hope not. Surely you can make Nate stay with the baby once in a while so we can party."

"Uhhh ... yeah. Maybe. Anyway, I knew you'd be up and I had to tell someone before I exploded, but I'll call later today, okay?"

"Absolutely. I'm really happy for you. Let me know if you need anything and poke your silly husband for me."

There was a grunt in the background, followed by "That wasn't nice!"

"I did. He's confused now. I'd better go."

"Drive safe and keep me up to date."

"Love you!" Joss hung up before Polly could reply.

Polly turned to look for Eliseo. He had disappeared into one of the stalls and she knew better than to press it.

Jessie had done what she could to help Jason, but it didn't take long for her to end up on a bench with two friendly donkeys begging for attention. Polly sat down beside her.

"I'm going back up to the apartment. You can come and go as you please. If you want to stay here for a while, that's fine."

"Thanks," Jessie said. She giggled as Huck pushed his head under her hand. "I have to get a job and find an apartment. Maybe I should do that today."

Polly put her hand on the girl's knee. "No. Not today. Maybe not even this week. Jessie, you've been through a lot. You don't have to rush right back out into the world and live on your own."

"But that's why I came out here."

"Is it what you want to do today?"

"Well ..."

"I'm really proud of you that you don't want to sit around and feel sorry for yourself and that you're ready to grab the world, but it's okay if you relax for a few days. You've been through more in a few weeks than most people will ever face in their entire lives. Take a breath."

"I don't want to be a burden."

"You aren't. Take time to learn about what Eliseo and Jason do down here. Then I'll introduce you to Rachel and you can help her in the main building. You can work with Eliseo in the garden and if Sarah needs help in the office, you can poke around there. I might ask you to babysit with Andrew and Rebecca sometimes and we'll just take it slow."

"Are you sure?"

"I'm sure. Get to know Bellingwood and then we'll keep an eye out for jobs that might come up. But don't worry. It doesn't have to happen today or tomorrow."

"Thank you very much. I never expected this."

"Do you want to stay here in the barn for a while?"

"Would that be okay?"

"Sure. I'll take my dog and head back. I know you don't have a phone yet, but Jason and Eliseo can reach me if you need something and can't find me."

Polly stood and patted her leg for Obiwan to follow. They went back up to the main building and she wondered about Lois Wexler. After calling Sarah last night, she'd completely forgotten about their guest. Hopefully Sarah had gotten the information that Aaron needed. Polly glanced up at the room, but it was still dark. She didn't know whether that meant the woman was gone or simply asleep. Lights were on in Sarah and Rebecca's room, but not in the room Ben and Amanda Bowen were using. It was good that Amanda had finally snapped out of her shock. Most everyone in Bellingwood was starting to find their way back to their regular lives after the tornado had spun the community out of control. Polly had noticed it last night when she was downtown. People were out and about - playing, chatting and thinking about anything other than the devastation that had hit the community.

There was no one in the apartment when she returned, so she fed the animals and went into her bedroom to take a shower. Polly was in the kitchen drinking a cup of coffee and eating a piece of toast when Jessie walked in, her face flushed and her eyes bright.

"What's up?" Polly asked.

"It was awesome."

"What?"

"We let the horses out into the pasture and then I played fetch with Tom and Huck. They love that red ball. They're like dogs. Demi rolled around in some mud and Jason told me I was going to have to brush him down later on. They'll really let me do that?"

"Oh, honey, if you want to spend time with those animals, they'll let you do everything."

"That was awesome. I'm going back this afternoon, if that's okay."

"You have no schedule to keep with me."

"I talked to Rachel. She said I could help her in the kitchen this morning."

"Wow, you're really digging right in." It occurred to Polly that Kelly Locke didn't know what she was talking about when she accused Jessie of having no gumption. She decided she couldn't think about it anymore. It just made her angry.

"I don't like to sit around. I start thinking about things and then I get depressed. I need to keep busy. If you have something you want me to do up here, just tell me."

"We're good, but thanks."

"I'm going to take a shower. I've never been in anything like that bathroom."

Polly smiled. "Me either until I had these built. I thought I was doing something wonderful for my guests, but I love them. If I'm not here when you come out, I'll see you later."

With no notice, Jessie rushed at Polly and hugged her. "Thank you," she said and ran out of the room.

"You're welcome," Polly said quietly.

CHAPTER TWENTY-SEVEN

Filing the last few pieces of paperwork, Polly turned back to her desk when her cell phone rang. She didn't recognize the number, though it was a Boston area code.

"Hello?"

"Polly, it's me, Bunny."

"Hi sweetie, how are you?"

"I'm wonderful! I had two dates this week with the same guy!"

"Do you like him? How did you meet him?"

"You aren't going to believe it, but Drea set me up."

"Really!" Polly grinned. As snarky as Drea was, she had a heart as big as the city they lived in. "Who's the lucky guy?"

"It's one of her clients and she set us up for coffee on Thursday and then he asked me to go out for dinner with him Saturday. We're going to a little concert series in Belmont this Thursday."

"Well, what do you think of him?"

"He's sweet and he's loaded. He's divorced and doesn't have any kids yet. It sounds perfect, doesn't it?"

"I'm happy for you, Bunny. I hope you have a great time with him."

"Me too and I am going to try my best to not go overboard. Drea told me that I can't plan a wedding until he asks me to marry him and if he doesn't ask me, then I can't make a scene about it."

"She's right. I hope this works out for you." Siccing Drea on Bunny for a few hours had done the silly girl a world of good.

"Will you come out to Boston and be my Matron of Honor when I get married?"

"You're planning, Bunny. Stop it. But of course I will."

Bunny giggled on the other end of the call. "Oops, you're right. I'm going to just enjoy the moment. So, do you think the universe heard me whining at you all last week and decided it had had enough of my pitiful behavior?"

"That makes as much sense as anything. It was wonderful to see you, though."

"I'm sorry that you didn't get to go on your honeymoon. I can't believe we flew out of there just before that tornado came through. CNN was showing video of it. I couldn't believe that I'd just been there!"

"It was pretty crazy stuff."

"I wanted to tell you about Brett, but that's not the only reason I called."

"What's up?"

"I know this won't surprise you, but last night I finally got around to emptying my suitcases. I found something weird in my travel bag. I can't believe I didn't notice it while I was there. But, it's just a little black kit - kind of like a first aid kit or something. Only it's not mine."

"Okay ... ?"

"Well, I think it came from that girl who drove up to Bellingwood with us. We were jammed in the back seat of that car and this must have dropped into my bag."

"Is it important enough that you want to ship it to me so I can give it to her?" Polly wasn't really even sure how long Lois Wexler planned to stay. She quickly jotted a note to herself. It had gone in and out of her mind to ask Sarah about the dates that Lois had scheduled, but each time she'd completely forgotten.

"No, I think it's more important than that."

"What do you mean?"

"I mean, there's a big roll of money in there and old lady jewelry. I think it's the real stuff, too. And then there are two big pill bottles."

"All of that could be hers."

"Polly, the bottles have bullets in them."

Polly deflated. "Crap," she said.

"I know, right?"

"Sweetie, are you going to be around this morning?"

"Yeah, I have a meeting with a client this afternoon, but otherwise I'm free."

"Let me ask some questions and I'll get back to you, okay? Don't do anything with that."

"Okay. Is it important?"

"It might be. I'm glad you called me. I'm so excited to hear about a great guy in your life, too."

"You'll call me back?"

"Yes. I love you, sweetie!"

"Love you too!"

They hung up and Polly dropped her head to her chest. That was unexpected.

"Sarah?" she called as she got up and went into the main office.

"Yes?"

"Did you talk to Aaron last night about Lois Wexler?"

"Yeah. He came over and got copies of her information. What's up?"

"So, when did she register?"

"It was a last minute thing. She called that morning to see if we had a room available and Jeff told me that if you needed it, you'd have already filled it up. She wanted it for two weeks."

"Have you seen her this morning?"

"I heard someone moving around up in her room last night. She's right above our room. I was awake about three o'clock."

"But nothing this morning?"

"No. Deputy Decker was here before you came downstairs. He

knocked on her door, but she didn't answer. Jeff went upstairs with him, so I don't know if they went in or not."

"Okay, thanks. All of this is happening under my roof and I know nothing!"

"What's happening?"

"She might be a suspect in the shooting of Ralph Bedford."

"I had no idea!"

It hit Polly that she'd probably said the wrong thing to a mother whose little girl was sleeping in the room right below a potential murder suspect. "She's dangerous, but mostly to old men, I think," Polly said. "You and Rebecca are safe."

That wasn't helpful either. The stalker who had pursued Henry and Polly a few months ago had held Rebecca hostage. She shouldn't have been involved at all, but in the end, her life had been in danger.

Polly leaned over and hugged Sarah's shoulders. "I feel like I'm a little dangerous to be around," she said, with a half-hearted chuckle.

"I'm trying not to be nervous about it."

"I'll bet she has cleared out. I saw her at Pizzazz last night with some old guy and that's why Aaron was checking on her. More than likely we've scared her off. Maybe even out of town for good."

"I hope so. It's kind of creepy thinking about a murderer living over my head."

Jeff came out of his office. "Now you're rubbing off on Sycamore House, Polly."

"What do you mean?" Polly spun on him.

"People are going to quit making reservations if they think they might get murdered here or might be living next to a murderer."

"That's not fair," she cried.

Sarah chuckled. "He's not being honest with you."

"Hush. You work for me," he said, wagging his index finger.

"Oh. Sorry boss."

"What did she mean by that?" Polly tugged on his shirtsleeve and winked at him.

"Nothing. She meant nothing."

"Sarah?" she asked.

"I only work here, but if this pile of reservation requests is growing because people think that Sycamore House might offer them a chance to see a murder happen while they're in town ..."

"So, I'm good for Sycamore House," Polly said, standing up a little straighter.

"Don't you think now would be a good time to let all of this talk about our owner finding dead bodies become legendary rather than everyday reality?" he asked.

"You might have something there," she responded. "I need to call Aaron, though. I'll be in my office." Polly slipped past him and went back into her office and shut the door.

She dialed a very familiar phone number and when Aaron answered, he said, "Polly, every time I see your name come up on my screen, my insides clench up and my head starts to pound."

"No bodies this time. Do you know who the old guy was with Lois Wexler last night?"

"Yes, it was Russell Gourley."

That name was familiar to Polly. But he wasn't a widower. She'd met his wife at some event Lydia hosted.

"Was she really his granddaughter? Because his wife is still alive."

"Actually his wife is in Maine for the month with their daughter and granddaughter. I went out to talk to him last night and he was very embarrassed about your little guest. She'd flirted with him and he just thought she was as cute as a button. When she told people she was his granddaughter, he figured that she was trying to save his dignity. He dropped her off at Sycamore House after they left Pizzazz and he went on home without her. They were planning to meet again this evening for dinner, but I think he's a little more wary now."

"Do you suppose she's already gone?"

"I don't know, Polly. I don't want her in my town any longer, but I hate the idea that she's going to move on to another community."

"My friend Bunny called me this morning."

"I remember her. Chatty little thing."

Polly chuckled. "Yes, that describes her. But I have a real reason for telling you about her call. I think that Lois Wexler inadvertently dropped a bag into Bunny's travel bag when they were driving up from Des Moines last week. Bunny didn't finish unpacking until last night and that's when she found it."

"Is there something interesting about the bag?"

"Well, she said there was money and jewelry in it, and two large pill bottles filled with bullets."

"That's very interesting. Please don't tell me this was a bag she carried onto the plane."

"Like Bunny would carry anything. I can't even imagine her carrying her purse. No, I'm sure she checked it through."

"Well, since I made friends in Boston a year and a half ago when you were out there with your friend, Joey, I'll ask for help."

"I told her I would call back this morning and let her know what to do."

A rumbling chuckle came from the other end of the phone.

"What's so funny?" Polly asked.

"Well, what I wanted to say was 'tell her that I'll make sure a couple of good looking Boston policemen show up at her front door to take custody of that bag,' but I decided that was probably out of line."

"Everyone learned what she was about in three short days, didn't they."

"Yes we did, but she seemed like a nice girl anyway. Tell her that someone will contact her. And tell her thank you."

"Will do."

"And Polly?"

"Yes?"

"If you see Lois Wexler anywhere in town, will you please try to avoid confronting her? I don't want to have to tell Henry that his lovely wife is in the hospital."

"I'll do my best, but you know as well as I do that I can't guarantee anything. Sometimes I feel like I'm wearing a magnet."

"Just promise to be careful."

"Like I said, I'll do my best."

"That's all I can ask. Do you have a building full of people again this week?"

"I think there are a couple of groups coming in again. We've cleared the classrooms and auditorium for them."

"Thanks for all your help. It means a lot."

Polly shook her head, even though he couldn't see it. "I don't understand what the big deal is, Aaron. People have done far more than I have this last week. I'm a part of Bellingwood. It's my home."

"Yes it is. We're glad you're here."

Well, she'd done what she could. She put the phone down and ran her fingers through her hair. It was frustrating to think about a murderer getting away with hurting Ralph Bedford. If she were Lois Wexler, she'd have ducked out of town as soon as possible. Bellingwood had to have frustrated the girl. She'd gotten nothing and apparently she'd lost a large chunk of what she'd had to Bunny's travel bag. And how did she plan to get out of town? She didn't have a car.

Polly jumped out of her seat and ran out of the office, then headed for the barn. She opened the door and pulled up short when she saw Jason and Eliseo. Both of them were startled to see her.

"What's up, Polly?" Eliseo asked. "You look like you've seen a ghost."

"What if she went back to Ralph Bedford's house to get whatever she could from him?" Polly asked. "She didn't get anywhere with Russ Gourley last night and Bunny called me this morning to tell me that she had a bag filled with money, jewelry, and bullets."

"You should call the Sheriff," he said.

"Yeah, yeah, yeah. I know. But she knows where Ralph's house is and it's not that far from here. She could have walked there in the middle of the night last night. No one would have seen her on those back roads."

"Call the Sheriff," he repeated.

"She doesn't have her own car. I'll bet she tries to steal Ralph's truck."

"Good luck to her. Unless you know how to start that thing, it's not going anywhere."

"If I ride Demi over there, she won't hear a vehicle coming down the road."

"You're not taking one of these horses into danger. And you shouldn't even be thinking about going yourself. This is what makes Aaron crazy and drives your poor husband to ... well ... he doesn't drink."

Jason was starting to laugh.

"What?" she demanded. "What are you laughing at?"

"You're going to go over there and if she's there, you're going to get yourself nearly killed until someone shows up to rescue you."

"When did you get so all grown up?"

"Call the Sheriff, Polly," Eliseo repeated again.

"Fine. I shouldn't have come down here in the first place." Polly sat down on the bench beside Jason and dialed Aaron once more.

"I haven't had a chance to get anything going yet, Polly."

"Eliseo won't let me go over to Ralph Bedford's house."

"I'm sure he has a good reason. Why do you want to go there anyway?"

"Because if Lois Wexler is looking for money, she didn't get any from him and she didn't get anything from Russ Gourley and Bunny has her stash. She doesn't own a car and has no way to leave town."

"Don't you dare go over there. I'll call Stu."

"How long is it going to take for him to get there? What if she leaves?"

"We'll deal with that. It's our job. Now, thank you very much for putting some pieces together, but stay away!"

"Fine. Can't I even watch?"

"Polly ..."

She heard the warning in his voice.

"Fine. Bye." She slumped back on the bench.

"You know, Polly, the Sheriff and his deputies solve crime every day without you," Eliseo said.

She lifted her upper lip at him and growled, then stood and headed for the front door. Before she walked out, she turned around and said, "You're no help."

Polly slowly walked to the main building and up to her apartment. She sat on the couch and pulled her laptop close and did a quick search. Something wasn't right, but at this point she didn't feel like bugging Aaron one more time. She ran down the back steps and out to her truck. She opened the garage door and saw Henry pulling into the driveway, so waited for him to stop.

"Where are you going this morning?" he asked.

"Out. Do you want to come with me?"

He shrugged. "I can drive. Get in."

Polly climbed into the cab of the truck and pulled her seatbelt on.

"Where are we going?"

She showed him the address and he turned around and headed out on to the highway. The house they were heading for was just beyond the hotel and winery.

"Why are we going here?" Henry asked.

"I need to check on someone. Don't ask too many questions or you're going to get mad at me."

He pulled into the parking lot of the hotel and stopped the truck. "No. We're not going anywhere until you tell me why."

"I want to make sure that Russ Gourley is okay. He got caught up with Lois Wexler last night and even though Aaron warned him to be careful, I just want to make sure that he's still safe."

"Why are we doing this and not one of Aaron's deputies?"

"Because they're going over to Ralph Bedford's place to make sure she isn't there robbing him blind."

Henry let out a breath. "You do know that if we are going to Gourley's place, that's where she'll be, don't you?"

"So if I'd gone to Ralph Bedford's house, she would have been there? Is that what you're implying? That I'm the linchpin?

Whatever I do is how she made her choice? Because I was on a tear to get over there first, but Eliseo and Aaron wouldn't let me."

"It sounds crazy when you say it, but Polly, I absolutely know that's what will happen. If you and I show up, this woman is going to find some way to try to hurt you."

"Then it's a good thing I have you with me."

Henry took out his cell phone and made a call. When Polly heard his first words, she huffed.

"Aaron? Yeah. I'm with Polly. We're going over to check on Russ Gourley. She says that she wants to make sure he's okay. I figure that if this is where Polly is trying to go, that's where the woman is going to be."

He listened and said, "Okay. Thanks. No worries."

Henry set the phone down on the console and looked at her. "Aaron already thought of it and has someone heading over to check on him. Polly, you are going to make me die a young man!"

"I know you guys are right, but damn." Polly got out of the truck. She had to pace. Things were happening and she was frustrated to be so far from all the excitement.

Henry joined her and put his arm around her waist. "I want you to be around for a very long time. You have to stop putting yourself in dangerous situations."

"I know, I know," she said and wriggled out of his embrace. It was too constricting. "Just let me walk off the adrenaline," she said. "I worked up a pretty good head of steam."

Henry chuckled and leaned back on the truck. "I'll stand here and watch you walk, then. It's not a bad sight at all."

Polly walked toward the far end of the parking lot, looking up at the empty sign. The insert for Sycamore Inn was ordered. That had been a fun purchase. She and Henry decided that they were going to stick with some of the colors and kitsch from the fifties. They'd found a company to reproduce the bright teal and red sign, with chasing white lights around its perimeter.

She glanced over her shoulder and saw Henry watching her, so she swung her hips a little and grinned when he let out a wolf whistle. When she arrived at the sign, she turned around and walked back. Polly considered an attempt at being sexy, but the last time she'd done something that silly, she'd bounced off a bathroom door sill and she didn't want to do that again.

Renovating this old hotel had been a great idea. Two of the homes across the street had cleaned up their yards this summer, one of them had even painted the exterior. She looked back at the hotel. They'd chosen to paint the outer door and window trim of each room in a different color. Henry hadn't been quite ready to acquiesce, but once it was finished, he agreed that it was a good idea. She winked at him.

"What?" he asked, leaning forward.

"Oh nothing. I was just thinking about what a good guy you were. You put up with my crazy ideas."

"Uh huh." He leaned back and leered as she approached.

"Henry?" she said.

"What, honey?"

"Something moved in that room."

"Which room?" He stepped forward and walked toward her.

"Room six. Right there." Polly desperately wanted to point, but knew she shouldn't.

"Don't look," he said and grabbed her arm. As soon as he touched her, he pulled her to him and walked her back toward the truck. They were nearly there when a shot rang out, shattering the glass window of the room.

"Damn it," he yelled and pulled Polly to the other side of the truck. They crouched behind the tire and he patted his pockets. "My phone is in the truck. Do you have yours?"

Polly took her phone out of her back pocket and swiped it open, then went to the last call she'd made and redialed.

"Polly, what now?"

"She's here!"

"Where?"

"At the hotel. Room six. She just shot at us. We're hiding behind Henry's truck."

Another shot rang out. This time it hit the ground in front of the truck, spitting gravel at them.

"My boys are on the way."

The call ended and Polly looked at Henry in shock. "I didn't do this!" she said.

"I should have known. If this is where you are, this is where she was going to be."

"Why didn't she just wait until we drove away? I had no idea anyone was in there. She could have gotten away cleanly."

Another shot skittered off the top rim of the bed of his truck.

"Are we safe?" she asked him.

"As long as it doesn't take very long for Aaron's boys to get here."

Polly heard glass shatter as one of the truck's windows exploded.

"I'm going to wet my pants," she said.

Henry pulled her tightly to him. "I love you, Polly Giller. More than life itself. We're just going to hover here like the cowards we are and let the authorities deal with the serial killer psycho woman in Room Six.

"What if she comes out and tries to steal the truck?"

"She can have it."

Sirens sounded. Polly couldn't tell where they were coming from, but was thankful to hear them. She and Henry clutched each other while they waited. First, one deputy's vehicle entered the lot, then another. A third drove to the back of the building. In all the chaos that accompanied their arrival, Polly realized she was shaking. Three more vehicles arrived, blocking the highway, and soon, she heard Stu Decker's voice ordering the person to leave the hotel room. There were no more shots and things grew quiet.

Vehicles continued to pull in from both the sheriff's office and the local police force. Polly couldn't believe what she was seeing. Just as one of them attempted to approach her and Henry, they heard a voice call out, "We've got her. She went out the back door and was heading for the vineyard."

All movement stopped and Polly and Henry stood up and watched two well-armed deputies haul a petite blond out to the front parking lot.

Polly's knees wobbled and she grasped the bed of the truck to steady herself. Henry put his hand on her back and she took a deep breath, trying to draw oxygen back into her body.

"Well, Miss Giller, it looks like you were in the middle of it once again," Stu said as he strode over to them. He stuck his hand out to shake hers and then Henry's. "Did you have any idea that she was here?"

Polly looked up at Henry, then back at the deputy. "No! I swear I didn't."

Henry sighed. "You all will learn someday that no matter where you think the murderer is, you're wrong unless you follow Polly around. Wherever she is - that's where they'll be." He turned to her. "The death of me. You're going to be the death of me."

"You don't have any guests in these rooms, do you?" Another of the deputies had joined them.

"No, we used them last week for temporary housing, but they're empty," Polly said.

"We'll need to close off that last room for a while. It's a crime scene now."

"I know. I know," she said and threw up her hands. "Whatever you guys need, just tell me."

Stu had stepped back to speak with some of the other law enforcement men and women, releasing most of them.

As they dispersed, Henry asked the young deputy. "Do you need my truck? The girl tried to shoot it up, but I'd like to get Polly home."

"We need to get the bullets out of it. Let me run you two back to Sycamore House and we'll let you know when we're finished.

"My phone's in the cab," Henry said.

"Just a sec." Stu went over to the cab of the truck and opened the door. It took a few minutes and he came back and handed the phone over to Henry. "I had to do some searching. That cab's a mess. Sorry about that."

Henry hugged Polly to him again. "At least we're safe. Thanks for showing up as fast as you did."

CHAPTER TWENTY-EIGHT

For the last five days, poor Henry had complained about missing his truck. And this evening he looked dejected as he pulled the passenger seat belt on. Polly was driving them to dinner.

He drove her truck when he needed to haul things and they'd brought the Thunderbird over so there were two vehicles, but Polly didn't feel comfortable driving his baby. The first time she needed it, he spent twenty minutes going over everything in the car with her. She'd finally reminded him that he had two more speeding tickets in his history than she did and that she'd never totaled a vehicle - something he couldn't say.

He stroked the car every time he walked past it. Polly was desperately afraid she would scratch it or bump something and knew that she was driving like a little old lady around town. She was going to be glad when his truck came home, too.

The week had sped by and here they were at another Friday evening. All of the people who had come into town to help were heading home again and few would be returning. All Polly could think was that people in the Midwest rocked. They helped when they were needed.

This afternoon Aaron had asked Henry and his family to meet at Sycamore House. When Betty and Dick arrived, Aaron explained that Loren's death could not be attributed to Lois Wexler. She had admitted to murders around the state and to trying to kill Ralph Bedford, but she had no idea who Loren Sturtz was. He was prone to believe her, especially since the bullet they'd recovered from Loren's body was not the same caliber as those used during the rest of her killing spree.

"Do you have any idea who might have done this then?" Betty had asked. "Are we in any danger?"

"I don't know," Aaron had replied. "We have no leads right now. You've told us everything you know ..."

"And that's not much," she said. "The old buzzard didn't want us around at all."

"He used his shotgun to scare me off the land once," Bill Sturtz said. "You did find that gun, didn't you? Just to be sure the man didn't kill himself with it?"

"Yes, we have that. It wasn't what was used to kill him," Aaron said. "I just wanted to let you know where we're at."

"Is that because you haven't let Polly loose on the case yet?" Bill asked, grinning across the table at his daughter-in-law.

Aaron looked over his glasses at the older man. "Don't you get her going. It's bad enough that she gets involved in solving these things on her own. She doesn't need encouragement from you."

"I'm right here," Polly said. "Sitting right here. It's not like I ..."

"Don't even," Henry interrupted. "You were the one who was hell-bent on getting to Ralph Bedford's house and then to Russ Gourley's. At least I was with you when the psycho murderer showed up."

"Whatever. I don't have any good ideas about this anyway. I was perfectly fine with it being the same person who was killing older men around the state. That would have wrapped things up quite nicely. Now people are going to worry." She reached over and put her hand on top of Henry's.

"I'd really appreciate it if you didn't think any more about it, Polly Giller." Aaron had given her a glare. "You don't have any idea what my life was like this week after Lydia heard about you caught in gunfire at the hotel."

"Oh, I had lunch with her on Wednesday. She was just fine." Polly looked for support from Marie Sturtz. "Wasn't she?"

Marie just nodded and smiled. "You do keep our hearts pumping, Polly."

"I didn't know she'd be in that hotel room," Polly protested. "How could I have known that?"

Henry's Aunt Betty laughed at them. "I think it's a good thing that this family has a spitfire running around causing trouble. We were getting too comfortable and set in our ways. I, for one, am glad you make Henry's life exciting."

"You're not helping, Aunt Betty," Henry said.

"Of course I am. Any time you need someone to give you support, just call me, Polly. I'll tell this stick in the mud to get over himself."

Polly laughed and Aaron had finally stood to leave. "I know that you all probably had better things to do this afternoon, but I wanted to tell everyone at the same time that we weren't any further along on the case than we were last week. Stu Decker would have been here today, but he's busy working with departments around the state, trying to coordinate everything with Lois Wexler's arrest. I may not be able to keep him after this case. He's going to be quite a hot commodity."

He walked to the door of the conference room, "Thank you for coming, and I am truly sorry for your loss. If you think of anything else or want to talk about this, feel free to contact me."

"We really like your hired man," Betty said to Polly after Aaron left. Eliseo had actually moved into Loren's house yesterday. They hadn't cleared Loren's things out, but Eliseo was so ready to get out of the little house in the middle of town, he was perfectly amenable to having Henry's family in and out of his new home during the day while he was at work.

"I'm glad. He's going to be happy out there."

"We invited him over for dinner tonight. Dick here thinks he's found a new fishing buddy."

"Don't you be stealing him from me," Polly said.

Betty's husband smiled. "I don't think we can do that. But everyone needs time at a fishing hole and I've got just the place to take him. If he gets tired of people in town, he can hide in the woods and never see a soul."

"Last night he was already working in the yard, gathering up all of that junk that Loren let fall to pieces. If the weather stays nice, he and Dick are going to do a big burn pile this weekend. You won't recognize the place before too long, Henry."

"It's going to take a while to deal with it all," Bill said. "I told him I'd bring the trailer up next week and we could load that metal out. Might even make a few bucks scrapping some of it."

Henry leaned over to Polly and said, "It's not enough that you are restoring Bellingwood, now you're sending your minions out into the country to start restoring things there."

"You give me more credit than I'm due," she said. "Stop it."

"I'm just glad that old house is going to get some tender loving care," Betty said. "At least I can finally get my hands on mother's things. There are a few antiques in there that she had had marked for you to have, Marie, and one or two that I'd hoped to share with my kids. I'd pretty much given up on it all, though. It will be nice to rescue them before they've completely fallen apart."

She had looked up and around the table. "It sounds like I'm glad he's gone." Betty's eyes filled. "I miss my brother, but I lost him a long time ago. This poor man wasn't the boy we grew up with, was he, Bill?"

Her brother had given her a warm smile. "No he wasn't. It's too bad our kids will never know the playful prankster you and I knew. And you're right, it will be good to get into Mother's home and rediscover her treasures." He touched his wife's arm and stood. "Henry, Monday starts another busy week. I think we should take the rest of the afternoon off and relax before the real world takes over again. Marie and I are going to take a little vacation this weekend. It's surprising how much I miss her when I'm not hovering around the house all day. We're packed and ready to go. Don't bother me until Sunday night, okay?"

Henry gave his father a surprised look and stood to shake his hand, "Okay then. I'll leave you alone until you come home. You are coming back, right?"

"Just as soon as I remind your mama why she married me."

Marie stood up as well and swatted her husband's shoulder. "You old reprobate. We're going to the gardens in Ames this afternoon and then heading over to Decorah and maybe Dubuque tomorrow and Sunday. We'll stay in touch."

Betty and Dick followed them out, leaving Henry and Polly alone.

"We're going to be like that when we get older, aren't we?" she asked.

"Oh lord, I hope not," he said. "They're just embarrassing."

"I like it."

"I'm going to be too busy keeping you alive to act like an old reprobate," Henry said. "But I like the idea of taking the rest of the afternoon off."

They hadn't ended up taking any time off. Since Eliseo had moved out of his little rental home, Polly had ridden over with Amanda Bowen to clean it while Henry and Ben packed up the few belongings the couple had left. They got them moved in and settled and then gone home.

Jessie had offered to help Sylvie and Rachel prepare for the wedding rehearsal dinner that was being held in the auditorium and then had agreed to spend the evening with Rebecca and Andrew. Sarah and Polly had gone to Boone yesterday for another chemotherapy treatment and the poor woman was absolutely worn out. Rebecca checked on her regularly, but Sarah was just as glad to have her daughter spend time upstairs.

Eliseo and Jason had driven to Ames to see Ralph Bedford every afternoon this week. He'd finally come awake on Wednesday, much to Eliseo's relief. He would be transferring to a rehabilitation center before he was able to return home. More than anything, he was mad as a wet hen that he'd been caught off guard by a pretty little girl. He identified Lois Wexler as the person who had shot him and was glad to find out that she'd been caught. Eliseo told Polly that when Stu asked if he would be willing to testify, Ralph managed to come fully alert, as if the morphine that filled his body wasn't even there. His eyes had been as clear as ever when he promised to do whatever it took to put that little hussy in her place.

~~~

Polly pulled into the parking lot at Davey's and Henry asked, "When are Joss and Nate supposed to come home?"

"Sometime this weekend. I talked to her last night. She's ready to be back."

"And she won't tell you about the baby? I can't believe she didn't send pictures."

"It's the weirdest thing," Polly said. "She won't tell me anything. I don't know if it's a girl or a boy or even what hair color the child has. Nothing. She keeps telling me that since they were surprised, I should be too."

"Okay," he said. "That's weird, though. Right?"

"I think so."

They were meeting Mark and Sal for dinner. Sal was flying to Boston on Sunday to close down her life and ship it to Bellingwood. She'd given her boss two weeks' notice and he was glad to let her use her vacation.

When they got inside, the hostess smiled and said, "They're already here, waiting for you." She led them into the dining room and Polly looked around to find Sal waving.

"We've got it. Thanks," she said and went on ahead.

"Hey sweetie." Sal jumped up and met Polly with a hug. "We ordered appetizers and a couple bottles of wine. Is that okay with you?"

Sal was the person who had taught Polly everything she knew about wine. That was more than okay.

"If you'd rather have a beer ..." Mark began.

"No, wine is good," Henry responded. "We're on vacation this weekend. My dad informed me of that this afternoon."
~~~

"Are you doing something special?" Sal asked. "Going away somewhere?"

"No way," Polly said. "We're staying home. I don't want to pack bags, I don't want to find sitters for the animals. I just want to be a slug."

"How is it with Jessie living with you?"

Polly gave Henry a sideways glance. He'd been wonderful about having a houseguest. Jessie wasn't intrusive, but she was always there. "It's been okay. I think that when she gets a job and isn't in the building all the time, it will be better for everyone."

"That poor girl. I thought my mother was tough to get along with," Sal said. "I can't imagine having a mother who didn't care whether you lived in the house or not."

"I had friends whose parents kicked them out of the house when they turned eighteen," Mark said. "The ones I felt terrible for were the kids who hadn't graduated from high school yet."

"That really happened?" Polly was aghast.

"To one of my classmates. It wasn't like they hadn't warned him. So, the day after his birthday, his things were neatly packed up and in the front hallway."

"Where in the world did he go?"

"Another buddy took him in. He lived in their basement until he was done with school and then he got a job and found his own place."

"No support from his parents?"

"As I recall, they paid for his car insurance for the rest of the year and his dad kept him on his health insurance for a while, but that was it."

"That's just so strange," Polly said. "I always knew I was welcome at home."

"Me too," Henry said. Everyone else laughed at him. "What?" he asked, genuinely confused.

"Puh-lease," Polly drew it out. "Your parents moved to Arizona so you could have the business and the house. Of course you knew you were welcome."

"Well, that's not a bad thing, is it?"

"No, it's wonderful, but not very many people get to experience that."

"The only reason my mother wanted me around was so she could control my life," Sal said. "I knew it was going to be safer to never let her have any control."

"And so you move to Iowa, just to make her crazy." Polly was teasing, but she knew there was some truth to it.

"No, I'm moving to Iowa because I couldn't stand living without my very best friend."

Polly and Mark looked across the table at each other. "Which one of us is it?" Polly asked. "You or me?"

"He's my hot lover." Sal leaned into him and ran her fingers up his chest. Then she sat up straight and wrinkled her nose. "Who comes home some nights smelling like horrible things." She waggled her well-manicured fingers and said. "These poor hands have done more laundry these last two weeks. I'm going to keep Nanette at the salon very busy."

"What are you looking at?" Polly asked, about to turn around. Both Mark and Sal had been watching the front door.

"Nothing," Sal said. "Oh, by the way. Maybe Jessie should go up to the salon and ask for an application. I saw on the door that they were hiring. I don't know what the job is, but it might be something."

"I'll tell her. Thanks. I wish I had something for her to do, but the only job I have available right now is running Sycamore Inn and I don't think she's ready for that. And besides, it isn't even really open yet."

"Just remember she's not a little girl," Sal said. "She's trying to live as an adult and you have to make sure you treat her that way."

Polly dropped her head. "I know you're right. It's hard not to see her as broken after all she's been through. I just wanted to give her this week to be anything she wanted to be with no pressure."

"I know you'll figure it out. I didn't mean to imply you would do something wrong."

"No, you're right."

There was some scuffling behind them and Polly turned around. Then she gasped and pushed her chair back.

"You're here! With the baby! Where's Nate?"

Joss was carrying a car seat and Henry jumped up to let her sit in his chair.

"He's right behind me."

"Let me see the baby," Polly said.

Before Joss pulled the blanket back, Polly saw Nate walk in carrying another car seat.

"What?" Tears began to spurt from her eyes. "Is this why you wouldn't tell me anything? You got twins?" Polly grabbed her friend into her arms and started to sob as she hugged her. "You have two babies? How did this happen? Why didn't you tell me?"

Nate had joined them and everyone shifted around the table to make room. Polly had wondered why there were extra chairs, but didn't think more of it after the initial thought flitted through her brain.

"Did you know about this?" she asked Sal.

"Maybe," Sal replied.

"We got home this morning and called Sal so that we could surprise you tonight," Joss said.

"I couldn't figure out why you were taking so long to come home. It's been five days! And I really couldn't figure out why you wouldn't tell me anything about the baby. The babies! Show me!"

Joss unbuckled one baby while Nate took the other out of her seat. Then he proudly said, "We'd like you to meet Cooper Oliver and Sophia Harper Mikkels."

"I'm not going to squeal," Polly said. "But I want to. They're beautiful!"

She reached over to touch the milk-chocolate cheek of the little boy in his mother's arms. She stroked his dark, black hair and couldn't help herself. Before she knew what had happened, a small coo had come out of her mouth. "Dear heavens, they're beautiful!"

Little Sophia opened her eyes and Polly was struck by the deep set beauty of them and the sharp lines of her little face.

"Do you want to hold her?" Nate asked.

"No, not yet. I just want to look at her. When did you know that you were getting twins?"

"I knew when I called you on Monday," Joss said. "But I couldn't say anything. At least not until we knew for sure that they were ours. And then I couldn't tell you on the phone because I wanted to surprise you with them. Are you mad at me?"

"How could I possibly be mad?"

Polly had lost her index finger to Sophia Harper's tiny little hand. "Look what she's done!" Polly exclaimed. "Her fingers are so tiny and they're wrapped around mine."

"Sal? Would you like to hold Cooper?" Joss asked.

Sal backed her chair up, stopping before she ran into the wall. "No, that's okay. I'll admire from afar. Babies and I have never been real friendly."

Mark looked at her. "I come from a big family. I hope you're not telling me it ends here."

"No, I'm not saying anything like that. But until I absolutely have to, I'm not ready to hold babies."

"This really is the wrong crowd, isn't it," Joss said, laughing.

"No. This is just perfect," Polly replied. She took her finger back and said, "Okay. If you stay really close and put the baby in my arms very carefully, I want to hold her."

Nate waited until Polly had settled herself in the chair and then placed his daughter in her arms. Polly looked down at the sweet face staring back at her.

"You know Sophia is Greek for wisdom, right?" she asked, looking up at Joss.

Joss nodded. "As soon as we saw her, we knew that would be her name. And do you know where we got her middle name?"

"No." Polly shook her head.

"In your favorite series, the Harper is the one who sings the stories that brings all of the clans together."

"McCaffrey's *Dragonriders of Pern* stories?" Polly asked.

"Yes. It seemed like the perfect middle name. She's wise and will have plenty of stories to tell."

"And Cooper Oliver?" Henry asked.

"That was my choice," Nate said. "I'm raising someone who loves food and wine. A cooper builds barrels ... like wine barrels. And Oliver comes from those who deal in olives. I thought that those two names would give him a strong foundation for feeding the world."

"That's great," Mark said. "Did any of our parents spend that much time on our names?"

Henry laughed. "No. My name came from one of my father's relatives. They couldn't have chosen a more boring name."

"Mine too," Mark replied, laughing. "What about you, Polly?"

"Mom loved the Pollyanna books. Dad wouldn't let her use the full name. Thank goodness." She looked down at the bundle in her arms. "Oh, Joss. How can you help but fall in love with this child?"

"We did the minute we met them. I'm glad to finally be home, though. I couldn't wait to have them in our own house and quit worrying about whether or not some nurse was hanging over my shoulder checking my technique when I changed a diaper or fed them."

Polly grinned. "That's funny. Were you a good student?"

"Not nearly as good as Nate. He's a natural at this. I'm going to be lost when he has to go to work."

"So, everything has changed because you have two babies. I didn't even think about that. Do you need another crib?" Polly asked.

"No. They sleep together. It's the cutest thing. Sometimes they reach out and touch each other while they sleep."

"Oh, you're killing me," Sal said. "That's almost cuter than even I know what to do with."

Mark took her hand. "I need to get you around more babies so you can find out how wonderful they really are. Maybe I'll take you with me when the cows are calving."

A snort burst out of Sal's mouth. "No, I'll figure it out on my own. I'm not ready for that either.

"Lydia and Andy are going to flip out when they discover you have twins," Polly said.

Joss looked over at her. "Please tell me that can wait until tomorrow."

"It can definitely wait, but you're going to have all the babysitters you need."

Polly held the baby back up to her daddy, who took Sophia and cradled her in an arm. "I think we should make a toast," she said. "To the newest and youngest residents of Bellingwood.

Mark and Henry poured wine into the glasses and Sal chuckled. "Not too many new moms get to drink. It looks like adoption is a great way to do this baby thing."

Joss smiled at her. "It's been wonderful. I wanted a houseful of children and starting with two right off the bat is perfect."

They passed around the glasses and Polly held hers up. "Welcome home Cooper and Sophia. Your family has been waiting for you and there are so many people who can't wait to meet you. We're glad you're here."

Glasses clinked together around the table and little Cooper Oliver gave a big yawn, settling back into his mother's arms.

"Your family keeps growing, Polly," Henry said, his eyes twinkling.

"It really does." She smiled down at Cooper. "I hope it never stops."

"Hear, hear," Henry replied, his words echoed by their friends.

THANK YOU FOR READING!

I'm so glad you enjoy these stories about Polly Giller and her friends. There are many ways to stay in touch with Diane and the Bellingwood community.

You can find more details about Sycamore House and Bellingwood at the website: http://nammynools.com/

Join the Bellingwood Facebook page:
https://www.facebook.com/pollygiller
for news about upcoming books, conversations while I'm writing and you're reading, and a continued look at life in a small town.

Diane Greenwood Muir's Amazon Author Page is a great place to watch for new releases.

Follow Diane on Twitter at twitter.com/nammynools for regular updates and notifications.

Recipes and decorating ideas found in the books can often be found on Pinterest at: *http://pinterest.com/nammynools/*

And, if you are looking for Sycamore House swag, check out Polly's CafePress store: *http://www.cafepress.com/sycamorehouse*

Made in the USA
Columbia, SC
11 May 2020

96425693R00153